Retaliation

A Julian Mercer Thriller

G.K. Parks

Copyright © 2019 G.K. Parks

A Modus Operandi imprint

All rights reserved.

ISBN: 1-942710-17-8
ISBN-13: 978-1-942710-17-2

For my mom and dad

ONE

"The things you say to these women," Donovan chastised. "It's a miracle your willy hasn't been lobbed off."

"Nah, mate, just my shoulder." Hans grinned, far enough along in his recovery to joke about the near-amputation. His eyes flicked to Mercer, who just entered the house. "Bas called, told us to meet here. What have you got for us this time, commander?"

"A missing MI5 agent." Mercer went to the closet and removed a roll of vinyl, propping it against the wall.

"Has there been a ransom?" Donovan asked.

Mercer shook his head. "This might not be a recovery. It may be a cleanup."

Hans swallowed. "Are we doing that now? Does Bas know?"

"He's aware." Mercer went into the kitchen and filled the kettle with water. His gaze dropped to the tile floor. His breath caught and his throat tightened. Squeezing his eyes closed, he waited for the images to pass. It was done, and yet, it didn't change a bloody thing.

"Jules," Donovan called, "do we have any intel?"

Steeling his nerves and quieting his emotions, Mercer returned to the sitting room. "MI5 gave us the classified mission log and Agent Owen Shepherd's personnel file. Our first priority is locating his sister, Lara. He reached out to her right before his disappearance. She might know where he is or what happened."

"Do we know where she is?" Donovan asked.

"No."

"What about the wankers at the Security Service?" Hans asked.

"They haven't been able to locate her. She disappeared around the same time Shepherd missed his check-in." Mercer unrolled the vinyl and with Donovan's help tacked it to the wall. Soon it would be covered in intel which they could roll up and move to their base of operations. "She's the key to figuring out what happened to Shepherd. We don't know if he turned or if he's blown, but she's his family. He'd want to keep her safe."

"Unless someone is leveraging her to use against him," Donovan said. "Maybe Shepherd turned because he didn't have a choice."

"Or whoever caused his disappearance also took revenge on his sister. Agent Owen Shepherd infiltrated a dissident republican group in Northern Ireland. Colin Flynn's group to be precise," Mercer said. "We can't discount anything at this point."

"Bloody hell. We're dealing with the fucking IRA," Hans said.

"The bulk of them went political," Donovan pointed out. "Maybe we can negotiate. He might see reason."

"Just because most of the loyalists agreed to the

accords, it doesn't mean the rest of the bloody lot did. Flynn's a terrorist, and we all know it. It doesn't matter who he identifies with. The tactics are the same." Hans ran a hand over his face. "MI5 thinks one of theirs turned and is now helping Flynn? Those pissers are one sorry lot."

"They don't know what's going on. That's why they hired us." The kettle let out a shrill whistle, and Mercer went to grab it. He returned a moment later with a cup of tea. "The only thing they know for certain is Shepherd has vanished. The surveillance units haven't spotted him. Nothing indicates he left Ireland. He must still be with Flynn. We just don't know if it's by choice."

"Bugger," Hans muttered.

"If it turns out Shepherd's a traitor, the Security Service wants plausible deniability in silencing him. They don't want to broadcast that one of their operatives crossed the line. It might sully their reputation."

"That's why they need us."

"Flynn could be holding Shepherd for information, or he killed him." Donovan reached for the laptop and opened the lid. "This is why Lara is our priority. I'll do what I can to locate her."

Mercer took a sip and put the cup down. "We're splitting up. As soon as Bastian gets here, we'll work out our travel arrangements. He has the file on Shepherd's family. I'll need you to check with everyone from Shepherd's past and find out what they know. In the meantime, I'll scout Flynn's stronghold."

"The hell you will," Hans said. "You can't go up against an entire cell alone."

"It's recon. Flynn will never see me."

"Are you daft? I'm our recon expert."

"I'm taking point. If you have a problem, you can

piss off."

"Pish. You need backup support. I'll be careful. No one will see us, let alone touch us. Going alone is sloppy, and you know it."

"What's sloppy?" Bastian asked, startling his teammates by slipping in through the back entrance.

"Jesus." Donovan placed the firearm back on the table. "You need to learn to knock, mate." He clutched his chest dramatically. "I'm having flashes of giving your eulogy. Bastian Clarke was not a very bright man, but he was a dear friend."

"Hardy har. Since you're so jumpy, I take it Jules has caught you up to speed."

"Aye." Donovan reached for the file, searching for details on Lara Shepherd. As soon as he found her last known address, he grabbed his coat. "According to this, she resides in Islington. Interesting choice given her brother's profession. I would have figured she'd live in a safer neighborhood." He eyed his gear and checked the contents of his pockets. It was hard to be prepared when he had no idea of the situation.

"Here are some area maps and security cam footage." Bastian passed a second folder to Donovan. "I went ahead and ran the basics. I also checked police records. No calls have come from her address or any of her neighbors. We have no reason to believe anything foul is afoot."

"Except for Shepherd's disappearance," Mercer said. "Initial assessment?"

"Looks clear. No reason to assume the worst," Bas said.

"You think she ran?" Donovan asked.

"Too soon to say." Bastian dug his computer out and flipped it open. "If she ran, Owen told her to. I'll figure out how he did that. According to her phone logs, she received a call from a public landline that lasted less than two minutes a few days before she and Owen vanished. It might be something."

"Keep digging, Bas. Donovan, you and Hans go to her flat. Question her neighbors. See what you can dig up," Mercer said.

Hans moved to stand, but Donovan held up his palm. "It'll be faster and less obvious if I go alone. With two of us, people might mistake us for coppers. And in that dodgy neighborhood, even the hint of the police will keep anyone from cooperating."

Mercer nodded, and Donovan left without another word. Bastian watched the younger man disappear. His eyebrows knit together in consternation. Normally, they didn't split up this quickly. Something was up.

"Is Donovan feeling okay?" Bas queried.

"He's afraid I'm not at my best." Hans rotated his shoulder, wincing. "Two more months of rehab is overkill. I'm field ready now."

"Hans, you should sit this one out," Bastian said.

"I can handle it."

Mercer stared at the recon expert. "Can you handle a rifle?"

Hans didn't answer. His shoulder couldn't withstand the recoil of a long gun, and the entire team knew it.

"Fine, you can assist, but you better tell us when you can't." Mercer took a final sip of tea and returned the cup to the kitchen. He gripped the edge of the counter and stared at the tile floor. "Forgive me, my love, but it looks like I'm leaving on another mission."

TWO

Julian Mercer remained at his post, a crumbling staircase which led to a basement shop in the center of Belfast. It was just after midnight. The cold rain had soaked through his clothes hours ago, leaving his boots soppy and his toes numb. He fought against a shiver as water ran down his back.

He stared through the icy fog of his breath. His eyes fixed on his target. Colin Flynn was practically IRA royalty with his entourage of bodyguards and lieutenants. Mercer couldn't help but wonder if the mission had already been compromised. Did Flynn know MI5 was monitoring his every move? Or were these IRA wankers really that oblivious?

Honestly, Flynn was powerful enough that he probably didn't give a fuck. He controlled most of Belfast. No one was daft enough to make a move on him. The terrorist was untouchable. He'd proven it time and time again.

To date, the bastard had made more people disappear than most Vegas magicians. And Owen

Shepherd might be another name to add to the ledger. Flynn owned the police. They never investigated these cases, and if they did, the details were kept quiet. MI5 had proven ineffectual in stopping him. That's why they sent Owen Shepherd undercover to infiltrate Flynn's rank and file. Obviously, that did not go as planned.

MI5, Mercer scoffed at the notion. The Security Service was the reason he was here. He didn't trust them any more than Colin Flynn, but he would fight on their side, at least until he found proof they were responsible. Then he'd see them burn to the ground.

After Mercer killed Thomas Vogel, the man who murdered his wife, Michelle, MI5 swept the details under the rug. The police had nothing to investigate, and the matter quietly disappeared. However, Mercer knew the real reason MI5 had taken precautions. It wasn't to protect him. It was to protect Vogel.

It was a cover-up, plain and simple. Powerful people knew what Vogel was, what he did, and knew about the team he ran, but since Vogel had been a decorated SAS operative, the powers that be turned a blind eye to the unsanctioned killings. And Michelle became another of his victims. Had MI5 acted swiftly, none of that would have happened. Michelle would still be alive. Mercer's life and career would not have been destroyed, and he wouldn't be here now, standing in the frigid rain, paying back a favor he didn't believe he owed.

Vogel killed Michelle, but he was only able to do so because other powerful men allowed the crazed killer to run amok. Mercer would see that they pay. Right now, he didn't trust anyone in government or the military, that included MI5. And since the Security Service forced him to assist, he'd use the opportunity to his advantage. The fact that they wanted to turn his team into a group of mercenaries, not that dissimilar from Vogel, made his stomach turn. Mercer and his teammates might kill, but they weren't killers. They were kidnapping and ransom specialists, not cleaners.

As far as Mercer was concerned, this proved his assumptions about MI5's complacency in Vogel's actions correct. Now he just needed the names of those in the know. His team didn't know of his personal vendetta or his real reason for agreeing so easily to the Security Service's request, and they never needed to. Ever since they left the Special Air Service, they walked a fine line between security specialists and mercenaries. This one case, so out of the norm but necessary due to recent complications, could change everything. And Mercer would be damned if he let it. They would not turn into the thing they despised. He wouldn't let that happen to his brothers.

Colin Flynn surrounded himself with the best—the most loyal and the most ruthless. Nothing was more dangerous than a true believer on a mission. And the pub was bursting with true believers, so Mercer held his position in an alcove across the street. He'd stay here all night if it meant locating Shepherd.

Boisterous guffawing filled the streets as the pub door swung open. It slammed shut, muting the sound as two of Flynn's men went to get the car. Two down. Mercer glanced at his watch. It was nearly three a.m. The usual time for Flynn to call it a night.

Mercer watched as Flynn's men performed their ritual check. As long as nothing appeared out of place, they would give Flynn the all-clear. That's what they did every night. Predictability would be the terrorist's death but not tonight. Tonight was a warning shot.

Mercer waited for the two bodyguards to get close to the car, a high-end SUV that screamed for attention and respect. Everyone knew it was Flynn's car and not to touch it, but if it belonged to any other plonker, the vehicle would have been stripped before the engine even had a chance to cool.

"In position?" Mercer's voice echoed in his own comm, and he cringed. The weather was wreaking havoc on their equipment.

"Affirmative," Hans replied.

Pressing a button on the detonator in his pocket, Mercer watched the SUV erupt in a ball of flame. The force of the blast knocked the bodyguards off their feet. The stout one with the ginger beard caught fire. The flames lapped at the back of his jacket and along his left arm. He screamed, surely from surprise and not pain since he wore far too many layers for the fire to have gotten to his skin so quickly.

But Mercer's attention didn't remain on the blaze. Instead, his eyes were drawn to the pub door. Two more of Flynn's men stepped outside to investigate the commotion while the IRA commander remained inside the pub, staring out the frosted front window and across the street.

Mercer took half a step forward, just enough for the streetlight to illuminate his silhouette. He wanted Flynn to know this was no accident. Turning on his heel, Mercer vanished down the dark avenue. He just taught Colin Flynn an important lesson–actions have consequences. No one was untouchable, not even the head of an IRA faction. At the end of the block, he climbed into his car.

"Keep him in your sights and don't get spotted. We need a location for his safe house," Mercer said. "Do not engage. I repeat. Do not engage."

Giving the rearview mirror a quick glance, he started the engine and drove a few blocks before turning on the headlights. Flynn and his crew were occupied, but Mercer didn't want to risk being spotted by one of Flynn's overzealous followers. It was imperative he get to his destination without being tailed.

Killing the engine a few streets away from Flynn's compound, Mercer checked his gun and put on the mask. He wore full blackout gear. The black mesh mask allowed him to see out and breathe but prevented anyone from seeing him. It was a bit of a hindrance but, in this situation, a necessity.

He screwed a suppressor onto the end of his gun. He had a knife in his pocket, along with a garrote. Based on MI5's intel, Flynn had at least two guards inside his home at all times and six others guarding the perimeter. It would be best to do this quietly, if possible. Grabbing the jammer, Mercer locked the car, hoping this would be a simple in and out.

Under the cover of darkness, he crept down the street, stopping at the gate in front of Flynn's compound. The wrought iron fence encompassed the entire property. Each metal piece culminated in a razor-sharp spike. Jumping the fence wouldn't be easy. Nothing about this bloody mission was easy.

Carefully, Mercer made his way up the fence, using his torso to roll over the spiky prongs. The Flak protected him from being impaled, and he silently dropped to the ground below. The compound had several spotlights positioned on the corners, ensuring no one could sneak up to the house. Shooting out the lights was always an option, but broken glass would attract attention. And Flynn would know the compound had been compromised. As a rule, the less Flynn knew, the better and the safer Shepherd would be, assuming the agent hadn't been turned or killed.

Mercer activated the jammer and waited. Flynn had a wireless security system, preventing anyone from approaching the house without being caught by the security cameras or sensor grid. Within moments, the comm buzzed and went dead. All wireless signals were blocked. He was on his own.

Doing his best to stay in the shadows and avoid the roaming eyes of the patrol, Mercer moved across the property and went straight to the side of the house. The meter pressed against the brick, and Mercer made quick work to disable the electricity. He barely heard the sharp pop before the lights flickered and went out. *Bloody good.*

He crept along the house. The rain no longer an annoyance but an ally in cloaking his approach.

Mercer waited at the side of the rear door. Now that they were in the literal dark, Flynn's interior guards might come outside to check the perimeter. According to the intel, the sharpshooter on the roof was only present when Flynn was conducting business at home, but the faction leader didn't have any plans in the works. At least none to which MI5 was privy. Still, the possibility remained in the back of Mercer's mind, and he glanced warily skyward.

When no one emerged, Mercer tested the rear door, finding it locked. He blew out a slow breath and reached for his tension tools. He teased the pins until the lock released fifteen seconds later. Palming his gun, he turned the knob. The rear door opened into the back of the living room. No one was inside.

In the pitch black, he listened for footfalls or voices but didn't hear anything. Could the place be empty? He lowered the night vision goggles and flipped them on, but the jammer kept them from functioning properly. Prepared for that possibility, he had memorized the blueprints. He didn't need to see to navigate. If Shepherd was inside, Mercer would find him.

Unwilling to waste time, he moved stealthily

through the dark house, relying on memory and sound rather than sight. MI5 provided surveillance photos of the exterior and a few glimpses inside the rooms that could be seen from the outside, but Mercer depended mostly on the research his team had done, the blueprints they'd examined, the work orders that had been filed, and Shepherd's reports. After completing his search of the main level, Mercer moved to the staircase.

Voices stopped him in his tracks. The spoken words were nearly indecipherable with their thick Irish brogues. Going upstairs was currently out of the question.

Mercer stepped back, ducking beneath the steps as a beam of light swept the landing above. He waited, but no one came down the stairs to investigate. If anything, it sounded like the men were arguing.

Without waiting to see who would win, Mercer followed his mind's eye to what should have been a descending staircase leading to the basement. The door was locked. It was the only locked door he'd come across. Something important must be in the basement. Could this be where Flynn was keeping Shepherd?

Since pained screams weren't coming from above, Mercer assumed Owen Shepherd wasn't being held and tortured upstairs. Perhaps downstairs. Unless he was dead. Or turned. Or...Mercer exhaled. He didn't have time to contemplate the possibilities, even though the voice in his head coming up with these infernal thoughts sounded a hell of a lot like Bastian. *Focus, Jules*, again his second-in-command's voice resonated inside his skull.

Light beams bounced down the steps, and Mercer felt his way through the house, unable to see much given the mask and the dark, but he circled around the guards and made his way back to the locked door. He approached cautiously, pressing his ear against the door to listen for sounds coming from within. However, he wasn't convinced the thick door wasn't soundproofed. If it was, he had no way of knowing what awaited him on the other side.

He set to work, feeling his way to unlocking the door using nothing but touch and muscle memory. The tension tools made the occasional metallic scrape as he manipulated them in the lock. This was taking too long. The exterior door had been child's play compared to this. "Come on," Mercer whispered.

The voices grew louder. Heavy footsteps approached from above. The intel was wrong. There were three guards inside. Maybe more.

The top step creaked. Boots descended the staircase. Mercer continued to work on the lock, forcing his breath to slow to keep his heart rate steady. The final pin clicked as the man rounded the corner. Fortunately, he didn't carry a torch.

In the dark, Mercer discerned his location by sound alone. As silently as possible, he opened the door and ducked inside. He hoped once the door closed, the lock would click back into place.

"Wha—"

Mercer heard the beginning of the question before the door blocked out the sound. But from the vibrations in the floor, Flynn's guard was just outside the door. He must have heard the door or seen something in the dark.

Mercer drew his silenced pistol and went down a few steps. This wasn't supposed to be messy. Flynn wasn't supposed to know anyone had been inside, but as the door swung open, Mercer knew that objective was no longer possible.

THREE

Mercer held his position. He was a meter and a half from the door. The staircase was narrow. Too narrow. Even with the suppressor, the gun would boom in the enclosed space. He remained still. The darkness worked in his favor. The guards were as blind as he was.

Flynn's guard remained at the top of the steps. He didn't have a torch, but the other one did. And he was approaching fast.

"Oi," the man with the torch called, and the guard turned, his motion caught in silhouette, "what are you doing there? Colin doesn't want us venturing into the basement without permission."

"I thought I heard something."

"Rubbish. Get your arse outside and check the power. The wires probably got wet with all this damned rain. It happens every bloody time we have a storm."

Mercer used the distraction to edge silently down the steps. The third step creaked, and he froze, keeping his weight evenly distributed for fear that the step might creak a second time.

"There," the first guard said. "Didn't you hear that?"

The other one scoffed. "It's an old house. They do that. Now get to it." The light grew brighter, but the door slammed shut before Mercer became visible.

Hurriedly, he descended the staircase before the men changed their minds and decided to investigate the noise. He couldn't risk navigating the unfamiliar room in the pitch black, so he remained stationary while he waited for the danger to pass. What was Flynn hiding that he didn't want his men to see?

Mercer crouched at the bottom of the steps. He listened while counting the seconds ticking by. He didn't have time for this. He placed a hand against the wall, feeling for vibrations. They grew weaker as the men upstairs moved away from the staircase and into another room.

Letting out a breath, he reached for the torch hooked to his belt and flipped the switch. The beam of light bounced off the pale tile floor. He swept the room. No one made a sound. He was alone.

Mercer moved through the basement. Wooden crates lined the walls. He cracked one open and peered inside. Russian artillery–assault rifles and grenades. He tried another one, finding more of the same. Another crate contained dozens of MAC-10s. Flynn was preparing for war. It would be a bloodbath.

Flynn had amassed enough firearms to outfit half of Belfast. And MI5 had no idea. Rebellion. Guerilla warfare. Arms dealing. Mercer wasn't sure what Flynn's plan was, but it wasn't good.

Abandoning the crates, he examined the items laid out on the metal tables in the center of the room— wires, batteries, rat poison, and glass canisters filled with nails. All the makings for a bomb. From the looks of things, several bombs. Did all terrorists read the same bloody playbook?

A scrap of crumpled paper sat at the edge of the table. Mercer picked it up. The top of the paper had a gold foil design, which seemed out of place in the dingy basement. The paper listed items along with quantities. Mercer folded it and tucked it into his pocket.

No wonder Flynn didn't want anyone down here. He didn't want to risk tipping anyone off to his plans. Flynn must have realized there was a spy in his midst. After all, this was his compound. The only men here were the men he trusted with his life. Maybe Shepherd hadn't been discovered or turned, but Flynn suspected someone close to him was a traitor. Did MI5 have a leak?

Mercer had to find Shepherd. The agent could provide answers. Unfortunately, time was running out.

The basement didn't have any windows. Based on the blueprints, there was only one way in and out. So what was behind the door in the far corner of the room?

Mercer listened for sounds coming from within. Once he was convinced it was safe, he opened the door. The room was empty except for rolls of plastic sheeting. No skeletons. No bodies. No torture chamber. And no clue as to what Flynn intended to do with the weapons and bomb materials.

Mercer closed the door and moved back to the staircase. He had orders to report his findings to the powers that be. This was MI5's op. He was just a tool in their arsenal, but he couldn't walk away now. He didn't trust the Security Service to intervene in time to stop a tragedy. After everything he'd been through, he didn't trust anyone outside his immediate team. That wasn't about to change with potentially hundreds or even thousands of lives at stake. Flynn was planning a massive attack. That's the only conclusion Mercer could come to after examining the items on the table.

Owen Shepherd would have answers, but there was no sign of the undercover MI5 agent. So Mercer would improvise. Being alone behind enemy lines meant only one life was at risk. His. And he found that acceptable.

Based on the long-range surveillance photos and blueprints, he knew it was unlikely Shepherd could be anywhere else in the house, assuming, of course, he was still alive. Perhaps Hans and Donovan were having better luck. After all, this was just one of many compounds Colin Flynn used for his operations. The rest were secret locations. Only rumors existed. Shepherd never reported anything official, and MI5 hadn't bothered to share their speculating with the private security team. That's why Mercer had blown up Flynn's car. The bomb was meant to force the faction leader to seek refuge at a secondary location. Shepherd might be there. If not, they would keep looking. It's not like they had any other choice.

But right now, Mercer needed to get upstairs. Flynn must have a computer. His office was on the top floor. Surely, Flynn had plans for the stockpiled weaponry. He might even have bomb schematics or targets listed. Maybe even buyers, if he was dealing in arms. Mercer had to find them. He needed the intel. He had to stop this, whatever this was.

He crept up the steps, halting outside the door. He couldn't hear anything through the thick walls, so again, he felt for vibrations. Nothing. As silently as possible, he eased the door open and slipped into the abyss.

He couldn't make out forms or shapes, so he relied

on his other senses. The smell of cologne and smoke tipped him to a nearby guard. He pressed against the wall. Peering around the corner, he saw the faint red glow from a burning cigarette. The beam from the guard's torch created a perfect cone-shape on the floor, but from the unwavering light and burning ember, the guard had no intention of going anywhere.

Mercer darted across the doorway and didn't stop until he located the staircase. He went up the steps, hearing his own thudding footfalls. Even with felt-soled boots, there was no way to completely diminish the sound on the hardwood steps.

Mercer emerged on the upper level. Nearly positive he was alone, he flipped on the torch and moved to the right. The upper floor branched in two directions. He entered the master suite, just as the lights came on.

Seamlessly, he tucked the torch away. It wasn't time to panic. He had at least ninety seconds until the guards returned. That was plenty of time.

He forced his breathing to slow and glanced around. He had to prioritize.

A desk and office chair sat neatly in the corner. Mercer ran his hand along the desk, finding a slight depression. He pushed down, and the monitor released, lifting out of the desk. He slid out a hidden drawer, revealing a keyboard.

Where was the bloody power button? After five seconds of searching, he turned on the computer. He waited, his gaze flicking to the doorway and back again. Thanks to the jammer, the security system remained inactive, as did the wi-fi and internet. Mercer wouldn't be able to get any outside help to locate the files or transmit them remotely from the computer without disabling the jammer and being caught on the security feed.

No matter. He removed a USB drive from his pocket and plugged it into the machine. He didn't have time to find the proper intel, so he'd copy all of it or as much as he could get in the next forty-five seconds.

While the USB blinked orange, he studied the room. A map of Ireland was pinned to the wall. He examined the stray markings. As far as he could tell, they didn't mean anything.

The sound of voices from below alerted him that the guards were on their way back, so he checked the rest of the room. There had to be another way out. He just couldn't find one that didn't involve breaking a window and jumping. He should have prepared for more contingencies.

Mercer unplugged the USB, hoping the files didn't corrupt in his haste. He set the computer to shut down and crouched behind the desk. Worst case scenario, he'd take out Flynn's guards. If he had to shoot one, he might as well shoot them all. At least then, he'd have the time to complete his search, but it would be best to avoid casualties for now. If Flynn knew someone was here, he might move up the timetable on his strike or he'd hurry to sell off the weapons. Without knowing the plan or Shepherd's whereabouts, it wasn't a risk worth taking.

Bloody hell, Mercer thought, tucking the gun away. Any deaths would have to look accidental or the result of a duplicitous traitor. And since Flynn didn't want his men going in the basement, he was already suspicious. Filing that thought away, Mercer focused on his current issue–finding an escape route.

The voices quieted. One of the men entered the master suite. Mercer held his breath. The guard glanced inside, muttering to himself.

Mercer waited, hoping the guard would resume his

normal patrol. Instead, the man strode into the room. He moved past Mercer, mumbling curses.

Is he bloody daft? Mercer didn't dare move. The guard had no reason to suspect the compound had been breached. Mercer made sure to make it look like a wire had come loose when he sabotaged the power. So why was the man in here? What was he looking for?

Mercer didn't wait to see what the man planned to do. As soon as the guard was far enough from the desk, Mercer slid around the side and darted out the door as silently as possible. The blackout gear would stick out like a sore thumb now that the interior lights were active again.

Mercer moved to the stairs, freezing in place when he spotted another guard near the bottom. He continued across the upper level, moving to the left of the staircase. He had to get out. Two guards were patrolling this floor, and from the sounds of it, a third was on his way.

The roof. There had to be access. How else would Flynn be able to position a sharpshooter up there? It'd be impractical to make a man climb a ladder up and down from the exterior. Plus, this compound was practically a miniature castle. Ireland was famous for its castles, and the compound's architecture mimicked the design perfectly. There had to be an interior staircase that led to the roof, but none of the research indicated one.

Mercer heard faint whistling and smelled rain. He followed the sound, hoping it was the wind and not another of Flynn's guards. At the end of the corridor, he entered a room with a balcony. The French doors rattled against the breeze. A puddle had formed on the floor. Someone had recently gone through the door.

"Hey," a voice bellowed from behind.

Mercer didn't turn. Instead, he moved at a steady pace. Luckily, he made it outside before the interior lights turned on. In the dark, the guard behind him didn't have enough time to determine what he was seeing, but he knew someone had stepped onto the balcony, and he had every intention of finding out why.

FOUR

Finding a ladder against the wall, Mercer grabbed a rung and swung his legs over the railing. As he started to climb, the balcony doors opened beneath him. He hauled himself onto the roof's small rectangular platform.

A guard stood on the roof, facing away from Mercer as he watched over the property. Mercer realized he was caught. With one guard on the roof and one on the balcony below, there was no escape.

"Brody," the voice below hollered, "the fuck you doing?"

"Eh?" Brody turned and snickered. "Really, mate, are you trying to scare me?"

Mercer didn't move, and when the voice below sounded again, Brody realized his mistake. The guard lunged forward. He was built like a rugby player and barreled into Mercer with the force of a bullet train.

Mercer's back collided with the waist-high wall. Brody pinned him to the brick and pummeled Mercer with jabs. Mercer forced the guard off him with an unexpected uppercut that knocked Brody back only centimeters.

Not giving the guard time to alert his colleagues, Mercer slid forward, his right hip sinking into the indention at Brody's pelvis. Brody reacted by trying to lock Mercer in a chokehold, but the former SAS operative expected it. Bracing one hand on Brody's elbow and the other around his shoulder, Mercer threw himself forward, pushing his hips back and sending the guard sailing over the ledge.

A sick, metallic thunk echoed as the guard below let out a surprised gasp. Mercer crouched beneath the waist-high ledge, afraid of being spotted and unsure if more guards were on the way. A string of curses and the static of a radio sounded beneath him, but the radio didn't work on account of the jammer.

"Brody. Shit." The French doors opened and shut with a clang.

Move. Get out now. Mercer crawled to the other side of the roof and peered down. Everyone was gathering at the front to help their fallen comrade. Mercer climbed onto the ledge. Without a ladder, a jump from this height would result in a broken leg at the very least.

He eyed the tree, a large oak with thick branches that sat a few meters away. In the dark, he couldn't make out much more than the general shape. Throwing caution to the wind, he sprung from his perch, arms outstretched, hands blindly searching for purchase. He felt the scratch of tree limbs against his gloves and mask and the impact of a branch against his chest. He tried to grab on, but the limb wasn't strong enough to support his weight. With a thunderous crack, it broke, and Mercer toppled the rest of the way to the ground. The impact knocked the wind from his lungs, and he gasped, desperate for air.

Unable to catch his breath, he silently choked in the growing storm. The side door opened, and two men raced out. They went around the front, oblivious to his presence. Mercer heard only a few of their words. "Tosser tumbled off the roof. Broke his ruddy neck on the rail."

Mercer climbed to his feet, turned, and ran for the fence. By the time he went up and over, black bubbles clouded his vision. He ran as fast and as far as he could. On the brink of collapse, he ripped the mask off his face, fell to the ground, turned on his side, and gasped. His lungs weren't prepared for a hit like that.

As soon as he was able to breathe again, he picked himself up off the ground and returned to his car. Turning off the jammer, he drove to Palace Barracks. His team would rendezvous at the Security Service. They had a lot to discuss.

*　　*　　*

"Jules?" Bastian scrutinized the commander's appearance and hunched form. "You all right?"

Mercer ignored the worried look. "Hans?"

Bastian swiveled his chair around to face the computer monitor. The Security Service provided him an office to use for the duration of the mission. Normally, the team hid away in a safe house, but this wasn't their op. They were handed mission parameters and a plan in an eerily similar fashion to their old military days. MI5 wanted complete oversight, and at the present, the former SAS were complying. "He sent coordinates for Flynn's current location. He's scouting it now. So far, no sign of Shepherd."

Dropping onto the couch, Mercer put his arms over his head and rested the backs of his hands on his forehead. A strange feeling of dread, possibly guilt, had wormed its way through him. He found the sensation rather disagreeable. Hans shouldn't be in the field alone. He wasn't ready. He was still recovering. But Bastian had to stay behind to coordinate, and Donovan remained in London to track Lara's movements. They didn't have much of a choice.

"How did it go? Did you find anything?" Bas asked.

"Flynn's bodyguard, Brody, tell me about him."

Bastian clicked a few keys. "Brody Devlin hooked up with Flynn six years ago, suspected of bombing a church, resulting in four fatalities." Bastian scanned further down. "He's not a good guy. Best to watch yourself around him." Bastian glanced in Mercer's direction. "I take it from your question it might be too late for that warning."

"Flynn had him positioned on the roof."

Bastian kicked off the floor, rolling his chair beside the couch. "You're covered in twigs." He plucked one off Mercer's chest. "And you're drenched. You're getting my couch cushions soppy."

Mercer brushed Bas's hand away, sitting up when a cough rattled through his chest.

"You need to change out of those wet clothes before you catch your death."

"You sound like my mum," Mercer retorted.

"Piss off. I'm not picking up the slack when you're stuck in bed with pneumonia."

"Is Partridge in?" Mercer coughed. When he pulled his hand away, he saw specks of blood. Wiping it on his trousers, he climbed off the couch. "I need to speak to him."

"He should be here soon."

"Colin Flynn is stockpiling weapons." Mercer tossed the USB to Bastian, along with the crumpled list. "See if there's any mention of it on there. And use your computer. We don't need extra eyes monitoring our progress."

Bastian gave Mercer a quizzical look but knew better than to question him. Removing his laptop from a bag at his feet, he turned it on and plugged in the drive. "Did you copy Flynn's whole hard drive?"

"As much as I could get. I'm going to get cleaned up. Let me know the moment Hans returns. Hopefully, he'll arrive before Partridge."

"I wouldn't count on it. And for the record, I'm not your secretary."

Mercer went down the corridor to the showers. Peeling off his wet clothing, he examined the fresh bruises among the still healing scars. It'd be a long road to recovery. He coughed again, an all too familiar stabbing in his lungs. It had only been a few weeks since the surgery. Clearly, this was a side effect from the pummeling he'd taken at Brody's hand and the impact from his less than agile drop from the roof.

It was of no concern. He'd be fine. He had to be field ready. Lives depended on him. His team depended on him. Honestly, if it hadn't been for them, he'd still be locked in his bedroom or dead on his kitchen floor, a fate he wouldn't have minded.

At one time, Mercer had a mission, an honorable one. But that was before his world came crashing down. When his wife was murdered, he lost everything. It took years, but he finally exacted revenge, but it wasn't enough. Ending the killer's life didn't take away his pain. Instead, it left him hollow and missing the lower portion of his left lung.

The hot water eased his aching body but did little for his mind. Stupidly, he thought once he found Michelle's killer and avenged her death, he'd find peace, but he didn't. Instead of living with the constant nightmares of her last few moments, he was now haunted by memories of the past, namely her insistence that he make the world safe. She was the reason he was here. He couldn't save her, but he had to try to save others. He and his team were K&R specialists for a reason. And right now, their raison d'être was to locate a missing agent and stop a terrorist plot.

"Jules?" Bastian banged against the door. "Mr. Partridge is waiting."

Mercer turned off the water and grabbed a towel. After dressing, he stepped out of the bathroom. "Did you find anything on the drive?"

"I'm still working on cracking the decryption. The majority of the files are password protected. Flynn didn't want anyone to see his plans."

"Keep me apprised. The intel goes through me first."

"What's going on?"

Mercer shook his head. He had no basis for his paranoid thoughts, but something told him not to trust the Security Service. "You'll find out at the briefing." He coughed again, pressing the towel against his mouth.

Bastian spotted the telltale red on the white cotton and quirked an eyebrow. "How long's that been going on?"

"It's fine."

"The bloody hell it is. Your lung was resected a month ago. It shouldn't be doing that."

"It just started. It'll be fine." Ignoring Bastian's inevitable protest, Mercer continued on his path to Liam Partridge's office. It was time the Security Service put their cards on the table concerning Agent Owen Shepherd's disappearance and the real objective of his undercover assignment.

FIVE

"We lost contact."

"When?" Mercer asked.

Liam Partridge slid the folder across the desk. "Agent Shepherd missed his last two check-ins. He's been dark for nearly a month."

"We were told ten days."

"That was four days ago. It's not uncommon for Shepherd to miss a check-in, so the first time it happened, we thought it was nothing. Flynn runs a tight ship. Sometimes, it's hard for Owen to get away. But when he missed the second check-in and didn't leave anything at any of the dead drops, we knew something was wrong."

"Has Flynn's behavior been unusual?" Bastian asked.

"Flynn's been exhibiting signs of paranoia. He's taking extra precautions when he travels. He's doubled his number of bodyguards."

"You should have told us that before I ventured into his house," Mercer said. "That might have been useful."

"I take it you met additional resistance. Were there any problems you couldn't handle?"

Mercer's cold hatred spoke volumes.

Bastian interceded. "Has Flynn ever been this cautious before?"

"Occasionally, but it's not typical behavior. Flynn's usually more relaxed. Something has him on edge. From the chatter we've heard and things Shepherd alluded to, we think the faction is planning something big. Perhaps that's the reason for Flynn's odd behavior."

Mercer studied the classified folder. "Any idea what it might be?"

"Probably an attack of some sort."

"You don't seem particularly worried." Mercer put the folder down. "Shouldn't you be?"

"We review credible threats every day and stop ninety-nine percent of them. There's no reason I should worry."

"You're an arse."

"What Julian means to say is you're wrong." Bastian hoped a bit of diplomacy would ease the tension. "Your intel suggests an imminent threat, and one of your people has gone missing. Those factors add up to trouble, mate."

"That's why we hired you," Partridge said.

"Why did you immediately assume Shepherd was compromised?" Mercer asked.

"He vanished. We haven't discovered his body or received any type of demand or threat. We don't know what else to think." Partridge looked uneasy. "During our last communication, Shepherd was agitated, erratic. He was upset. I don't know what caused it, but he was acting like Flynn."

"We'll need additional details regarding Shepherd's

mission parameters. Your case notes, observations, the works," Mercer said. Liam Partridge was the operation runner and Shepherd's handler. If anyone knew what was going on, it'd be him.

Partridge looked even more uncomfortable. "You have the reports. You've already read them. Any other details are classified. You'll need clearance."

"We have it. And if we don't, you better make sure we get it."

"I'll make sure you have everything you need."

"Tell us about Shepherd's family," Bastian said. "Has he tried to make contact with anyone outside the Security Service? His sister, Lara, is his emergency contact. Surely, you must know where she is."

"I don't know much about his sister. Owen never spoke of her to me. Everything I have is centered around his ex-wife, Grace, and their son, Harry. They were his life. He had photos of them in his office. I never imagined they'd get divorced, but shit happens in this life."

"When's the last time they spoke?" Mercer asked, sensing a pattern. "Was it before he went undercover?"

"They split several months before that. Owen never told me exactly what happened, but he said it was the strain of the job. Maybe she cheated or grew tired of the long hours and extended assignments. The last time they spoke was nearly a year ago."

"Anyone else in his life?" Bastian asked.

"Like a girlfriend?" Partridge asked.

"Like anyone," Mercer said.

"Owen's parents are dead. According to our records, Lara's all he has left. When he disappeared, we tried to locate her. But she wasn't at the address we have on file. We pinged her phone, but it's off. Our intel might be outdated."

"Or she disappeared too. She should have been moved into protective custody the moment you lost contact with Shepherd. What about his wife and son? Have you taken measures to keep them safe? Or have they vanished as well?"

"Grace and Harry are being guarded. No one can get to them."

"Too bad you can't say the same thing about Owen's sister," Mercer quipped.

"I'm not a fortune teller. I can't see the future, Mr. Mercer. By the time we realized something peculiar was afoot, Lara was already gone. She might have went missing before Owen did, but we have no way of knowing. As I said, it's possible she's perfectly fine and we have an old address and phone number on file."

Bastian and Mercer exchanged a look. "We'll need your files and any details you have on Shepherd's family and his undercover identity," Bastian insisted. "Actually, all of his known aliases."

"I don't see how that's relevant," Partridge said.

"It doesn't matter." Mercer eyed him. "If you expect us to locate your missing agent, you'll give us what we want. He distanced himself from his wife for a reason."

"Ex-wife," Partridge corrected.

"I don't bloody care about labels. They have a child. Shepherd will take measures to protect the boy."

"Of course." Partridge pressed the intercom button and requested the additional details be brought to his office. "If Shepherd's been turned, I expect you'll take care of it."

Bastian's expression soured. "We don't do that."

"Need I remind you of the terms of our arrangement, Mr. Mercer?" Partridge asked.

"You need not." Mercer stifled another cough and

rubbed his chest. The burning sensation was getting worse. "I'll do whatever is necessary."

"Excellent. So what did you find in Flynn's compound? It must have been something big for you to request Shepherd's reports and files."

Mercer strode to the window and stared out. Partridge put him on edge. Maybe it was the operation runner's cavalier attitude toward a missing agent or his seeming indifference to Flynn's capabilities. But something told Mercer he needed to get his team out of this building and away from Partridge as soon as possible. "We should have had every bit of intel from the beginning. Giving us nothing but mission parameters will not result in anything except more deaths. Should anything happen to my team, I will hold you responsible."

"What did you find?" Partridge smiled, a sick, amused look that might have been a muscle tic. "You wouldn't be making thinly veiled threats if you weren't afraid of what you found."

"There's nothing thinly veiled about it."

"Jules," Bastian whispered, his voice a warning, "what happened inside?"

"Brody Devlin's dead. He fell off the roof and broke his neck. At least another three men were patrolling the interior. I didn't get a look at them."

"I'll have Devlin removed from the watchlist." Partridge made a note. "I take it Flynn will know someone was inside."

"Perhaps, but Flynn already knows someone's on to him. I suspect he knew that before you even called us. But if he didn't, he knows now. We turned his car into a fireball. He knows someone's out to get him, and from what I've seen, he's leery of his own people."

"What makes you say that?"

"He doesn't want anyone in the basement, not even

his personal guards." Mercer studied Partridge, but he couldn't get a read on the man. "Was Shepherd sowing seeds of distrust between the faction leader and his followers, or is something else brewing?"

"You'll have to check the official reports. I can't recall. Does Flynn have any reason to think his compound was breached tonight?"

"We're in the clear. Brody's death was an accident. It looks like he took a tumble."

Again, the sick grin. "Sure, he did."

"What do you know about Colin Flynn? Why did you send Shepherd to infiltrate the faction?" Bastian asked.

"Flynn's an arms dealer by trade. He started making noise years ago. He and his people bombed a few churches. We attributed over a dozen deaths to his faction. That's why we sent Shepherd in to keep tabs on Flynn. Since he went under, there's only been one bombing. The device detonated prematurely and killed Flynn's wife and two small children. Since then, he's been quiet."

"We'll need Shepherd's report on that incident," Mercer said.

"I'll get you the files we have." Partridge picked up the phone again.

While he spoke, Mercer turned and rested his palms on the desk. The hint of gold foil caught his eye, and he slid the papers around in the tray to reveal a shiny, expensive piece of stationery in Partridge's inbox.

"You said Flynn might be planning an attack. Any idea what his target might be?" Mercer asked when Partridge put the phone down.

"Shepherd said Flynn was planning an attack. He didn't have time to give us details. He said he would tell me more during his next check-in, but we lost contact. We haven't spoken since. It could be anywhere. Or anything."

Mercer and his team didn't have the resources to take out an entire faction, particularly one as well-armed as Flynn's. Ignoring his instincts, Mercer said, "Flynn is stockpiling munitions. Guns, grenades, bombs. Whatever he's planning has the potential to be massive."

"How do you know this?"

"The crates are in his basement."

Partridge stared in horror. "Since Flynn's exhibiting signs of paranoia, a body on the property might force him to move the materials or rush the timetable for his strike. We need surveillance teams to sit on his compound."

Mercer dropped into a chair beside Bastian, flicking his gaze to the tray. "You realize a team is already monitoring Flynn's movements."

"What team?" Partridge asked.

"My team."

Partridge scoffed and relayed his request up the command chain. When he hung up, he looked at Mercer and Bastian, as if confused why the two men remained in front of his desk. "Well?"

Mercer bristled but forced his emotions to remain in check. "Why Flynn?"

"What?" Partridge didn't comprehend the depth of the question. "He's a terrorist."

"Then why haven't you done anything to stop him?"

"We need evidence. Proof. It's Northern Ireland. There are dozens more out there just like him. You've seen what happens, the kinds of things they can achieve. You know shutting down one cell won't stop the problem. That's why we placed Shepherd on the inside. Even if we shut down Flynn, his rival, Mathias Murphy, would step up and take over. It'd be trading one problem for another."

A knock sounded at the door, and an assistant handed the files to Partridge. The operation runner flipped through the stamped folders before holding them out to Mercer, who ignored the gesture. Bastian took them, finding several details blacked out.

"What about dead drops?" Bastian asked. "You said Shepherd hasn't tried to make contact. Do you have anyone monitoring them, just in case?"

Partridge rubbed a hand down his face. "Yes, but there's been no communication."

Mercer stared at Partridge. "You sent me into the lion's den. Did you honestly believe Shepherd was being held at Flynn's compound?"

"That was our best guess. Shepherd's told us about meetings, about men disappearing into the house, screams coming from locked rooms, and Flynn returning with bloodied knuckles. It made sense, particularly since we don't have eyes inside, and the last time surveillance spotted Shepherd was when he was entering Flynn's compound."

"Did Shepherd ever give you names or descriptions of these men who Flynn allegedly tortured?"

"No, but a few of them were Flynn's own guys. Colin doesn't put up with liars or thieves. He'll make an example out of anyone who crosses him." Partridge leaned forward, pointing at a folder, and Bastian handed it to him. "These are hospital reports. These two men supposedly had an accident in the men's room, but according to our intel, Flynn did this."

Mercer read the reports. Unless the men were hit by a car that crashed through the wall of the men's room, this was no accident. He put the folder down. "Is Shepherd a coward?"

"How dare you insult my friend and a respected member of this agency."

"So what is it then? You believe Shepherd woke up one day and decided to turn his back on everything he ever knew?"

"What else could it be? We haven't found a body. Owen hasn't made contact. By now, wouldn't we have heard something?"

"Not necessarily," Bastian said. "The dossier you gave us on Flynn, is that everything you have?"

"Yes."

"Why do you think Shepherd turned?" Mercer asked again. "Does it have to do with his wife? Fear for his own safety? Or is Colin Flynn that charismatic?"

"Being surrounded by fanatics spouting dogma might have made him change allegiances. It happens. Sometimes undercover operatives can't separate themselves from their covers. They become friendly with the enemy. Shit happens. The only support they have undercover comes from the inside. They band together. It's not that dissimilar from Stockholm Syndrome."

"But you said Shepherd was upset the last time you spoke. He was acting erratically," Bastian pried. "What exactly did he say or do?"

"Shepherd is normally calm, soft-spoken, not easily excitable. But the last time we spoke, he was jittery, frantic. He said something happened to Flynn. That Flynn was going to retaliate." Partridge's eyes darted back and forth. "The transcripts should be in that folder. You can read his exact words for yourself."

"But you don't know what happened or who Flynn intended to target?" Mercer asked. The story was making less and less sense.

"No."

Mercer grabbed the transcript and skimmed it. "This can't be all he said."

"That's it." Partridge stood. "Now, if there's nothing else, gentlemen, I have to get a team briefed and ready to monitor Flynn and his known hangouts."

Mercer opened his mouth to voice another accusation, but Bastian gave him a sharp look.

"Let us know when they are ready to move out so I can recall my team," Mercer said.

Partridge shook Mercer's hand. "I expect you'll find Shepherd swiftly. With an attack imminent, we'll need whatever intel he can provide."

Mercer gave a tight nod and strode out of the room. Partridge was a paper pusher. Either he screwed up and was covering his own arse, or he was incompetent. Still, Mercer found it hard to believe that two years of undercover work resulted in such thin files. What was Shepherd really doing on the inside? Could he be a double-agent? Or did Partridge bury the real reports and transcripts?

SIX

"I want Hans out of there now."

"Jules, we still have a mission," Bastian reminded him.

Mercer sunk onto the couch. The dull ache in his chest had turned into a constant burning. He coughed again, feeling as though he were choking. After clearing his airway, he took a few deep breaths, and the pain eased. Hopefully, that had been the worst of it. "Have you spoken to your contacts at Thames House?"

"Not since they handed us this assignment."

"That needs to change. We'll take the first ferry back." Mercer glanced out the window, watching the slow rise of the sun. The storm had stopped almost an hour ago. As the sun's rays met the wet pavement, every flat surface cast a blinding orange reflection. "I'm recalling Hans. I don't want him getting seen. He'd be outgunned in a firefight. You and I both know his shoulder can't handle the recoil of the long guns. If something were to happen..." Mercer stopped, rephrasing the thought. "I can't let anything else happen to him. To any of you."

"We do this for a living," Bas reminded him.

Mercer picked up the radio. His own had been damaged in the storm or when he took that tumble from the tree. "Pull back. We'll meet at the ferry."

"Already on my way," Hans replied.

Hans started to offer additional details, but Mercer interjected, "Wait until we have a secure line."

"Aye, commander."

"What do you think is going on?" Bastian fingered the crumpled note from Flynn's compound. "Odd, isn't it?"

Mercer gave Bastian a sideways glance but didn't offer any suggestions or explanations. "We have much to discuss." He jerked his chin at the laptop. "Have we made any progress?"

"Still working on it. Flynn's serious about his security. This will take a while."

"Pack up. It can finish elsewhere."

After collecting the files and a few belongings, Mercer stepped into the outer office. Bastian grabbed his computer bag and other peripherals and joined the commander. While the two waited for the lift, Bastian chatted with the secretary. Mercer studied the plaques and framed photos on the wall. Aside from a few commendations for exemplary service, the items were of little interest. Nothing indicated Owen Shepherd had been anything other than a dedicated professional, and dedicated professionals didn't allow their allegiances to flip-flop. There only two reasons Shepherd would change sides. He was threatened or blackmailed. And since he remained missing, possibly presumed dead, Mercer's blackmail theory didn't hold much water.

The elevator dinged, and Mercer stepped into the

car. Bastian bid the woman goodbye and joined him inside. Once out of the building and safely past the gate, they checked for a tail and switched cars. Bastian swept everything for surveillance devices, finding their belongings and the vehicle clean. Then they went to meet Hans at the ferry.

"Is the op over?" Hans asked, settling onto the bench beside Mercer. "Did you find our missing agent?"

"Not yet. We're taking a detour." Out of habit, Mercer turned to look for their missing fourth member, unaccustomed to Donovan not being with them.

"Have you heard from Donovan?" Bastian asked.

Mercer shook his head, as did Hans.

"Hopefully, he's having better luck than we are." Bastian took a seat across from them, his back to the water.

"How did it go?" Mercer asked Hans.

"Flynn holed up in an abandoned boathouse for most of the night. At daybreak, he headed for a flat. A woman answered the door. She seemed friendly. I'd guess that's his mistress. Probably wanted to make sure she was safe after we blew up his ride."

"At least we know of two more locations Flynn uses. There might be something there worth investigating," Bastian mused.

"I scouted the perimeter but didn't get a chance to check inside. It's hard to observe and track at the same time, but I got photographs of the buildings and some shots of several faction members."

Mercer reached for the digital camera and scanned the photos. "Good work. Did you notice any bombs or weapons?"

"None." Hans rubbed his shoulder. "No sign of Shepherd either. But it's hard to see much from the outside. Anything could be in there. Or anyone."

"We'll go back and check," Mercer decided.

Bastian moved away from the railing and leaned closer to his comrades, keeping one eye peeled for possible interlopers. "How's the shoulder, Hans?"

"Wet. Sore." Hans stretched. "Otherwise fine. You know I would never compromise any of our lives. I can handle this. I'm in tip-top shape."

"Probably about as fine as Jules."

"We have bigger problems." Mercer uncrumpled the list and handed it to Hans. "That came from Flynn's compound. I spotted the same stationery on Partridge's desk. Did you see anything like it at the pub or Flynn's other locations?"

Hans shook his head.

"I noticed that too," Bastian said. "But it was in Partridge's inbox. We don't know where it originated. I don't believe it was his. I believe someone left it or had interoffice mail deliver it to him."

"Until we know how it arrived on his desk, we can't speak freely in front of him. He can't be trusted." Mercer stared into the horizon. "No one at the Security Service can."

"Jules," Bastian grumbled, "you're being paranoid."

"Is he?" Hans asked. "A terrorist shouldn't use the same letterhead as MI5."

"Precisely," Mercer agreed. "Partridge isn't telling us everything. Even the newest files are redacted. That's why we're heading home. Our friends at Thames House might have a different story to share."

"We need to pick up Donovan. That'll make it easier to follow and surveil." Hans cocked a confused eyebrow. "Unless you're thinking about throwing in the towel."

"No," Mercer said. "But I do have a new assignment for you. When we arrive in Liverpool, Bastian and I will head to Thames House. Our contacts there should be able to shed light on these redacted files and give us additional details on Agent Shepherd and Mr. Partridge. I need you to assist Donovan. It's been four days. If he doesn't have a lead on Lara Shepherd by now, tell him to come home."

"Okay."

Mercer studied the other man, seeing the slightest indication that Hans favored his left side. "Once that's done, I'll need you to remain at home base. Bas already started decrypting Flynn's hard drive, but it'll take time. Get started on that. We need every drop of intel you can find on Grace Shepherd and Harry, Owen's ex-wife and son. Aside from Lara, they are his weak points. If Flynn discovered Shepherd was a traitor, the faction might go after his family. They might have already done something to Lara. It would explain her disappearance. Shepherd would have known his family would be leveraged against him if his true identity was discovered. It might have been the reason for the estrangement and divorce. I'm wagering he had contingencies in place. Find out what they are."

"You think the divorce is a ruse?" Bas asked. "Isn't that a tad extreme?"

"Perhaps."

"Isn't the Security Service guarding his family? That's SOP in these types of situations," Hans said. "Shouldn't that be enough of a contingency?"

"You mean like how they kept an eye on Lara?" Mercer asked.

"I shouldn't be stuck at home base. I should be out tracking," Hans protested.

"In case you haven't been paying attention," Bas said, "Jules is off on another of his paranoid tangents." But despite the dig, Mercer saw the same fears reflected in Bastian's eyes. They were just downplaying the possibility of an internal breach, one that had existed for quite some time, to sideline Hans without making it obvious.

"What about Flynn and whatever he's planning?" Hans asked. "We aren't leaving that up to MI5. No one with posh stationery like this should be taken seriously when it comes to security matters."

"We'll see how it goes at Thames House before making a decision." Mercer leaned back and closed his eyes. "We have two hours until we arrive at the port in Liverpool, and with traffic, probably a four hour drive back to London after that. I suggest we rest while we can."

*   *   *

Thames House held the London branch of the Security Service. Mercer looked out the window. It was overcast, making the glass reflective. Without turning away from the window, he watched someone in a suit enter the outer office with a file box containing intel on Flynn's faction and pertinent mission logs. He handed the items to the secretary, nodded a greeting to Bastian, and disappeared out the door.

"Is that it?" Mercer asked.

"Yes, sir," the secretary said. Bastian signed the form and took the box, frowning as he skimmed the tabs. "Is there anything else I can do for you, Mr. Clarke?"

"No, love, I appreciate this."

Without another word, he and Mercer left the MI5 offices. Stepping outside, the two scanned the area for potential danger. As they headed down the street in the direction of their waiting vehicle, Bastian leafed through the classified files.

"Not here," Mercer said.

Bastian shut the lid and tucked the box against his side, resting his hand over the top. "Do you think Hans made it back to home base yet?"

"Let's hope so. I don't want him running around half-cocked with Donovan."

"Donovan won't allow it. He's just as protective as you are."

"I suppose."

"Any reason we're using your home as home base?" Bastian asked. "We never discussed assignments at your house until now."

Mercer's cheek twitched. Things used to be different. Perhaps one day they would be again. But for now, it was the only place he wanted to be. He could feel Michelle's presence there, and even though it made his heart ache, he needed to feel the pain. It was all he had left of her, and he didn't want to be without it. "We'll be leaving soon enough, so don't get used to it."

The two men climbed into the car, taking a different route to their destination. Even though the last threat they faced had been permanently removed, they still acted as if they were behind enemy lines. It was best not to allow anyone to get the drop on them, particularly after their last two bouts. The team had barely recovered, and now, they were off again. It was the life of a security specialist, but this wasn't their typical mission. This was something much worse.

"You saw the letterhead," Mercer said.

"Aye." Bastian scrounged around in the glove box for a bag of pretzel sticks. Taking one out, he bit down, practically sighing in relief.

"What do you make of it?"

"Jules, we don't know enough yet. Let me delve

into the rest of the files before I give you an opinion. For all we know, it's the hottest item sold in every shop in Belfast. It might mean nothing."

"You can't seriously believe that."

Bastian shrugged.

"Don't just look into the files. We need intel on every agent involved in Shepherd's op. Any name that pops up in regards to Colin Flynn needs to be examined. Someone's dirty."

"It could be Shepherd." Bastian saw the protest on Mercer's face. "Hear me out. He lost his wife. He doesn't see his son. We have no idea if he speaks to his sister, but Partridge didn't think they were close. He might not have anything left. Maybe he lost it all to the job. And since Flynn suffered the devastating loss of his own family not too long ago, Shepherd might have commiserated with Flynn. It could have turned into more than that."

"Losing family doesn't turn you into a terrorist. From what I read, Flynn's responsible for killing his own wife and children. The arrogant prick brought the explosive into his home. He built it there, and it detonated. He killed them, just like he's killed dozens of others." Mercer rubbed the grit from the corners of his eyes. "Shepherd wouldn't comfort a man like that."

"You're projecting."

"Piss off. Flynn knows the faction is compromised, and after last night, he'll have more questions than ever. We need to take advantage of this. We need to convince him he's being hunted."

"How exactly?"

"It depends on what Donovan found and what you can pull from those files, but an introduction might be in order. Maybe I can offer Colin Flynn something he desperately needs."

"I don't like the sound of that."

Truthfully, neither did Mercer. But without Owen Shepherd's intel, the only way to find out where and when Flynn planned to strike would be to get the intel directly from the source. Someone had to infiltrate the faction, and Mercer didn't trust anyone at MI5.

"What are we telling Hans?" Bastian asked.

"That also depends."

"On what?"

"How desperately we need a fourth man. Do you think he could shoot left-handed?"

"You could ask, but in a pinch, I doubt he'd risk it. He'd shoot right-handed, and the recoil might do more damage. He needs to be careful. The first time he recovered, he stood a better chance. Now, after what happened," Bastian shoved another pretzel stick into his mouth, "he might only get forty percent function out of that arm."

Mercer clenched the steering wheel harder. "It's my fault. I won't let any harm befall him again. He's staying behind and compiling our intel. We'll figure something else out."

"Jules," Bastian began, but one stony look from the commander silenced him. "He won't be happy about it."

"I don't care if he's happy. Someone needs to work behind the scenes, and I need you in the field. We won't give him a choice." Mercer parked the car and surveyed the area. Deciding it was secure, he took the box and headed for the front door.

When they entered, Hans was already hard at work behind the computer. "You took your bleeding time getting here. Let me show you what we've found."

SEVEN

"Pressure cooker bombs." Mercer taped the intel to the vinyl sheet.

"Not just schematics, but orders. Flynn bought in bulk. According to these records, he has enough equipment to build twelve devices," Hans said.

Recalling the basement, Mercer said, "I only saw three. They might not have arrived yet."

"Or he already moved them to their intended locations," Bas said.

"Or he sold them," Hans suggested. "He might be outfitting the other factions."

Bastian propped his computer next to Hans' and wired the two machines together. "I'll see what I can pull up from his stored internet files. This would have been easier if you hadn't deactivated the internet, Jules."

"I couldn't bypass the security system without doing that. And finding Shepherd was the objective, not thwarting a terrorist plot."

"Looks like we have a new objective." Bastian stopped mid-keystroke. "We haven't worked a recovery like this since we left Her Majesty's service. If you want to pass, it's not too late to tell MI5 to bugger off."

"You probably should but not on my account." Mercer studied the intel taped to the wall. "I gave my word. I will see this through."

"Jules, we aren't cleaners. We do not perform wet work. And it seems that's all Partridge is interested in."

"Makes him look guilty, eh? I wonder what he's hiding. Whatever it is, Owen Shepherd must know about it, and Partridge doesn't want it coming to light." Hans looked at Mercer. "Is that what you're thinking, commander?"

"Not exactly. Do you think Shepherd's been turned?" It was something Mercer hadn't seriously considered, instead choosing to believe MI5 housed a sinister villain who sold out good agents and authorized needless killings.

Bastian bit his lip. "It's too soon to say. I'm still compiling the dossier, but the Security Service has special teams to handle this sort of thing. MI5 has no reason to involve us, lest they be nothing more than vindictive tossers. I think they want to remind us of our place, Jules. Two birds, one stone."

"Shitheads," Hans mumbled.

"I'll cooperate until it's no longer in my best interest, but you need not concern yourselves with this." Mercer plucked a surveillance photo off the wall. "MI5 wants me. I knew their price for wiping my record clean, so I can't very well complain when they call in their chits. But the two of you can walk away. Donovan too. We're dealing with the bloody IRA. You know how vindictive the Irish are. And Flynn's a proven sadist. You shouldn't risk your lives needlessly."

Bastian considered Donovan's absence and glanced at Hans. "Jules is right. You have your mum to think about."

"Pish."

"And your lady friends."

Hans grinned. "This is what we do, and the birds love a good story. This ought to get me laid throughout Ireland. Plus, Donovan would tell you to piss off. We do this together or not at all. And frankly, mate, not at all isn't a bloody option right now. Mass casualties aren't something I can have on my conscience."

"Agreed," Bastian said. "Face it, Jules, we're like the bloody Musketeers. All for one."

"Bad example, Bas. One of them was a traitorous bastard," Hans said.

"He must have worked for MI5," Mercer quipped.

"Catching up on the classics?" Bas asked.

Hans snorted, a mischievous grin on his face. "While I was in the hospital, one bird, in particular, liked to read to me, at least until we found a better use for her time."

Mercer returned the photo to its place on the wall. "When was Shepherd last sighted?"

"A member of the support team spotted him three weeks ago. He was with Flynn. He didn't try to make contact." Hans' index finger scrolled across the mission report. "If Flynn made him then, Shepherd's probably been cut to bits, and Flynn's disposed of the pieces."

Mercer nodded, more to himself than the team. "Any word from Donovan? We need to find out what happened to Lara. I'd prefer a briefing in person."

"He's on his way back," Hans said. "He hasn't

found her, but he might have a lead."

Bastian clicked a few keys. "I have a spider. Several actually. I set one to search for any transactions on her credit accounts and metro card, but there've been no hits. I'll set another to monitor social media in case she pops up in the background of anyone's photos. You know how much people love posting stupid shit on the internet. I might work miracles, but this is going to take a lot of time and computing power."

"We don't have the time, but we're out of options. Like Hans said, we have to stop Flynn from enacting whatever plan he has in place. We can't allow him to commit mass casualties, and we need to locate Shepherd." Mercer turned to Hans. "I need you to coordinate everything from here. You'll be our eyes and ears. We need you on overwatch, soldier." He heard faint scratching at the kitchen door. "And someone has to take care of Cynthia until she goes home."

"You want me to dog sit?" Hans asked.

"No, but I expect you to multitask. And I'm in no mood for an argument."

"Yes, sir."

Bastian flipped through the dossier. "MI5 put Grace Shepherd and Harry into protective custody. I'll get their location and pass it on to Donovan as soon as he returns."

"I can do it," Hans said.

"Agreed." Mercer checked the time and dropped into a chair. It wasn't common for him to act so blasé in the middle of a mission, but the intel was off. He could feel it. He just couldn't put his finger on what was wrong with it.

"Are you sure you're up for this, Jules?" Bastian asked. "Maybe you should have a medical consult."

"I'm fine. I just need a minute to think."

"Why does he need a consult?" Hans asked.

"This morning, he was coughing up blood."

"Shit."

"I'm fine." Mercer stood. "I just need a few minutes of peace and quiet to think. We're missing something." He went into the bedroom and removed his wedding ring, pressed it against his lips, and tucked it into the trinket box on the dresser. His gaze fell on one of his wedding photos, and he sighed. The thought of leaving triggered another stabbing pain in his chest.

He couldn't tell what was physical and what was emotional. It didn't matter. He had to last long enough to bring Shepherd home and stop Flynn from killing hundreds.

Several ideas coalesced, and Mercer returned to the main room. "Did Shepherd make contact with Grace or Harry before he disappeared?"

"No," Bastian said.

"Then he didn't tell Lara to hide either. If he had, he would have warned his wife to take care of their son. That would have been his first priority."

"Unless he hates the boy," Hans said. "Nothing indicates Shepherd should be father of the year. Based on their divorce proceedings, he wasn't husband of the year either."

Mercer didn't buy it. "What about communications between Lara and Grace?"

Bastian checked the files. "Nothing in the last two years."

"Since Owen infiltrated Flynn's faction." Mercer rubbed his palms together. "Flynn took Lara or had someone else take her. It's the only explanation for her disappearance and the reason for Shepherd's frantic and erratic behavior during his last check-in."

"So Flynn knows Shepherd is working against him,"

Bastian said.

"In that case, they're probably both dead." Hans pushed away from the desk, needing to move.

"According to MI5, Flynn makes examples of traitors. He would have made Shepherd's death a spectacle to rub in MI5's face. Owen Shepherd is still alive." Mercer was positive. He just had no idea where the man might be. "Where's your camera, Hans? I need to see the photos you took of Flynn's safe house. There might be something there, some clue. We attacked Flynn last night. He'll want to know who's gunning for him. And the first person he's going to ask is Shepherd."

"We need to get back there," Bastian said. "Shepherd could be in the boathouse."

Mercer took the offered camera and flipped through the photos. Pulling out a map, he marked the location and checked the files for additional details. The map hanging on the wall in Flynn's office indicated only a few locations. The stray markings might be targeted sites, or they could be Flynn's other compounds. Mercer placed the marks on the map and circled the known locations of Flynn's operations and the bar he frequented. They lined up with the pre-existing marks. "Now we have a starting point."

EIGHT

"There's no sign of Lara," Donovan said. "I searched her place. As far as I can tell, she didn't take anything with her. I didn't see signs of a struggle or a break-in either. It's almost as if she vanished."

"What about the post? Has her mail been collected?" Bas asked. "Maybe a neighbor knows something."

"I spoke to her neighbors. No one remembers hearing or seeing anything suspicious. She never mentioned going on a trip. Her mail's piling up."

"The Security Service has to know something. They should have observed the same things you did. People don't just walk away from their lives and take nothing with them," Mercer said.

"Unless she didn't have a choice." Hans scribbled down an address and hung up the phone. "I'll ask Grace and Harry if they have any idea where Lara might have gone. Her disappearing act must connect to the call she received from the public line. Maybe Owen reached out to his sister and told her to flee."

Mercer squinted, analyzing the expression on

Donovan's face. "What is it?"

"It's probably nothing, but her place was clean, practically pristine."

"Like someone picked up after making a mess?" Bastian asked.

Donovan shrugged.

"I want to see for myself." Mercer turned to Hans. "Did the Security Service give you Grace's location?"

"No, mate. They said they'd take me to her."

Mercer jerked his head toward the door. "Get going."

"Right-o. Anything else I can do? Maybe pull a rabbit from my hat?"

"No, that's plenty. Just be careful. Flynn's people could be monitoring Grace and Harry."

"MI5 calls it a safe house for a reason," Hans said.

"But we don't know if the agency has been compromised," Bas warned, "so be cautious."

Donovan studied the intel taped to the vinyl sheet. He didn't speak again until Hans was gone. "You should know, there were two chaps who seemed particularly interested in Lara's flat. They were outside when I arrived, and I spotted them again when I left." He held out a blurry photo he had taken. "They're either MI5 or Flynn's guys."

"Let's find out." Bastian took the offered photo and scanned it into the computer.

"Either way, I didn't like the looks of them. I tried to circle around, but they were careful. They might have realized I was on to them."

"Do you think they're still there?" Mercer asked.

"I don't know, but they weren't there for me."

"Let's find out who they are and what they want." Mercer grabbed his gear and tossed his car keys to Donovan. "You drive."

Mercer attempted to doze. He'd barely slept since

he agreed to be MI5's errand boy, but sleep didn't come. It was probably for the best. Most nights held nothing but heart-wrenching torment.

"Don't get too close," Mercer said, opening one eye. "We don't want to tip them off."

Donovan turned down an adjacent street and parked at the end. "How do you want to do this? Quiet or loud?"

"We'll start off quiet."

"And go out with a bang."

Donovan and Mercer crept along the side of the building. Donovan pointed out the waiting sedan with the two blokes inside. A pair of binoculars sat atop the dashboard.

"How long do you think they've been here?" Mercer asked.

"I have no idea, but it's odd timing. Could it have anything to do with striking against Flynn last night?"

"Impossible to say. They might have already been here. You don't suppose they're police."

"Undercover, perhaps." Donovan reached for his phone. "I asked DCI Yancy if he knew of any ops in the area, but he said no."

"Is he back on active duty?"

"Not yet, but we don't have many contacts in the police service. He was at the top of a short list."

Mercer studied the vehicle. It was an odd color, a dark green, and a more expensive make than what the coppers drove, even the undercover variety. "They're not cops." Mercer reached for his gun.

"Does that mean you're going to shoot them?"

"Only if they fire first." Picking up a rock, Mercer threw it at the rear window with enough force to break it. The glass didn't shatter, but it cracked, causing the two men to spin around in their seats. The passenger exited the car, looking around for the person responsible. The driver, a man with jet black hair, joined him, and they circled the car. "They won't be distracted long. Let's move."

"What is it with you and property damage?"

Mercer and Donovan went down the sidewalk and up the steps to Lara Shepherd's flat. To save time, Donovan used a bump key, opening the door instantly. By the time the men gave up their search for the person responsible for breaking the rear windshield, Mercer and Donovan were inside without anyone being the wiser.

The exterior of the building, along with the rest of the neighborhood, was worn and old. Mercer expected to find peeling paint and cracked plaster, but the apartment was pristine. Even the walls had a fresh coat of bright white paint.

"Told you it was clean," Donovan said.

"Any indication how recently she had the work done?"

"No hits on her credit card, and I don't recall any recent trips to the hardware store." Donovan went into the kitchen. The appliances were dated, but they appeared as if they'd never been used. "How exactly does Bastian gain access to a person's credit card information? Isn't that a major privacy violation?"

"Don't ask." Mercer went into the bedroom. The closet had an adequate amount of practical clothing. Trousers, blouses, a few smocks, and several pairs of shoes. They were all the same size, indicative that they belonged to a single resident. Picking up one of the shoes, Mercer examined the sole. No scuff marks or signs of wear. Everything was new. He went into the bathroom to find a collection of toiletries and makeup that had rarely or never been used. "Check the pantry."

"Are you feeling peckish?" Donovan opened the

cabinet. "We have protein bars, snack mix, bottled water, and canned goods."

"And the fridge?"

Donovan gave him an odd look and opened the door. "She hasn't been shopping lately." The only items inside were condiments.

"Check the expiration dates." Mercer examined the rest of the cabinets and the closets.

"Nothing's expired." Donovan turned to watch Mercer conduct his own search. "You do realize I already did that."

"She doesn't live here," Mercer said. "It looks like she could, but she doesn't. She's never worn any of the clothes. I doubt she's used any of the items in the bathroom either."

"You don't think someone repainted and purchased new items?"

"Why go through the trouble?"

"To conceal a crime, be it murder or an abduction." Donovan glanced out the window, but the men in the green car were still waiting outside.

"They wouldn't have bought new clothes or toiletries. They would have taken whatever she needed or disposed of anything covered in blood spatter. Doesn't this look familiar?"

Donovan scrutinized every nook and cranny. "I don't think we've encountered a scene like this before."

"No, not a scene. This is what we do. The way we set up our safe houses. Check for a false back. Maybe she used this place to stash something important."

"If that's the case, why would she have this flat listed as her primary address? It would defeat the purpose." Donovan tapped against the walls and other solid surfaces.

But his words fell on deaf ears as Mercer returned

to the bedroom and ripped the room apart. Beneath the area rug, Mercer discovered a loose floorboard. He pried it up, expecting to find something hidden, but nothing was inside.

"It's a slick," Donovan said from the doorway. "Any idea what it contained?"

Mercer examined the dust that coated his fingertips. "It could have been anything."

"Do you think Owen hid something away?"

Before Mercer could answer, the front door slammed against the wall, leaving a blemish against the blinding white. Donovan aimed into the hallway, and Mercer glanced out the window. The men were no longer in the vehicle.

"Toss out your guns. Come out slowly with your hands in the air," a gravelly voice announced from the other room.

"The hell we will." Donovan edged around the corner, but the men had taken cover behind the kitchen counter. From this angle, he couldn't get a bead on them. "What do you want to do, commander?"

More than anything, Mercer wanted to know who they were. From the words they uttered, they didn't sound Irish, but they could have taken care to disguise the telltale brogue. They weren't coppers. The bobbies always announced themselves, usually before issuing orders.

Unfortunately, Mercer and Donovan only had their side arms handy. The flash grenades and other nonlethal artillery were in the car. Silently, Mercer signaled for Donovan to remain on standby as he made his way to the door. He stepped into the hallway. He had no intention of complying with their demands, unless the men gave him a good reason, and Mercer couldn't come up with any acceptable excuse to surrender his weapon.

One of the men watched him from behind the counter. Only a tuft of black hair poked up above the muzzle of his handgun. From this distance, it appeared to be a nine millimeter. Mercer didn't take his eyes off the firearm.

"Drop the weapon," Black Hair instructed.

Mercer took half a step forward. "What do you want?"

"Drop your weapon. And get on the ground."

Just as Mercer stepped past the corner, where the hallway opened into the living room, movement caught his eye. He jerked backward as the second man swung an assault rifle like a baseball bat. Mercer felt the whoosh of air as the rifle narrowly missed. Before the man could swing again, Donovan fired.

The assault rifle dropped to the floor, and the man crumpled to his knees. A pained yelp escaped his lips, and Black Hair opened fire. Mercer shoved Donovan back into the bedroom and slammed the door shut. Remaining low to the ground, they dragged the dresser in front of the door.

"That won't hold them for long," Donovan said as bullets shredded the wooden door. He helped Mercer lift the mattress off the bed and stand it up in front of the dresser. It absorbed the bullets, stopping the spray from peppering the room and its occupants. "I said we'd go out with a bang. I didn't realize it'd be quite this literal."

Mercer went to the window, but it was nailed shut. He aimed at the glass and turned his head away. He fired twice and dove through the broken window. He rolled and came up in a crouch. Donovan at his heels.

A woman and her child stood across the street, staring with bewildered fascination. Mercer ignored them and darted toward the parked car.

"Keep an eye out."

"Copy." Donovan kept his gun at his side, but he'd return fire before anyone had the chance to blink.

Mercer found the doors to the sedan unlocked. He scanned the interior for any indication of the shooters' identities. He didn't find anything, but from the half-filled bottles and number of takeout containers, they'd been sitting on Lara Shepherd's flat for days, if not weeks. He popped open the glove box.

"Jules, we have to move." Donovan fired at the men. They retreated behind the metal front door. Donovan's bullets made a loud clang as they impacted against it.

"Fine," Mercer tucked the registration slip into his pocket, "let's go." He darted across the street. Once he made it across, he provided cover fire, allowing Donovan to follow. As Donovan raced down the street toward their waiting car, Mercer shot out two of the green sedan's tires.

"Julian," Donovan called.

Mercer got into the car, and Donovan drove away. Mercer turned in his seat, watching the two men emerge in time to see their departure.

As soon as he was convinced they weren't being followed, he pulled out the RF reader Bastian kept in the glove box and checked for trackers. The car was clean. The two men hadn't seen Mercer and Donovan arrive, so they didn't know to check the car.

"Who do you think they are?" Donovan asked.

"Definitely not police." Mercer pulled out his phone and dialed the direct line to report the shooting. Someone, probably the woman, had already notified the authorities, and units were on the way. Mercer disconnected the battery and tossed his phone out the window as they continued down the street.

"They can't be IRA. They didn't have the accent,

and if they abducted Lara to use as leverage, they wouldn't be casing her place," Donovan said.

"That leaves MI5."

"Why would they open fire on us? That's insane."

Mercer thought, but nothing about the experience made sense, least of all the slick in Lara's bedroom. Slicks were hiding places used by covert operatives. They held valuable items—money, passports, fake IDs, basically anything one would keep in a go-bag. "Do you think those men are seeking intel Shepherd might have hidden at his sister's place?"

"Do you think he would keep something at her home and jeopardize her safety?"

"Maybe he didn't have a choice. Since his divorce, he doesn't have a place to live. He was undercover when the proceedings were finalized. He doesn't have a flat of his own."

"But what could he possibly be hiding that would warrant a shootout?" Donovan watched two police cars zoom past them. "Bullets bring the police. Everyone knows that."

Mercer fished the scrap of paper out of his pocket and read the information. "We need to determine who those men are. That should lead to figuring out what they are after."

"I tagged their car. I don't know if it'll be much help, but it was the best I could do on such short notice."

"If it moves or they send someone to collect it from police impound, we'll know about it. It might lead to something. But let's hope we get answers before it comes to that."

NINE

"We should have performed an R&R," Mercer said.

"We didn't have time. There were witnesses," Donovan said. "We did the best we could."

"A retrieval and rendition would not have solved the problem," Bastian said.

"At least we'd know who those men are and what they want." Mercer stalked the confines of the study. "They could be working with Flynn or MI5. They might even know where Owen is or what became of Lara."

Donovan watched the commander pace. "They wouldn't have come quietly. And the lady and her son were witnesses. The bloody bobbies would be all over our arses before we even found a place to conduct the interrogation."

Bastian bit down on a pen cap, breaking the plastic in half. "From what you said, I don't think Flynn sent them."

"They have to be MI5 then," Mercer said.

"Why would they fire on us? We're on the same

side. They would have identified themselves," Donovan argued.

"Could be a few bad apples. Perhaps Shepherd identified an internal leak." Mercer tapped the photograph they took of the gold stationery since the actual item was being delivered to their police contacts.

"Now you're jumping to conclusions." Bastian let out an exasperated sigh.

"Whoever they are, they've been trained," Donovan said.

"It's doubtful they're MI5, but the car is registered to a ghost. That doesn't help us determine who they are." Bastian gnawed on a shard of the broken cap. "The photo you took doesn't match anyone in MI5's records. I'm not getting any pings in the criminal database either. I don't know who these blokes are, but their mugs aren't in the system."

"Are you sure?" Mercer leaned over Bastian's shoulder. "Doesn't facial rec normally take days?"

Bastian resisted the urge to roll his eyes. "I entered additional parameters to speed up the process. I'm looking for connections to Shepherd, so I've narrowed the search to only include men who fit the description and are known associates of Colin Flynn or connected to MI5."

"They could be lowlife crooks from one of Shepherd's previous investigations," Donovan offered. The firefight had left him anxious. He hadn't stopped moving since they returned to home base. He stared out the window, watching traffic outside. "I don't think they have any idea who we are."

"They wanted to question us," Mercer said. "That's why they told us to toss out our weapons." He replayed the event in his mind. Donovan fired first, an automatic reflex to someone attacking a teammate.

"They aren't MI5 or Metropolitan Police. I doubt they're Interpol agents."

"They didn't identify themselves." Donovan stepped away from the window and studied the intel again. "The good guys don't usually open fire without provocation."

"You provoked them," Bastian pointed out.

"After they tried to bash in Jules' skull."

"They pinned us in the bedroom, Bas. They blocked the exit. They would have come in hot had we not escaped," Mercer said. "Aside from the elite tactical units, policing agencies do not respond like that."

"Even if they were an elite unit," Donovan said, playing devil's advocate, "we aren't terrorists. We didn't have a hostage. For all they knew, we were nothing more than burglars. That was too much firepower to throw at a couple of thieves."

"There was nothing in the flat worth stealing. Whatever was hidden in the floor was already gone." Mercer thought for a moment. "But they didn't know that."

"Or they were after us and not the contents of the empty slick."

Bastian clicked a few more keys. "The tracker you placed on the green sedan shows it was moved to a police lot. Since it's part of an active crime scene, the bobbies will examine every inch of it. They'll find something."

"What about the shooters?" Mercer asked. "Are they in custody?"

"No arrests were made."

"I shot one of them," Donovan said. "That would have hindered their escape."

"Not bloody well enough," Mercer muttered.

"He must have bled inside the apartment. Perhaps they left a trail. Worst case, the police will collect the evidence and run the DNA. Everything you've said indicates these men connect to a criminal enterprise. That means they should have records. The police will get it sorted." Bastian opened a new window. "But I'll check hospital records to see who's been admitted in the last hour for a GSW."

"Anything?" Mercer asked impatiently.

"I need more than two seconds." Bastian spit out the pen cap while he typed. "I don't see anything, but I'll continue to monitor. Paperwork isn't always instantaneous, but we should assume the injured shooter will seek medical care from less public sources."

Mercer picked up the dossier they'd been given on Colin Flynn. "The shooters have to connect to Flynn. It wouldn't make sense otherwise, unless Lara Shepherd has her own enemies." He sorted through the growing pile of documents. "What do we know about Lara?"

"She studied to be a linguist at university but dropped out before completing her degree. Her income is erratic and unstable. Honestly, her entire professional background is a bit dodgy. It appears she works as a temp. I've found some old listings on job sites. She worked as a nanny and a dogwalker. She tutored and has done mostly office work." Bastian handed the paperwork to Mercer and returned to the searches and analyses he was conducting.

"Probably explains why she lives where she does," Donovan said. "It's unlikely she can afford a safer neighborhood. Any legal troubles or run-ins with the law?"

Mercer skimmed the pages. "None. She's clean, but she lives on the fringe. Not quite off the grid, but not really on it either. Those men have no reason to watch her place, unless they're after her brother."

"I'd say that's a safe assumption." The computer at the end of the desk beeped, and Bastian checked on the progress. "Brilliant. We've broken through Flynn's encryption." He clicked a few keys. "There's a lot to assess."

"What about the stationery? This gold paper stock can't be that common. Have you found anything on it?"

"I'm not a bloody octopus. I only have two hands." Bastian shoved a computer toward Mercer. "Start searching. Your fingers aren't broken."

Donovan intervened before Mercer could say a word. "Hans started looking into it." Donovan opened a few recent files. "We have the manufacturer and distributor." He turned the computer around for Mercer, who dropped into a chair and read the information.

"Make a note," Mercer said, "we'll need to check records for these shops." He listed three stores in Belfast that sold that particular item. "We'll need purchase orders and surveillance footage. It can't be a coincidence Flynn and Partridge use the same posh paper. I want to know what the connection is."

"So do I," Donovan agreed.

Bastian whistled, pushing away from the desk. "I need a drink."

"Make that two," Donovan said.

Bastian poured. Donovan's hand shook as he reached for the offered glass. The worst part about firefights was coming down from the adrenaline high. It led to jitters, nausea, and inevitably the human body shutting down for a few minutes or hours to rest. It was always the best and worst part of any op. If the mission was a success, it meant some much deserved rest. But if things hadn't gone as planned, it left one vulnerable. No one was immune to it, but there were ways to stave off the effects for as long as possible. However, since they weren't in any immediate danger, Donovan deserved the opportunity to unwind and sleep for a few minutes. They'd be back in the field soon enough.

"Why don't you bunk down in the guestroom?" Mercer suggested. "I'll let you know when we're ready to move out."

Donovan ignored the comment and stood behind Bastian, swirling the scotch around in the glass. "What's on Flynn's hard drive?"

"Bomb schematics. A veritable array of targets. Shit."

"Speak, Clarke," Mercer said.

"Flynn's an arms dealer. We know as much from MI5's records, but it's not just handhelds. According to this, he has a couple of fifty cal machine guns he's planning to unload or has already unloaded. Lots of Teflon rounds, armor piercing, and hollow points," he scrolled down the page, reading off more equipment and types of weapons, "but the real kickers are the chemical weapons."

"Chemical? As in?" Mercer waited. It could be anything from nerve agents to lung toxicants.

"Sarin, chlorine gas, and VX."

"Bloody hell." Mercer rubbed a hand down his face. "You said he had a list of targets. What about a timetable? When is he planning the attack?"

"How widescale?" Donovan downed his drink in a single gulp.

Bastian continued to work through the intel. "There's no way to tell. But I don't think he's selling the WMDs. He's planning to keep those for his own use."

"Like the pressure cooker bombs," Mercer said.

"With the proper disbursal method, he could load

one of those up with sarin, VX, or even the chlorine and increase the death toll exponentially," Bastian said.

While Bastian searched for details on the terrorist plot, Mercer analyzed the target list. The locations Flynn had scouted were all popular public places. And the research Flynn had performed was nothing more than checking online tourist sites. None of the locations were personal. None of them spoke of a political, religious, or social agenda.

"It could be fearmongering." Donovan dug into MI5's files for any hint as to when or where Flynn would strike. "He could detonate one device and hold the city hostage until they meet his demands."

"What are his demands?" Mercer asked, glancing at Bastian. "Did you find a manifesto?"

"No." Bastian crunched on a piece of ice. "These files are broad. Vague. The only detailed information I found are the spreadsheets. They appear to be business in nature. An inventory of the items he has for sale. Prices. A list of incoming shipments. Apparently, he's waiting on a few crates of MAC-10s. Do you think FedEx is delivering?"

"No." Mercer's mind drifted to the boathouse Hans had scouted, the secondary location Flynn had fled to after his SUV exploded. "He must be getting illicit shipments from overseas. Probably from the Russians. They still have some influence in Afghanistan, even though they officially pulled out in the '70s. But those connections still exist. And with the weapons caches that have been delivered as the war continues, private dealers have made millions selling off the artillery that's been left behind as various nations have recalled their troops."

"I'll make some calls and see if I can track down Flynn's source." Donovan grabbed a phone and went into the other room.

Mercer stared at the pages in front of him, not seeing any of it. His thoughts were on the items in the basement. Flynn's laboratory, that's what one of the bodyguards had called it. Now Mercer knew why. "Shepherd must have found out. If he's alive, we need to find him. We have to stop this."

"Maybe it's not as bad as it seems."

"Don't be a bloody optimist. It won't serve any of us."

The front door slammed, and Mercer spun. Hans held up his palms. "Only me."

"What do you have?"

"Not much, I'm afraid. Grace hasn't spoken to her husband in nearly a year. She said one day Owen cut ties. He told her he didn't love her and never wanted to see her or the boy again. The few times they've communicated since has been mandated by the courts or necessary for their custody agreement." Hans licked his lips. "Owen said he didn't want to have anything to do with Harry. He set up a trust that pays child support and alimony, but he has no contact."

"When did this occur?"

"Right before Owen went undercover. He burned his bridges, mate. He has no reason to come home. I'd say it's possible he switched sides."

Mercer wondered if Hans was thinking clearly. Hans' own sordid past with a missing father and abusive step-father might be coloring his perception of the situation. "Or he did all of that to protect his family in case his cover was compromised."

"Why are you giving this bloke the benefit of the doubt at every turn? Owen Shepherd's a piece of shit. He abandoned his family. He abandoned his post. He probably sold out his bloody country."

"Where's his sister, Lara?" Mercer asked. "Did he

sell her out too?"

Hans shrugged. "I don't know. Maybe they planned something together. Maybe they both want to stick it to the Crown. Maybe they went over to the dark side."

"Find proof."

"You mean aside from that scrap of paper?"

"Did you bring it to the police?"

"DCI Yancy promised to have someone print it for you. We'll know tomorrow who's touched it." Hans practically laughed. "I never thought I'd live to see the day a bobby was indebted to us."

"Desperate times." Mercer pasted a printout of Flynn's inventory on the vinyl sheet and highlighted the chemical weapons. "Regardless of your feelings, we need to find Shepherd. There's a good chance Colin Flynn is planning a chemical attack."

"Bollocks."

TEN

Mercer took a step back. "This isn't right. What is going on?" He reached for his phone and chartered a helicopter. They didn't have time to wait for the next ferry, nor did they have six hours to waste on the commute. "We're leaving in thirty. Pack up and grab whatever gear you think we'll need. Make sure you have full blackout. We'll need stealth. Donovan, you're coming with us. Hans, I need you to stay here and keep us apprised of the situation. Let me know what the bobbies find, and whatever you do, do not engage."

"What if they engage with me?"

"Don't let them." Mercer met his eyes. "I'm serious."

"Yeah, yeah." Hans waved Mercer away, wondering how Bastian managed to pull off so many tasks simultaneously while the rest of the team was in the field.

With their bags in hand, Mercer, Bastian, and Donovan left for the helipad. Chartering a private flight was costly, but Mercer wasn't concerned about the money. They didn't have time to make the long, slow trek back to Belfast, and taking a commercial flight required too many extra steps regarding their gear.

"We might have asked MI5 for a lift," Bastian mumbled as they loaded the bags into the back and climbed into the chopper.

"No time." Mercer slid into one of the seats and strapped himself in. A flood of memories from his days at the SAS ran through his mind. At least they wouldn't be rappelling down or jumping from this helicopter.

Bastian exchanged a few words with the pilot while Donovan settled in and closed his eyes. They'd have to refuel in Manchester or Liverpool before crossing to Ireland, but they should arrive in under four hours. Once they landed, Mercer wanted to hit the ground running. They had to find those weapons and stop the attack. It was possible Flynn had no immediate plans to strike, but given Shepherd's rushed and upsetting final communication, Mercer decided it was best to err on the side of caution. They needed answers. Hundreds of lives depended on them. This was no longer about MI5's deceit. This was about stopping a terrorist attack.

Mercer closed his eyes. He had to rest now. It might be his last opportunity until the mission ended.

He emitted a strangled groan and jerked awake, his breath coming in heaving gasps. Bastian grabbed his shoulders and pushed him back against the seat.

"You're okay."

Mercer blinked, swallowing and nodding. "Aye." He peered out the window, seeing a few yellow lights in the distance, a stark contrast to the pitch black. "How much longer?"

"Twenty minutes."

Mercer glanced to his left. Donovan remained motionless, his eyes closed. The sound cancelling earbuds and white noise provided him with some much needed tranquility. Mercer wondered if the younger man was asleep or deep in meditation. It didn't matter either way.

"I didn't realize you were still having nightmares." Bastian pulled a piece of licorice from his jacket pocket and chewed on the end.

"They aren't nightmares."

Bastian clapped him on the shoulder and leaned back in his seat. "Next time you see Michelle, tell her I miss her too."

Mercer pressed his lips together, barely nodding. They were a sorry lot.

*   *   *

"Colin Flynn's extremely careful." Donovan picked through the discarded shipping containers. "Or paranoid."

"He came here for a reason." Mercer watched the water lap against the dock.

"I'd say he came here to arm himself." Bastian filled a vial with dirt samples. "We blew his SUV sky high. He and his men retreated to this location in the hopes of setting up an ambush. But this isn't the most secure location. I doubt Flynn used it to hold Shepherd. Although it is secluded enough for torture, and it would be a brilliant place to dispose of a body."

Mercer peered into the murky water. "We'll keep it in mind."

Donovan pointed to the single entry point. "Strategically, it's damn near perfect. Unless Flynn's attackers were coming by water, there's only one way in. It's a chokepoint. He could pick off his enemies as they enter."

"And if he was overrun," Mercer climbed into the small speedboat, "the getaway vehicle is waiting. He'd have the perfect escape plan."

"But the walls are flimsy. The wood's ancient, practically rotted. A few sharpshooters with thermal goggles could pick him off from the outside." Bastian brushed his gloves on his trousers and eyed the exposed ceiling beams.

"Not everyone thinks like us." Donovan joined Mercer in the boat, and the two searched the storage areas. Aside from several guns and a few bricks of C4, they didn't find any suspicious containers or items marked with a skull and crossbones.

Giving up the search, Mercer stepped out of the vehicle. "Whatever was here is gone now. Flynn must have moved it. He might have come here to lure out his attacker, and when that didn't happen, he figured the location was compromised or feared for his girlfriend's safety."

"I'd wager this is where he receives his shipments," Bastian said. "His supplier must know about this place and Flynn's routine. Perhaps, Flynn filched on a payment. Our stunt outside the pub might result in a case of mistaken identities."

"Flynn's a paranoid fucker. He doesn't know who to trust." Mercer gave the boathouse a final look. "Let's move out."

They followed the route Flynn had taken the previous night, arriving at the luxury apartment building. Security cameras covered the doors. The windows were barred with a card scanner on the front door. The lobby had someone working the front desk and more cameras throughout the interior.

Mercer stayed out of sight. He couldn't afford to be caught on any of the feeds. "Does Flynn own the building?"

"No, but he owns one of the apartments. According to the rental agreement, the tenant is Alana Reilly. She's his paramour," Bastian said.

"Was he shagging her while the missus was alive?" Donovan asked.

"I don't know. It's possible, but he didn't buy the apartment until months later. I'm not saying Colin Flynn was ever a family man, but it is a possibility."

"I doubt he's learned from his mistakes." Mercer gave the building another look and returned to the car. "No amount of locks or security measures will keep her safe from the monster he is."

"What do you want to do, Jules?" Bastian asked. "It's too late to check the stationery store. I'll have to access those records in the morning once they reboot the system."

"Let's scout a few of the marked locations from Flynn's map. They could be targeted sites or established safe houses. He could have stashed Shepherd at one of those spots. Since MI5 is onto him, Flynn might keep Shepherd alive in case he needs him for something."

"Like access to a government building?" Bastian asked.

"Perhaps." Mercer sighed. "We should split up to cover more ground. Stay in radio contact. Should you encounter any resistance, notify us immediately. Let's move out."

Donovan nodded and climbed behind the wheel of another car.

Ever since the Good Friday Agreement, Belfast had become a relatively safe city with low crime rates and lots of tourism, but the RIRA and CIRA remained active in the region, and Flynn's faction was no different. For the most part, their paramilitary activities had been contained or prevented by policing agencies, and Mercer wasn't about to let that change. Colin Flynn wanted to destroy everything, starting with Owen Shepherd.

"We're looking for a needle in a pile of needles." Bas hunkered down and used the scope to scout one of the locations from the map. "This one doesn't look any different from the last two."

"Donovan, anything?" Mercer asked.

"I can't tell, but I'm not seeing any guards." Donovan squinted into the binoculars. "Wouldn't Flynn have guards keeping Shepherd detained?"

"Not necessarily," Bas replied. "We don't know the state of his hostage."

"Or Shepherd's whereabouts or what's going through Flynn's mind." Mercer glanced at the time. Flynn would be at the pub. It was the only place he routinely went. "Donovan, keep searching. Run through the rest of the locations. If you don't find Shepherd, we'll pass the locations on to MI5 anonymously so the Security Service can monitor the area. We're already spread too thin."

"Aye." Donovan's tone held the slightest question, but he wasn't going to second guess Mercer in the field.

However, Bastian didn't have the same qualms. "I thought we didn't trust them."

"We don't, but I have a plan." Mercer tucked the scope away and headed for the car. "Meet me outside the pub, Bas. I'll need you set up in the parking garage across the way to watch my back."

As Mercer approached Flynn's bar, the phone rang. He hit answer, knowing there was only one person who would be calling. "What do you have, Hans?"

"Yancy called. The prints came back on that paper stock. Colin Flynn definitely touched it."

"No shit."

"Yeah, well, that's the only identifiable print the coppers pulled. And it gets worse."

"Meaning?"

"The tossers who fired on you and Donovan have gone to ground. The police are still processing the scene, but they have no leads."

"What about blood?"

"They're running it through the system, but it'll be a few days." Hans hesitated, and Mercer sensed there was more bad news. "The police released the vehicle. Someone with government credentials showed up and took possession."

"Bollocks."

"It wasn't MI5."

Despite Hans' insistence, Mercer couldn't fathom any other possibilities. The men who shot at him, who were staking out Lara's apartment, had to know Owen Shepherd and his assignment. Everything about this screamed conspiracy.

"Who was it?"

"Yancy is working on it."

"Tell him to work faster." Mercer fought the urge to hang up, wanting to make sure Hans had finished relaying the updates.

"I'll keep you apprised."

"Brilliant." Mercer tucked the phone away and slammed his palm against the steering wheel. "Balls." He'd have to take matters into his own hands.

He peered out the window, watching a few stragglers wander the streets. Drinking was a daily event. It would be hours before the pubs emptied. However, Mercer didn't feel like waiting. He just hoped the patrons at Flynn's pub were mostly faction members, or things might get awkward and complicated.

He left the rental car parked on the corner and walked around the neighborhood, assessing vantage points and possible terrorist strongholds, but it was a small commercial street with a few rundown pubs and shops. The location was perfect to avoid attracting attention, and tonight, that would work in Mercer's favor. He circled a few more times and returned to his car.

"Bas, where are you?"

"Just pulling up."

"I'm going inside. Follow my cues. And let it play out."

"I don't like the sound of that."

Mercer waited forty-five seconds, and then he entered the pub. It was quiet compared to the other neighborhood pubs.

Colin Flynn sat in the corner. A few women crowded around him, but he only paid attention to the pale blonde seated beside him. She had her hand on the inside of his thigh, claiming her territory. A few of Flynn's personal bodyguards, men Mercer recognized from MI5's files, sat at nearby tables, keeping one eye on the boss and the other on their emptying glasses.

Two men on the other side of the room sat up a little straighter when Mercer entered, so he took out his phone and pretended to check for text messages. He approached the bar, placed his order, and sidestepped down the short hallway to the men's room. It was empty.

Mercer was relieving himself at the urinal when one of the men stepped inside to join him. Mercer zipped up and went to the sink.

"Nice night," the man said, unzipping. He had a Celtic cross tattooed on his left inner forearm.

Mercer nodded, catching a glimpse of the forty-five in a shoulder holster beneath the man's jacket. Flynn's guards weren't as lax as they appeared. This man might cause a problem. Mercer would have to keep an eye on him.

"I've never seen you before." The man finished his business and moved to the sink.

"I've never been here before."

The English accent caught the guard's attention. "Why are you here?"

"Work brought me to Ireland. Thirst led me to the pub." Mercer met his eyes. "Is that a problem?"

"There are other places to drink."

"This seems as good as any."

Turning, Mercer stepped out of the men's room and took a seat at the bar. A few seconds later, Celtic Cross returned to his table and whispered to his friend. Obviously, they were leery of strangers. Amusedly, Mercer wondered if it had anything to do with last night's explosion.

The bartender placed the shot glass beside the pint. Mercer smiled, waiting to catch Flynn's attention before downing the shot. Normally, it would have been dropped in the glass, but Mercer detested the combination. Plus, had he ordered it forthright by the name the Americans called it, an Irish Car Bomb, he would have been thrown out of the pub or shot. Still, he wanted to make his intentions known, and from the icy glare in Flynn's eyes, Mercer had gotten his point across.

ELEVEN

"I've got eyes on you," Bastian said. "Are you sure about this? You order another one of those and I might have to shoot you myself."

Mercer smirked, gesturing to the bartender for another. He remained off to the side, not quite in the corner, since that area was already occupied by Flynn's men, but close enough to overhear pieces of their conversation.

The terrorist was nursing his fourth Guinness. The woman with the pale blonde hair hung on his arm and every word, but Flynn was growing bored with her. The other ladies had left, and the remaining one thought she and Flynn should do the same.

"Not tonight, eh?" she asked.

Flynn kissed her cheek. "Too much on my mind, love. Killian will take you home."

"I can take myself, Colin. I don't need to be handled by your friends. I'm not stupid. I know what you're doing."

"Alana, do as I say." He signaled for Killian, the

man with the Celtic cross tattoo. "This is for your own good."

"Nothing you do is for my benefit, Colin. It's for yours."

Flynn grabbed both of her wrists in one hand and pulled her close. "That isn't true, love." He stared into her eyes. "Now kiss me goodbye."

She did as he asked and allowed Killian to escort her from the bar. "Following," Donovan said in Mercer's ear.

Mercer cast a sideways glance at Flynn, who was now facing the bar, his sole focus on the glass in front of him. "Birds," Mercer mumbled.

Flynn cocked his head to the side. "Excuse me?"

"Nothing, mate. Just an observation. They need to be kept in their place." The words tasted sour on Mercer's tongue, but he knew Flynn would have a response. The terrorist would either appreciate the caveman attitude, or he'd tell Mercer to bugger off.

"I don't see how my business is any of yours." Colin Flynn put the glass down and swiveled in his seat. "I don't recall seeing you before. Who said you could drink in my pub?"

"You own this place? It could use some work."

"You English are all alike, staking claims to territories that aren't yours. Telling us what to do. Why don't you piss off while you still can?"

Mercer turned back to his empty glass and stared at the bartender who had yet to bring him a refill. "Barkeep, another shot."

The bartender poured, doing his best to mind his business. As soon as he placed it on the bar, Mercer dropped it into his remaining Guinness, watching the surface bubble, like a bomb.

"Oi," Flynn took a step toward Mercer, "you think that's funny? Who sent you?"

Mercer tipped the glass back and chugged the contents before slamming it down on the counter. He caught two of Flynn's guards moving in from the other side before Bastian's warning sounded in his ear.

"No one sent me," Mercer said.

"Rubbish." Flynn leaned in closer. "Who are you?"

"No one of any importance. Just a security specialist."

"You're a bleeding mercenary. Do you have any idea who I am?"

"Someone in need of better security," Mercer slid a business card with nothing but a phone number across the bar, "and a new car."

Flynn pulled something out of his pocket and held it down at his side. Mercer didn't turn to see what it was. Bastian warned him it was a dagger. Flynn nodded to the men on Mercer's other side, who remained poised to strike, but on their leader's orders, they stayed where they were.

"That was you last night? You came at me?" Flynn asked.

"No, mate. I was working in the area and heard what happened." Mercer glanced at the twitchy bodyguards. "You've upset some very powerful people. They're coming for you. From what I hear, so is MI5. If I can get to you this easily, I hate to see what your enemies have planned."

"Why should I believe you?"

"I don't care either way. But I came here for a reason. May we speak in private?"

"Speak now and fast before I slice out your tongue."

"As you wish." Mercer didn't turn to look at the men again. Instead, he stared into Colin Flynn's ice blue eyes. "As I said, I just finished a job. There were unforeseen circumstances, and I lost most of my equipment. From what I hear, you have connections.

Figured I'd replenish my stock before I push on. I could use a dozen semi-automatic handguns. Clean. Untraceable. A few assault rifles, and a Dragunov. I'm prepared to pay top dollar if you can deliver now. A storm's coming, and I want to be gone before it arrives. I don't have time to waste."

Flynn's expression remained unreadable. And then he laughed. "You insult me and then ask for a favor. Fucking English dog."

"Fine." Mercer put some quid on the bar. "Word of advice, mate, you might want to consider relocating for a while. From what I hear, your life is about to get complicated."

Flynn put a hand on Mercer's chest and shoved him back onto the barstool. "Are you threatening me?"

"It's not me."

"Who?"

"It could be anyone. I'm sure you've heard the whispers. Your faction's been infiltrated. Are you sure you can trust any of these lads?"

"Piss off." But something in Flynn's eyes told Mercer he wanted to hear more.

"Surely, you must realize one of your own men planted that bomb. No one could get that close, and you know it. You're Colin fucking Flynn. You command an army."

"Aye."

"I imagine that wasn't the first close call you've had lately. And if I'm right, it won't be your last."

The wheels turned in Flynn's head. Mercer knew the seeds of distrust had already been sewn. Flynn knew his operation was compromised. It's the reason he acted the way he did and why he didn't allow his men to wander into the basement. Perhaps he'd been tipped to MI5's infiltration, either by Shepherd or a traitor farther up the food chain. But the fear of the unknown was the only reason Mercer was still alive. Flynn wanted answers.

"There've been other strange occurrences, unexplained happenings, delays, issues arising for no real reason, haven't there?" Mercer asked. "You need to get your house sorted. I shouldn't have wasted my time asking for a buy. You have bigger problems."

The insult angered Flynn, who grabbed Mercer by the collar. "No one would betray me. What have you done? Who do you work for?" Flynn pressed the blade against Mercer's neck.

"At the moment, no one. My job's done. I'm passing through."

"How do you know so much about me?"

"Everyone knows about you. That isn't to say I haven't been approached by parties interested in your demise. However, I have no desire to enter a fight I'm not prepared to win. Instead, I thought it best to warn you, extend an olive branch."

Flynn pressed the knife's edge harder into Mercer's Adam's apple. "Who approached you?"

"Information isn't free."

"Maybe I should loosen your tongue."

"Go ahead."

Flynn cursed. "What do you want?"

"Guns would be nice."

"Let me put it this way. If you don't answer the question, you're a dead man."

"That's not how this works."

"I'm the one with the dagger. You don't dictate terms."

"This is my profession," Mercer said. "I possess vital information crucial to your survival, and dare I say, Alana's survival as well. You know who you've screwed. It's just a matter of time. You need protection, and these wankers aren't enough, especially when one of them has sold you out. I hope Killian's loyal and better trained than the rest of your guards."

"Answer the fucking question." Flynn pressed his weight into Mercer and forced him to bend backward over the bar.

"You want answers, and I want to get paid. It's that simple."

"How about I cut until you start talking?"

Mercer laughed. "Do you honestly believe I'm stupid enough to walk in here without hiring someone on the outside to watch my back?" He tapped his thumb twice against the bar, and Bastian turned on the laser sight. The red dot danced across the dagger's edge and Flynn's hand until it caught the terrorist's attention. Then Bas shifted his aim, letting the laser sight linger in the center of Flynn's skull. "You have two seconds to drop the knife, or my man drops you."

Bastian shot to the left of Flynn's ear, close enough that the bullet grazed the cartilage. One of Flynn's men ran to the door and fired into the dark night. The crack of the sniper rifle boomed a second time, and the man let out a howl at the same moment his gun clattered to the floor.

"That was a warning shot. The next one won't be," Mercer said. "Unlike you, I know who I can trust, and I come prepared. If you'd be so kind, Mr. Flynn." Mercer glanced down at the blade pressed against his neck, and Flynn lowered the weapon. "Tell your men to sit down unless you know which one's a traitor. In which case, I'd be glad to eliminate him for you, free of charge, as a show of good faith."

"You're playing a deadly game."

"No," Mercer tugged on his shirt front and freed himself from Flynn's grip, "I'm showing you my capabilities. You need me, Mr. Flynn. You need my protection."

"You think this is a fucking job interview?"

"Job interview, negotiation, whatever you prefer. But they're coming. If you want my help to stop them, you'll find me next time."

"Why should I trust you?"

"You shouldn't, but if I wanted you dead, I wouldn't have wasted my breath or stepped inside this bar. You'd already be dead." Mercer glanced at the faction members. "And so would they." He tapped the business card he placed beside Flynn's hand. "Consider my proposal. You have twenty-four hours, if I don't hear from you, I'll move on with or without new gear. We both know you need better security than some drunken fucks who can't shoot straight. And unlike your trusted inner circle, I have a better grasp of understanding your enemies."

Turning, Mercer walked out of the bar. One of Flynn's men tried to follow, and Bastian fired a warning shot a few millimeters in front of the man, halting him in his tracks.

Mercer continued down the street, climbed into a black sedan with rental plates, and drove past the bar. "Bastian, get out of there," he instructed, keeping an eye out for a tail.

"Leaving now," Bastian replied.

"Donovan," Mercer said, adjusting the microphone on his radio, "Flynn will send someone for Alana, or he'll go to her himself. I want to know where they go. Do not get spotted."

"Aye."

Mercer ditched the car beneath an overpass and waited for Bastian to pull up. He climbed in before the vehicle came to a full stop. It wasn't safe to dawdle now that he'd angered the terrorist leader.

Bastian rubbed a hand down his face, the tremor

hidden by the motion. "Have you gone mad? What are you going to do if he calls?"

"Answer."

"Why do I even ask?" Bastian drove south, away from the pub and Flynn's known strongholds. After forty-five minutes, they stopped at a deserted spot near the shore. No one was following them. "You realize this is a ridiculous plan. What happens when he figures out who you really are?"

"Isn't everything in place?"

Bastian had created a believable alternate persona based on Mercer's background and history, but instead of turning to K&R and personal security, he tweaked the records to indicate Mercer was nothing more than a soldier of fortune. A mercenary for hire with a passport that matched timeframes and destinations for several high-profile deaths and murders.

"Yes, but if Flynn has someone inside MI5, he'll discover the truth. The lies won't hold up."

"Should that happen, I guess I'll have to tell him my side of things."

"So he can put a bullet in your head?"

Mercer stared into the darkness. "He won't."

"After that stunt, he will out of spite. He'll piss on your grave just to prove his bloody point. Honestly, Jules, I'm not sure he won't kill you anyway."

"He won't." The look in Flynn's eyes told Mercer everything he needed to know. "Colin Flynn knows it's true. His faction isn't secure. He doesn't know who to trust. He needs outside help. And this is the only way we're going to get close enough to find out what he's planning. Unless he leads us to the weapons, we might not find them in time."

"What about Owen Shepherd? Did you forget about him?"

"I did not. This is also the fastest way to find out what happened to Shepherd and if he's responsible for MI5's breach." Mercer tapped the screen on his phone. "Odd. Flynn's still at the pub. He hasn't left. I thought that'd be the first thing he'd do. He must be scared."

"Or stubborn. You're sure you placed the tracker securely?"

"Positive."

Bastian reached across for a bag of crisps and tore the package open. After working off the nervous energy, he put the bag down and wiped his hands on his trousers. "Let me see that. You're probably doing it wrong." Mercer handed him the device, and Bastian performed a quick diagnostic. "Remind me again how you talked me into this. Oh, that's right. You didn't put the matter up for debate."

"I didn't see any other way."

Bastian bit down angrily on another crisp. "No, you bloody didn't." He blew out a breath. "Is this really for the best?"

"We don't have time to be cautious. The chemical weapons are unaccounted for, as are nine other bombs. Flynn has more artillery than I care to think about. If the bastard has his way, blood will flow through the streets. I won't allow that to happen."

"We won't allow that to happen," Bastian corrected, but he gave Mercer another look and sighed. "How much of this is about Flynn, and how much is about your distrust of the Security Service?"

"They're the reason we're here. They started this op but couldn't finish it. We will. And with any luck, we'll recover Shepherd in the process. Traitor or victim, it doesn't matter. We will bring him home." Mercer's thoughts went to Lara, which inevitably led back to Michelle.

Bastian knew Mercer better than anyone. To the rest of the world, he was unreadable, but to his teammates, he was an open book. "You have to let it go, mate. It will consume you. It did once, and I won't stand by and see it happen again. If you let this eat at you, eventually, you'll be no better than Flynn."

"I won't kill innocents."

"Can you even tell who's innocent anymore?" Bas asked.

Mercer watched the waves break and crash violently against the rocks. "I need you to go back to Palace Barracks and find out what's going on inside the Security Service. Flynn will reach out to the traitor. I need you to intercept the communication and flush out the arsehole."

"Did the police find any helpful prints on the paper stock?"

"No, but regardless, that bloody scrap of paper indicates someone from MI5 is working with Flynn. It could be Shepherd. But if it isn't, it's someone else, and that means no one's safe, not even us. Visit the shops and get their records first thing in the morning. We need to know who we can trust."

When the blip on the screen left the bar, Bastian started the car and drove back the way they came. Colin Flynn was on the move.

TWELVE

"Bas, go," Mercer insisted. "We'll handle this. I need you to handle the rest."

Bastian let out a few mumbled expletives, exchanged a frustrated glance with Donovan, and headed for the car. After making a few quick stops to the three shops, Bastian would arrive at the Security Service just after nine. Hopefully, it'd be early enough to plant a listening device or two. Plus, it was a reasonable time to show up and demonstrate that he and Mercer were dedicated to their mission, even after their abrupt departure the previous day.

Donovan pointed at the map. "This is the route they took. They returned to Alana's flat. The guard hasn't left yet."

"Killian," Mercer said. "Do you find it odd he hasn't left?" Mercer studied everything about Flynn, but Alana was the only weakness he found. She was the only one not directly connected to the faction, and even Mercer had trouble believing she wasn't another of Flynn's radicals.

"He's following Flynn's orders. Hans said the guard

remained with her last night too."

"They could be having an affair."

"Perhaps, but Flynn's afraid to leave her unguarded."

"And you're sure the bastard doesn't have anyone else in his life?"

"I don't think so. You've read the dossier. Flynn doesn't get close to anyone. He couldn't protect his family, so I don't believe he'd risk making the same mistake twice. He tries to keep Alana separate from his business, but his life is the faction."

"He shouldn't have taken her to the pub the night after the explosion."

"Probably not, but he had to make a show of strength in front of his followers. That's the best way to do it."

Mercer knew exactly how to convince Flynn to trust him, but he had to be careful not to internalize any of it. It's the reason Bas was being particularly insufferable. He feared Mercer would start to empathize with the terrorist. But he wouldn't. This was a job, and he'd never been one to socialize with mass murderers. The thought sickened him. He'd have to take care to separate what little remained of his sanity from their objectives, or else he'd kill Flynn just as easily as look at him.

He loathed men like Colin Flynn. Despite Flynn's motivation, the tools and methods the terrorist used were deplorable. His acts weren't about justice or revenge. They were about anger and destruction. Flynn was a firebomb, destroying everyone and everything in his path. Mercer was a scalpel, only excising the malignancy while doing his best to leave the healthy tissue alone.

"Donovan, stay on her. Don't be seen. Lose the car afterward. Take every precaution," Mercer instructed.

"I'll let you know when to make a move. And when you do, make it obvious."

"You realize, if this backfires, Flynn will assume you're responsible. He'll do his worst."

"Should that happen, we'll at least have a fighting chance of determining what happened to Owen Shepherd. But I have no intention of tipping Flynn. He doesn't trust anyone, not even his own people. All we need to do is cultivate his suspicions and point them in the direction we need."

"Still, you're an outsider and a Brit. As a rule, he hates both."

"It doesn't matter how much he hates me, as long as he believes he needs me. Give me ninety minutes to arrive at the inn and get settled. I'll need the alibi. We're fortunate he followed the crumbs I left and put eyes on the inn. If not, things would be a lot more complicated."

Donovan hit the timer on his watch. "Make contact when you want me to move in."

"Will do."

"If I don't hear from you, we'll come get you."

"And to think, Hans is missing all the fun."

Mercer climbed into another dark sedan and drove down the street toward the inn. Flynn controlled most of the village outside Belfast, so his presence would be noted and reported back. After all, that was the point.

Taking the room key, Mercer went up the steps. At this early hour, the inn felt abandoned. Mercer let himself into the room, checked for surveillance devices, and stretched out on the bed. He cleaned his handgun and screwed on the silencer in case he had any uninvited guests with which he could not reason.

"Have they left yet?" Mercer asked.

"Twenty minutes ago," Donovan replied.

"All right. Move in."

Mercer started to doze when he heard a burst of static followed by Donovan's voice. "It's done."

"Good. Get out of there. The chopper's waiting at the heliport. See what you and Hans can dig up."

"Best of British."

Mercer removed the radio from his ear and tucked it into his pocket. His gaze fell on his phone, but Flynn wasn't calling yet. Mercer wondered how long it would take him to discover someone had broken into Alana's flat. The security system should have sent out the alert by now. Mercer checked the location of the red blip on the screen. Flynn hadn't left his house, or he'd changed clothes. Realizing there was nothing else that could be done, Mercer rolled onto his side and closed his eyes, keeping the gun tucked beside him.

A few hours later, Flynn kicked in the door to find Mercer's silenced weapon pointed at his face.

"You should have called first." Mercer sat up, keeping his gun aimed at Flynn's head. "I thought you weren't interested in what I had to say."

Flynn glanced into the hallway before pulling the door closed behind him. He held up his palms to show he wasn't armed and took a seat at the small, round table. "Put that down, unless you plan on using it."

"I haven't decided yet."

"Should anything happen to me, my mates will find you. Eventually, they'll kill you, but before that happens, they'll kill everyone you've ever loved."

Mercer holstered the gun. "It's a little late for that."

"Is it, Julian? I'm sure if they look hard enough, they'll find someone you still give a shit about."

"Does this make us even, since you know who I am? That must mean you also know my capabilities."

"Frankly, I'm surprised someone hasn't put you down like the rabid dog you are. Doesn't the Queen have a kill squad to deal with renegades?"

"Who says they haven't tried?"

"Is that why you left merry old England?" Flynn turned and spat, as if the word was an affront to his existence. "So you're a soldier of fortune now, but instead of moving on after your latest contract, you decided to what? Hunt for a new job?"

"You're the biggest arms dealer in the region. I needed gear. I told you that."

"You also told me someone wants me dead, but you didn't accept the assignment. I want to know who tried to hire you."

"I don't know. I have an online dropbox. It's anonymous. I received the offer and declined."

"Let me see it."

"Fine." Mercer grabbed his phone and tapped a few keys. He held it out, watching as Flynn read the message. "Now you understand my dilemma."

"Whoever this is threatened to kill you if you didn't perform. Why should I believe this isn't a ruse to follow through on the hit?" Flynn asked.

"I'm not daft. And I don't appreciate threats. You are an enemy I do not wish to have. Even if I ended you, the men who are loyal to you would hunt me to the ends of the earth. I have no intention of looking over my shoulder the rest of my life." Mercer considered his words. "More than I already do. Instead, I figured you might want to take care of this yourself. Or we could work together."

"So you want revenge?"

"That's not how I work. This is business. Emotions do not factor into it."

"You're a negotiator by trade, eh?" Flynn reached into his pocket. "How much do you want?"

"$100,000."

"Pounds Sterling?"

Mercer practically let out a hiss. "Since you know

who I am, you should know I hate the empire as much as you do, possibly more. I have no desire to remain here. My fees are in U.S. dollars. It makes it easier to travel, to disappear."

"Tell me what you know."

"Someone wants to take the weapons and armaments you've acquired and use them to wage their own war."

"Sure," Flynn said skeptically.

"That's why one of your rivals wants you dead. It's cheaper and easier to obtain cases of Russian assault rifles and the necessary materials for a dozen or so pressure cooker bombs when you don't have to worry about being caught or flagged. Your black market connections are stronger and better than those of the other faction leaders. Everyone knows you're the real power in Northern Ireland. The only real power left since the accords." Mercer knew men like Flynn. They were driven by power. They liked having their egos stroked, particularly by other formidable men. "Interpol and MI5 have cracked down on the black market arms trade. It's getting harder and harder to find reliable sources. Buying or stealing from you is the only option. I doubt they want to pay for something they plan to take."

Flynn didn't speak. He let the words and implications sink in while he studied Mercer, unsure if he should trust someone who'd once been valued by the British government before being cast aside like toxic refuse. Finally, he said, "Another faction. It must be Mathias Murphy. He's been making threats to dismantle my operation and take control of my territory. I squeezed him out years ago. I should have killed him when I had the chance."

Mercer played it cool. "Probably."

"That fucker."

"Mr. Flynn, you're missing the point. Someone close to you has other loyalties. How else would they have gotten close enough to blow your car sky high?"

"Someone in my crew is working with Mathias." Flynn had gotten the thought stuck in his head. "Who betrayed me?"

"I don't know."

"You will find out."

"When I discover the traitor's identity, I'll hand him over to you, but I have to get paid first."

Flynn sensed this might be a trap. "Working for me won't be so cut and dry. You'll do what I say. Follow my orders, and whatever job I need you to perform, you will."

"In that case, my fee will be much greater. I have little desire to get involved in a blood feud."

"You'll take what I give you." Flynn narrowed his eyes. "And I want the names of your associates."

"I hired a shooter to accompany me last night. It was a one-time deal. The fact that I'm not dead means I'm not stupid. I know how to survive. Being alone forces one to rely on nothing but himself and his instincts. When necessary, I hire the best and pay them a substantial amount for their time with the guarantee of their anonymity. It's not the same as loyalty, but it does guarantee a certain degree of trust. You've grown complacent. Your guards are fat and drunk. At least one of them is selling you out to your enemies. I'd wager its more than one. You know you need me, and because of that, you'll agree to my terms."

"Bloody hell." Flynn rubbed a hand through his hair. "That's your hard sell, eh? I pay you enough, and you'll be my lapdog?"

"I prefer guard dog, but that's how this business works."

A devious smile curled the corners of Flynn's lips. "I need something solid. Some piece of proof. I have no reason to take you at your word. Your word isn't worth shit. Bring me something concrete."

"I already have." Mercer clicked a few more keys, opening one of the files he'd taken from Flynn's computer. "This was circulating on the dark web. I don't know where it originated, but I doubt you'd broadcast this to the world." He held out the device, watching as the color drained from Flynn's face.

Flynn hit delete and handed back the device. "Someone will pay dearly."

Mercer entered a few details before sliding the device across the table again. "My services don't come cheaply."

Flynn stared at the waiting account transfer form. "Fifty thousand now, and if I find out your intel's unreliable, you know what will happen."

"And the rest?"

"That will come later, when we work out final payment." Flynn entered his bank account information and passed the phone back to Mercer. "It looks like you're serving a new master."

Mercer forced his face to remain neutral as he said, "Yes, sir."

THIRTEEN

Mercer remained at the inn for the rest of the day. He knew to avoid contact with his team. Flynn would be expecting that. Despite the money transfer, Colin Flynn did not trust him. And until he gave Flynn a reason to, he'd have to be cautious.

The only suspicious item Mercer had with him was his radio. It was a means of contacting the team, but it could be a noose. The moment he stepped foot outside the room, Flynn would have it searched. So Mercer crushed the earbud beneath his boot and flushed the tiny device down the toilet. Bastian would not be pleased to lose another piece of equipment, but the team knew to expect radio silence. Someone, Bastian, most likely, would scout Flynn's known locations to make sure Mercer was safe. As soon as Flynn became a bit more trusting, Mercer would leave intel at one of their predetermined dead drops. But that wouldn't be for a while. It was best to assume he was in this for the long haul.

Around nightfall, Mercer ventured out of his room.

He planned to grab a bite and check out Flynn's pub, but when he exited, he found Flynn waiting outside. The terrorist sat in the rear of a stark white SUV.

"Get in."

Mercer nodded and opened the back door.

From the weight of the door and the thickness of the windows, the SUV was meant to withstand a fair amount of firepower. Its construction seemed sturdier than the last SUV Flynn had, but it wouldn't be any more difficult to blow this one up if necessary.

"Give me your gun," Flynn ordered.

Mercer noted Killian watching from the passenger seat. If he didn't comply, he wouldn't make it out of the SUV alive, so he removed the Sig Sauer from his holster and held it out to Flynn.

Flynn checked to see if it was loaded, examined the sights, and aimed at Mercer. "I'm going to hold on to this for a while." Flynn wore a double-shoulder holster and tucked it into the empty slot on his right side.

"Where are we going?" Mercer glanced out the tinted window.

"You wanted a job, so I have a job for you."

The drive was quiet. No one spoke. Mercer paid attention to every turn and street they took. Despite spending hours studying maps and scouting Belfast, he was unsure of their destination.

When the SUV came to an abrupt halt, Mercer turned to Flynn. "You need a dock worker?"

"Something like that." Flynn opened his door and stepped out. "Let's go."

Mercer obediently followed, finding it odd Killian and Flynn's driver remained in the vehicle. Perhaps Flynn didn't want them to overhear what they had to discuss.

Mercer kept an eye on the periphery. As they

headed into a shipping warehouse, he couldn't help but feel he was walking into a trap. No one from his team had checked this location. It wasn't on their radar. Flynn didn't have it marked on the map in his office, and public records didn't indicate he controlled anything near the port. Either the intel was wrong, or Flynn's associates in the import/export business were letting him borrow the warehouse.

"Don't be shy." Flynn hit the light switch. "You mentioned someone wanted access to my guns. Only a few people know where I keep them, so it stands to reason one of them must have betrayed me."

"Possibly." Mercer eyed the freight containers. Most of the shipping labels were in Russian or some other Cyrillic language. According to the labels, the boxes contained foodstuffs. Since imported food was highly regulated, it didn't make sense to use those containers to import illegal arms, unless Flynn had people in customs.

"This way," Flynn instructed, an amused glint in his eye.

Mercer found it disconcerting, but he followed Flynn through a doorway into a separate, walled-in office. A man was shackled to the desk bolted to the floor. A piece of duct tape covered his mouth. His head shot up the moment the lights came on. Mercer recognized him from MI5's files–Kevin Aglin, suspected of terrorist activities across Europe and at least half a dozen murders.

"You believe he betrayed you?" Mercer asked. Unlike most men who found themselves in these situations, Aglin didn't appear frightened.

"Aye."

"Who is he?" Mercer circled the captive. He didn't see any surveillance devices. Did Flynn believe shackles were enough to detain prisoners? If so, Owen

Shepherd could be anywhere.

"It doesn't matter."

"Yes, it does. He might not be working alone."

"I've gotten the answers I need." Flynn removed the gun from his left side and held it out to Mercer. "Kill him."

Mercer examined the gun. It felt light, even for a thirty-five. He met Aglin's eyes, seeing an intrigued spark in them. "Fine." He aimed and pulled the trigger. As he suspected, the gun was empty. He cocked his head to the side, feigning confusion. Ejecting the magazine, he found it empty. "Explain."

Flynn nodded to Aglin, who flipped open one of the shackles on his wrist and then the other before removing the tape from his lips. He climbed to his feet and stepped closer to Mercer. They were roughly the same height and build.

"I wanted to see if you could follow orders," Flynn said as Aglin took the gun from Mercer's hand.

Mercer didn't take his eyes off Aglin. "Did this prove anything?"

Flynn shrugged.

"So he's not a traitor?"

"No. Kevin's family. He's one of the few men I trust completely."

Aglin loaded the gun and tucked it into his waistband. "You looking to cause trouble for Colin?"

"On the contrary. I'm trying to prevent it," Mercer said.

"We'll see about that." Aglin rubbed the corner of his mouth. "The trouble didn't start until you showed up."

Mercer glanced at Flynn. "If you don't require my services, I'll leave you be."

Flynn clapped Mercer on the back. "Enough of this. You passed the test. Now, we drink."

The three of them clambered back into the SUV. The back seat was barely large enough to fit the men comfortably. Mercer studied his companions, feeling naked and exposed without a weapon or Bastian's nagging in his ear.

"Colin," Aglin whispered, "I didn't find anything at Alana's."

Flynn gave the other man a sharp look. "We'll discuss that later."

Mercer turned away from the window. "Mr. Flynn, is there something I should know?"

"You'll know what I want you to when I want you to." He sunk back into the seat. The look on his face kept Aglin from speaking, and neither Killian nor the driver made any attempt to communicate.

Mercer understood team dynamics. For someone Flynn considered a brother, Kevin Aglin didn't comprehend the fundamentals about speaking in front of outsiders. Mercer filed that thought away for later consideration, cleared his throat, and gave Aglin a friendly smile. "No hard feelings, mate. It was nothing personal. I was just doing as I was told."

"No worries," Aglin replied, but the sentiment wasn't sincere.

The SUV stopped outside the pub. Flynn waited for Killian to check the perimeter before opening his car door. Mercer waited patiently on the sidewalk. He scanned the area, but he didn't spot any friendly faces. Bastian might be positioned somewhere nearby, but the analyst was smart enough to remain hidden. However, something told Mercer he was on his own.

"Julian," Flynn called as the rest of the men went inside, leaving only Killian to monitor the exterior, "you order another drink like you did last night, and I'll let the boys draw straws to see who puts a bullet in your head. Is that understood?"

"Yes, sir."

"Good." Flynn gestured for Mercer to go ahead, so he could whisper something to Killian.

The trick to any infiltration was to appear to belong, so Mercer went to the bar, ordered a pint, and took a seat. He scanned the area. Broken bottles would make useful weapons, as would the pool cues near the back of the room. The pub had two pool tables which he had barely noticed the previous evening. The rack of cue sticks stood against the corner at the back of the room. However, the racked balls caught Mercer's eye. One of those wrapped in a scarf or sock would make a decent weapon.

None of Flynn's men approached. In fact, they treated Mercer like a leper. It might have had to do with threatening to have them shot less than twenty-four hours ago, but there was nothing he could do about it now. However, from the constant leers, there was a good chance he might not make it out of the room alive.

Eventually, Flynn took a seat beside him. With a nod, Flynn dismissed the men, leaving only Aglin, Killian, and the driver waiting in opposite corners of the bar. The three of them were armed, as was Flynn.

"You still don't trust me." Mercer finished his beer. "That's smart. I wouldn't trust me either."

"Tell me about the man you hired, the one who shot off the tip of my ear." Flynn fingered the bandage.

"Not much to tell. He's another mercenary I crossed paths with in Africa. He happened to be working a job in the area and had a few hours to spare."

"What's his name?"

"You would have him killed, and that's bad for business."

"Maybe I should kill you. You seem bad for business." Flynn removed the Sig and pressed it against the hollow beneath Mercer's jaw. "It'd be easy enough, eh? Unless your man arrives to save your sorry arse again."

"No one's coming. Go ahead and shoot." Mercer waited, understanding this was about Flynn reestablishing his dominance and saving face. "I can't stop you."

Flynn laughed. "Bang." He put the gun on the bar and grabbed a bottle of whiskey. He hooked two glasses with his fingertips and put one in front of Mercer and poured. "Drink."

Mercer lifted the glass and swallowed. Flynn refilled it, emptying the rest of the bottle before grabbing a fresh one from behind the bar. He topped off Mercer's glass and filled his own. Flynn took a long sip, deflating as he swallowed. His shoulders sagged, and he rested his head in his hands. For once, Colin Flynn appeared overwhelmed. The stress was getting to him. Mercer could use that.

"Last night, someone broke into Alana's flat," Flynn said. "You were right. Someone is trying to fuck with me, so I want to know how you knew they'd go after her."

Mercer took another sip. They were finally getting down to business. "Was she hurt?"

"No. She left before the bastard broke in. She's fine." Flynn eyed Mercer over the rim of his glass. "I'm waiting."

"It made sense."

"Bollocks. You knew. Were you behind it?"

"Bloody hell. I was here with you last night, remember?"

"And after that?"

Mercer felt warm. Too warm. He blinked, painting

a smile on his face. "Honestly, I was working on my exit strategy. The way I figured it, you'd either hire me or kill me. I had a fifty-fifty shot and needed a contingency."

"Who's to say I won't do both?" Flynn laughed, and Mercer found himself laughing along with the terrorist. "Were you responsible for the break-in?"

A telling buzz went through Mercer's mind. "No, mate. I'm not insane." His eyes rested on the whiskey glass. Flynn didn't drink from the same bottle. "Bugger."

"Hmm?"

Mercer held the smile, hoping to appear oblivious. "I need to piss. Excuse me."

The moment he stood, he knew he was in trouble. The buzzing in his head turned into an intense pain, and the room spun. It took all of his concentration to navigate his way from the bar to the men's room without stumbling. The floor which appeared solid last night now pitched worse than a sailboat caught in a hurricane.

He pushed the door open, grabbing the edge of the sink before collapsing to the floor. What did Flynn put in that whiskey? Shoving a finger down his throat, Mercer gagged and choked before vomiting into the sink. Well, mostly into the sink. He heaved again, but it was too late.

He tried to straighten, but the floor lurched upward from beneath his feet. He fell backward and stared up at the blinding ceiling light. The door opened, and Aglin and Killian entered.

"Looks like you had too much, mate," Aglin said.

"What did you do to me?" Mercer asked.

"Nothing yet." The men hoisted Mercer to his feet and dragged him into the back of the SUV. The driver was already in the front, and Flynn was in the passenger seat.

Everything blurred. Mercer struggled to hang on to consciousness. His limbs weighed him down, heavy and uncooperative. He was barely aware of being hauled out of the SUV and dropped onto a cold tile floor.

Flynn knelt down and smacked his cheek. "Wake up."

Mercer blinked, his tongue thick in his mouth. "What did you do to me?" The words came out garbled.

"I gave you a little something to loosen your tongue. I have a few questions that need answering. And you're going to answer them truthfully. What you say will determine your fate, but first, I need to make sure no one's listening in. You said I shouldn't trust anyone, but I want to trust you. You just need to prove yourself."

Flynn nodded to Killian, who took Mercer's shoes and belt before stripping off the rest of Mercer's clothing. "Colin," Killian said, "he's been tortured recently. I'm not sure how well he'll respond."

"That won't stop me from giving it a go." Aglin grinned, a sick, demented look that Mercer vowed to wipe off the man's face.

Flynn examined the recent bruises and fresh scars. He slapped Mercer lightly on the cheek to get his attention. "How did this happen?"

"Knife," Mercer said without thinking. A quick answer didn't cause the jolt of pain to shoot through his skull, but he'd been interrogated enough times to know when and how to lie. As a general rule, it was usually best to deny everything, but he needed Flynn to trust him, which meant the terrorist needed to get enough of the truth so he'd believe everything. And Mercer wasn't in any condition to withhold everything, just the important details.

"I can see that." Flynn stood. "I don't want to hurt you. I want to protect you, like I do the rest of my family, but I don't know you. I don't know why you're here or what you want. Answer Kevin's questions and this will stop. I will stop it. Do you understand?"

Mercer squinted, forcing himself to nod. His body was sluggish, just like his mind. He couldn't fight back, and Flynn knew it.

Aglin examined the various scars, finding the deepest one and pushing the pads of his fingers into it. Mercer screamed. Whatever cocktail he'd been given wreaked havoc on his nervous system and pain receptors. Or he was always in this much pain and wasn't aware. Aglin retracted his fingers, watching the ribs spread as Mercer gasped and rolled onto his side, the tile floor cold against his overheated flesh.

Aglin poked at the wound again, and Mercer howled. Flynn's eyes came to rest on the recent bruise, courtesy of Brody Devlin. "Stop," Flynn instructed, kneeling beside Mercer. "It looks like you have plenty of enemies. I can hold them off, but you have to tell me who's coming for me."

"I can take care of myself."

"You don't have to. Why did someone do this to you?" Flynn tapped the bruise.

"Side effect of my work."

"What is your work?"

"Whatever has to be done." Mercer watched as Aglin picked up the belt and tugged on it a few times before folding it in half and slapping the thick leather against the wall. The thwack echoed against the hard, smooth surfaces.

"Why did you turn your back on your country? Why did you leave the SAS?" Flynn wiped his hands on his trousers and made room for Aglin.

The bodyguard used the belt like a whip, striking Mercer across the chest. The former SAS operative screamed, nearly blacking out. He had barely recovered when Aglin moved down to his knees.

Aglin let the belt dangle to the floor, building up the anticipation and dread before swinging hard. The leather cut into Mercer's thighs. It stung, drawing blood and causing welts to form.

"Another operative killed my wife," Mercer spat. "The SAS let it happen. They," tears welled in his eyes, his skull on fire, "betrayed me. They tried to blame me."

Aglin swung the belt again, gentler this time. The metal clasp hit against Mercer's tender bits. Mercer jerked, hissing. Before this was over, he might be castrated.

"Wait." Flynn put a hand on Aglin's arm before the guard could inflict another blow. The terrorist watched Mercer swallow down the sob. "You lost your wife?"

"Yes." Mercer bit back another sob. Once he regained his faculties, Colin Flynn would pay.

"Who blew up my car?"

The truth blared through Mercer's mind like a trumpet. Truth serum didn't exist, but whatever concoction Flynn mixed into the whiskey made the power of suggestion nearly overpowering. "I don't know. Probably someone Mathias Murphy sent," Mercer managed through gritted teeth. The name surfaced from MI5's reports and Flynn's prior musings. "He wants what you have. He wants the power. He thinks you've grown lazy." Mercer's mind drifted to Shepherd, but he locked his jaw to keep the truth from spilling out.

Flynn rubbed his mouth, circling Mercer's naked body. "Did Mathias try to hire you?"

"Yes." The single word lie was easier to get out. "I think so."

"What about your government contacts? MI5 wanted you to do their bidding. I've seen their requests."

"Fuck them." Mercer tried to push off the floor, but between the vertigo and slight muscle paralysis, he couldn't gain any traction. "Fuck them all."

"Good, you're finally being honest." Flynn crouched down near Mercer's face. "I just have a few more questions, and then we'll get you cleaned up."

FOURTEEN

The interrogation continued for hours. Mercer could feel his grip slipping. He wasn't sure what he was saying. He couldn't discern dreams from reality. What was happening? When he couldn't fight the drugs anymore, he stopped speaking. He'd rather die than jeopardize his team. But Flynn didn't appear angry. He wiped the blood from Mercer's chest and spoke softly to his men.

Mercer was vaguely aware of being dragged back to the car. When he blinked again, he was naked outside the inn. Killian and Aglin carried him down the hall and to his room. He caught a glimpse of Flynn. The faction leader was on the phone. Then everything went black.

Mercer woke with a blanket thrown over him. A woman, the brunette who'd spoken to Flynn two nights ago, rinsed the washcloth in a basin of water before washing the blood from Mercer's chest. The hot water stung, and he hissed.

"Shh," she soothed. "The worst is over now."

Mercer looked around the room. He was back at the inn. His Sig rested on the table. Flynn leaned against the dresser. For a moment, Mercer feared what he had said. What did he tell Flynn? Was the team in jeopardy? Was the op scrapped? But he had been trained to withstand torture and drugs. He would have died before sacrificing his team or their mission. He relaxed only slightly, desperate to recall the lies he told. He'd need to know what he said to stick with his story.

"How are you feeling?" Flynn asked.

Mercer wasn't sure what game the terrorist was playing now. He tried to sit up, but his head spun. His limbs felt like gelatin, and he didn't know if he had full control of his faculties.

"Easy." Flynn brought a glass over to the bedside table. "Drink this. It'll help."

"No, thanks."

Flynn let out a dramatic sigh and took a sip from the glass. "It's not drugged, see?"

"Piss off."

"Maura, get fresh water and clean bandages." Flynn waited for the woman to step out of the room before he spoke again. "My wife was also killed. My children too. It's a hard thing losing your family. And it's even harder to relive it."

Mercer squinted, recalling the story he had told. Operatives were trained to resist, but when they were pushed beyond the brink, they were trained to disclose useless information. And that was the story Mercer had shared. "I'm sorry," Mercer managed, even though his thoughts were far from sympathetic.

Flynn nodded, lost in his own nightmare. "I should have stopped Kevin sooner. For that, I apologize. But you need to see things from my perspective. A stranger walked into my pub, shot at me and my people, and claimed he was there to buy guns. We both know that wasn't the truth. You came to me for a job. Don't waste your breath denying it."

"I go where the work is."

Flynn laughed, "And this was the day after someone blew up my car and I lost one of my guards."

"Someone was killed?" Mercer asked. The lie filled him with relief that he was back in control of his thoughts.

"It was an accident." Flynn waved it away like it was nothing. "But I didn't know if I could trust you. Now I know I can." He picked up Mercer's cell phone and held it out. "You gave me the intel I wanted on Mathias Murphy and his crew. Now let me pay my debt. Enter your bank account information. You've earned your fee."

Mercer entered the number just as the woman returned. She took a seat on the opposite side of the bed and continued to clean and dress his wounds. "I can take care of myself," he said.

She withdrew, her eyes meeting Flynn's who gave a barely perceptible headshake, and she resumed her ministrations.

"Let her tend to you," Flynn said, leaving no room for argument. "Maura's a nurse. She'll get your head straight and make you forget the unpleasantness of these last few hours. By the morning, this will be nothing more than a memory of a bad dream."

Instead of arguing, Mercer handed the device back to Flynn, who transferred another $50,000 into the account. Bastian would be monitoring their accounts and know where to look to gain access to Flynn's. With this information, the team could make a list of Flynn's buyers and discover any potential informants or leaks inside the government. Maybe the last few hours were worth it.

"You have your money. You can walk away if you want, Julian, but as you pointed out, I'm in need of outside help. And I don't think things will end well for you if Mathias were to discover you came to me with a proposition." Flynn put the phone on the nightstand. "I'll let you think about it. We'll talk again in the morning."

Mercer tried again to dismiss Maura, but Flynn had given her orders. She wouldn't disobey the faction leader. After bandaging his chest, she pushed the blanket away and tended to the cuts on his thighs. When she touched him, he grabbed her wrist.

"Leave me be."

She pulled her arm free. "I'm making sure there isn't any permanent damage."

He didn't have the energy to fight. He sunk back against the pillow, watching her through his lashes. His head felt like it'd been knocked around Wimbledon. He needed the fog to lift and the invisible weights to leave his limbs. And despite everything, Maura's tenderness helped.

The faction leader knew precisely what he was doing. It was psychological manipulation. Basically, Flynn intended to trigger a quasi-Stockholm Syndrome. The torture and drugs would break a man, pushing him to the brink, and then Flynn stepped in, called off the attack, stopped the pain, and heaped rewards on Mercer, along with promises of more to come. It was an apology and a bargaining chip. Flynn was shrewd. Maybe Owen Shepherd did turn.

Mercer sighed, a wheeze traveling through his chest and culminating in an angry cough. She cleaned him up and covered him with the blanket.

"Colin's right," she said as she collected the medical supplies. "You should drink something. I don't quite care for that rattling in your chest." She picked up the stethoscope and pressed it against his left side. "That bastard really did some damage. You need to take care of yourself. I suggest you steer clear of Kevin Aglin. He won't forget you tried to kill him, and he'll hold a grudge until the day he dies."

"I've noticed."

She chuckled. "You would have." She stepped toward the door. "You need anything, tell Colin. He'll send for me."

"Do you always do what he says?"

"Aye. He's going to save us all. He's one of the few left who's willing to fight. I don't see how everyone's already forgotten what it used to be like, how terrible it was, but he hasn't. I'd do anything for that man, and you'll be hard-pressed to find anyone around here who won't, including Kevin." She jerked her chin expectantly at the glass, waiting for Mercer to take a sip. "If Colin hadn't intervened, Kevin would have torn you to bits. Colin must see something worthwhile in you. That's rare. He wouldn't have saved you otherwise, so you can trust that he won't hurt you again. He's just fighting for the cause. It'd be best if you remember that."

She shut the door, and Mercer dropped back against the pillow. Between the drugs, the beating, and everything else, he was spent. Reluctantly, he drained the glass, wondering if the contents would kill him in his sleep or if Flynn would come back and put two behind his ear.

Hours later, voices outside the door roused him. He climbed out of bed, stiff and sore. He dressed, ignoring the sting of the lash marks. He field-stripped his Sig, making sure each piece was in working order before reassembling it and pressing his ear against the door. A quick glance at his watch showed it was just after oh nine hundred. By now, Bastian would be frantic. He had to find a way to get a message to his team.

"Are you sure?" Mercer recognized the voice as Killian's. "You saw the marks. The scars. He's accustomed to torture, and based on his record, he's doled it out a time or two. How can Colin believe the intel he gave was good? He would have said anything last night to save his skin."

"I don't know, mate. No one's ever been able to resist before. You watched him break. Half the town heard him wailing and begging to die," another voice replied. "I don't think anyone could fake that. But it's not our call. It's Colin's, and he believes Mercer is valuable."

"We'll see." The voices quieted, as if the men were walking away from the door. "Keep an eye on him. The moment he crosses a line, Colin needs to know about it."

Were those two idiots attempting to disseminate misinformation? Perhaps they wanted to test Mercer to see if he was a snitch. Or they were clueless and didn't realize he might hear them through the door. Regardless, he was tired of games. The one last night could have killed him. He had to be more careful. Lives depended on it. Bastian's, Donovan's, and Hans' lives depended on it, not to mention countless others.

Mercer took a seat on the bed. The buzzing headache was growing in intensity. He needed water. He needed to flush the remnants of the drugs out of his system. He went to the bathroom, rinsed the glass, and drank. He'd wait at least an hour before leaving the room.

Colin had men waiting for him, and Mercer didn't know how he wanted to proceed. He had to commit to the soldier of fortune persona, but after last night, Mercer couldn't be sure what he said or what impression he made on Flynn. He'd have to sell it even harder now. Unfortunately, he had no idea what that would entail. He possessed very few details concerning Mathias Murphy, the rival faction leader. Painting him as a scapegoat and enemy wasn't a smart move, but in the heat of the moment with Flynn already convinced of Mathias's treachery, Mercer didn't have much of a choice.

He needed to contact his team. He needed facts. They needed to perform a threat assessment. His words might have inadvertently triggered a war between the two terrorist factions. Perhaps the authorities should intervene.

When he couldn't wait any longer, he stepped out of his room. Killian and Flynn's driver sat near the front desk. Mercer moved past them, doing his best to ignore them. When he stepped out into the mid-morning light, the sun's reflection off the white SUV nearly blinded him.

"Mercer," Killian called, "Colin told me to take you wherever you want to go."

"Why should I get in a car with you?"

Killian shifted slightly, making the gun on his hip apparent. "You don't have to, but it would be in your best interest. I suggest you hear Colin out."

"Mr. Flynn said I could walk away."

"Go ahead, but it's a long walk to the airport or ferry."

Mercer felt his pockets, realizing his car keys were gone, as was the sedan he rented. They must have taken it the previous night to check the navigation system and search for devices or clues as to his loyalty.

"You'll take me to Mr. Flynn?"

"Aye." Killian clicked the remote unlock, and Mercer climbed into the passenger seat. The second guard, the driver from last night, remained inside the inn. As Mercer suspected, he would toss the room to see if circumstances changed in light of last night's events.

Mercer slipped on his sunglasses and pretended to pay little attention to their surroundings. His head ached, but it was nothing compared to the way he felt last night. They passed a café on the corner. "Mind if we stop for breakfast?"

Killian ignored him and continued to drive. In broad daylight, the area around Flynn's compound looked residential and inviting with lush vegetation and well-kept lawns. They drove through the front gate, and Killian parked in the driveway. He left the SUV far enough back, so a sniper on the roof could pick Mercer off with a single shot. However, Mercer ignored the possibility. If Colin Flynn wanted him dead, he'd do it himself.

"How long have you worked for Mr. Flynn?" Mercer asked.

"I don't work for him." Killian led the way up the steps. "We grew up together. We work together."

"I see." Mercer resisted the urge to point out the obvious, that Flynn was top dog and everyone else was expendable. Right now, he needed to garner favor with the other faction members, not make enemies.

Killian held the door open, and Mercer stepped through. The house looked a lot different with the sunlight shining through the windows. "Straight back. He's in the kitchen."

Mercer moved forward, turning his head to look around. "What's up there?"

"Keep moving."

"Fine." Mercer went down the hallway, finding himself in the living room, just off the kitchen.

"Julian," Flynn greeted from the table, "I'm glad

you decided to join me." He gestured to an empty chair. "Please, sit down. Alana, bring our guest a plate. He must be famished."

Mercer took a seat, watching Flynn nod to Killian, who headed back the way he came, reactivating the security system on his way out. Mercer listened, but there were no other sounds anywhere in the house. Did Flynn dismiss the rest of his bodyguards?

Alana placed utensils and a plate in front of him before helping herself to a heaping serving of bangers and mash. "Dig in," she said.

Mercer waited for Flynn to push the serving plate closer before he helped himself. The kettle on the stove whistled, and Alana flew out of her chair to grab it. She was rather impish, petite and svelte. But there was a fire in her eyes.

"Tea?" She filled Flynn's cup and held the kettle expectantly in front of Mercer.

He waited for the faction leader to take a sip before he said, "Yes, please." If only Bastian could see him now. The analyst would think Flynn had beaten manners and etiquette into him.

The hot tea calmed the ache in Mercer's chest, and he closed his eyes. With Flynn, he didn't know what to expect, but he needed to stay grounded and alert. When he opened his eyes, he found Flynn studying his face.

"You wanted to speak to me?" Mercer asked.

"We have business to discuss." Flynn nodded to Alana. "Thank you for breakfast, sweetheart."

She untucked her bare feet from beneath her and got up to clear the plates. Flynn pushed his plate away and rested his forearms on the table. She cleared his place and hers, giving Mercer a curious glance. "Are you finished?"

"Yes. It was lovely."

While she took his plate to the sink, he refilled his teacup. His eyes remained glued to Flynn. As Alana made another pass by the table, Flynn reached for her hand and brushed his lips against her knuckles. Mercer couldn't discern if that was his way of staking his claim or if he really was madly in love. Even violent men possessed the capacity for love and compassion, but Mercer learned long ago it was easier to carry out a mission when he didn't humanize the target.

"Go upstairs," Flynn instructed, and she left the room. "Have you made up your mind, Julian?"

"I haven't decided yet. As a rule, I don't work for men who drug and beat me."

"That's a good rule, but these aren't normal conditions." Flynn picked up a folder. "The fact that you're here means you need work or fear retaliation."

"From whom?"

"Mathias, most likely." A sick smile twisted Flynn's lips. "You get itchy when you don't have a job lined up. I understand what drives you. You want payback. And I'll let you have it. Once you find out who betrayed me, you can take your pound of flesh before I finish the job." Flynn opened the folder and placed a classified MI5 document on the table, detailing Owen Shepherd's mission.

"Where did you get this?" Mercer's stomach twisted in knots, and he regretted having eaten.

"I'm connected. I have to be." Flynn leaned back. "You might be wrong about Mathias. MI5's full of deceptive bastards. They might have approached you under the guise of being one of my rivals. You see, MI5 has infiltrated my ranks. Perhaps, they've done the same to Mathias's faction. They would love to pit us against one another. If we kill each other, they won't have anything to worry about. So before I take action, I need you to find out everything you can. I won't go to war without proof, and I need to know who amongst us has betrayed me. So do it quietly. Can you handle that?"

Mercer read the briefing notes, finding they lacked the agent's name. It only listed code names. "Tell me where you got this."

"That isn't important. You have your secrets, Julian, and I have mine. Last night, you told me what these bastards did to you, to your wife. I'm giving you a gift. Find the problem, and exterminate it. Kill as many government agents as you like. I have no love for them, and it will save me time later."

"I don't work for free." Mercer remained still as he fought off the nervous twitch. Shepherd had been compromised. For Flynn to possess notes on a classified briefing, the source was inside Palace Barracks. Owen Shepherd was probably dead by now, or he'd been forced to flee. Were the men outside Lara's flat part of the faction or cronies working for the government traitor?

"I'll pay you another fifty."

Mercer dragged his gaze from the document. "On one condition."

"Go ahead."

"You tell me how you came upon this piece of information."

"It fell into my lap."

"That's not good enough."

"It has to be. Why the sticking point?"

"Clearly, you have a source on the inside. Why can't you ask him who's been planted inside your group? You can cut out the middleman, and I'll be on my way."

"My source is dead. He asked too many questions, so I had to kill him. Is history going to repeat itself?"

Mercer glanced toward the door. "Last night, you said I could walk away."

"You can, but I don't think you will. You understand my vision. Maybe you want to be a part of it beyond the scope of this one job. I need men like you, Julian. Men who've experienced the heartbreak and deceit firsthand and want to stop the cycle."

Mercer paused, as if giving this serious consideration. Hopefully, Flynn believed he held the power position. If he did, that meant he didn't realize the tables had turned. Originally, Mercer approached him for a job, now Flynn was refusing to let Mercer go. With that type of insistence, the faction leader wouldn't notice he was being played. That meant Mercer and his team had a fighting chance of stopping a strike and finding out what became of Owen Shepherd.

"Fifty thousand. No strings attached. The body count is at my discretion. If I don't want to get my hands dirty, I won't. And if I decide to leave, I will."

"Just make sure you find out what master the bastard is serving before we part ways," Flynn insisted. "If it's Mathias, I have to know. And if it's MI5, they'll get what's coming to them. But I will not wage a needless war. I don't have the time or firepower to waste. I have my own plans to carry out." A spark lit behind Flynn's eyes. "Maybe you'll help me with that."

"The last thing I need is to be labeled a terrorist on top of everything else Her Majesty has already accused me of, but the damage has been done. They deserve to pay."

Flynn smiled. "Bloody good. Get some rest. I'll need you completely recovered. And I'll pass word along. My men won't bother you again. You're one of us now. You'll be treated like the rest." Flynn's eyes went cold.

"I trust you'll keep our arrangement private. Should I find out this is a ruse, last night will seem like a tickle party compared to what you'll face."

Mercer nodded, wondering how much Flynn actually trusted him.

FIFTEEN

After leaving Flynn's compound, Mercer returned to the inn. His belongings were ever so slightly out of place. Clearly, they'd been searched. It was a good thing he had destroyed the radio, even though he regretted being out of contact with his team. A large gift basket sat atop the dresser, filled with muffins, dried meats, bottles of booze, and other essentials. Who knew terrorists sent gift baskets?

Mercer disassembled the package, but he didn't find any surveillance devices. However, after last night, he had no desire to consume anything Colin Flynn sent. After emptying the basket, Mercer tossed the uneaten foods into a bag and brought the liquor and basket to the front desk. After that, he took the bag of food with him. On his walk, he stopped to feed the ducks and squirrels. When they appeared unharmed, he continued his aimless trek and gave the bag to the first homeless man he found.

Then he ducked into a café across the street. He took a seat at the window and watched the man gorge himself on the baked goods and meats. Mercer finished his tea, aware of the two men following him. He recognized them from Flynn's pub. Obviously, Flynn didn't completely trust him. Until he did, Mercer wouldn't be able to contact his team.

"Bollocks," he muttered into the ceramic. His watchful gaze remained on the homeless man who seemed just as healthy as he'd been before eating a good portion of the gift basket. Apparently, the food hadn't been tainted. Now Mercer knew for certain Flynn didn't want him dead, at least not yet. That was progress. Maybe Flynn really did want to convert Mercer into a true believer.

Leaving a few quid on the table, Mercer left the café and went into a nearby shop. Bastian had contingencies in place, dead drops and check-ins that no one would ever find unless they knew where to look. Mercer couldn't risk leaving anything obvious, believing the two men keeping track of him might find it by mistake, so he went to one of the shelves, found some superglue, and used it to stick a coin, face up, to the back of the shelf, hidden behind boxes of cereal.

After selecting a few items from the aisle, Mercer went to the counter and paid. Bastian would know where and what to look for. Heads up meant Mercer was safe, and Flynn's men would never be the wiser. Even if they found the coin, they'd think a kid had glued it to the shelf as a practical joke.

Confident his team would find the message and realize he was alive and not in need of a rescue, Mercer returned to the inn. Flynn told him to rest, and it would not be wise to disregard orders this quickly. Now Mercer's biggest problem was convincing Flynn's men to voluntarily surrender the intel he needed. The chemical weapons were Mercer's main priority. Even if he couldn't get the list of targets or the date and time of the attack, he'd be able to limit the casualties by destroying the chemical weapons. Flynn would want to keep them close, but after the explosion that killed his wife and children, the terrorist wouldn't keep them inside his house. Would he?

Mercer reached for a pen and paper and sketched out a map. Flynn had taken him to a warehouse and some other facility to conduct the interrogation. But Flynn had to possess other properties, control other locations. And some arsehole at MI5 knew about it. Despite Flynn's insistence that the connection was dead, Mercer had trouble believing it. Every one of his instincts screamed Liam Partridge was working for Colin Flynn.

Bastian was already suspicious. Perhaps he had found damning evidence. It was pointless to speculate, so Mercer returned to the task at hand.

He had just tucked his rudimentary map into the vent and screwed the grate back in place when someone knocked on his door. "Yes?"

Killian stood in the hallway, his hands in his pockets. "Colin thought you might like to join us for dinner and drinks."

"Fine."

"Are you ready?"

Mercer pulled the door closed without giving the room a second glance. He doubted they'd find his sketch, and even if they did, it was a vague doodle. Meaningless to everyone else.

Dinner went off without a hitch. Flynn spoke to his lieutenants and closest friends. Mercer only caught a few surnames and didn't dare ask any questions. The group was seated around a large round table in an upscale restaurant. Alana remained at Flynn's side. The faction leader placed his left hand on her thigh when they sat down, and he had yet to move it.

No one spoke of their extracurricular activities. They barely spoke about anything aside from the food, wine, and some good-natured ribbing. It felt like a scene from a mobster flick.

"Oi, Julian, was it?" Aaron asked. "How long are you planning to stick around?"

Mercer glanced at Flynn, who had grown quiet. "We'll see. I move around often. I find it best to keep the authorities a few steps behind."

Aaron grinned. "Aye, so do we."

"Speaking of," Alana dug her nails into the back of Flynn's hand, "are you done sending me off with a babysitter?"

Flynn's eyes remained on Mercer. "Not yet, love."

She let out a huff. "Let me guess. You're going to force me to stay under lock and key?"

"You can't very well go home. The place is a ruddy mess. If you want, you can stay with your brother. But I much prefer having you close." Flynn sounded exhausted by the old argument.

Alana turned to Killian. "What do you think?"

"I think you're safer at Colin's than you are with me, but I can pull out the couch if that's what you want. I just want you safe and happy, Al. That's what we both want."

Mercer stared down at his plate, pretending to have no interest in the domestic squabble. But until now, he didn't realize the familial connection. Alana and Killian were siblings. That must be why Killian thought of Flynn like a brother, a soon-to-be brother-in-law, if one wanted to be literal. That information might be of use. Killian had a lot more at stake than his relationship with Flynn. He had his sister to protect. That's why he'd go to the ends of the earth to keep Colin Flynn safe and to keep his illegal activities off the radar. It also meant Killian knew more than anyone else in the faction.

Mercer found his mark. Now to turn Killian into an asset.

*   *   *

Despite Mercer's best efforts, Killian kept his distance while maintaining a watchful eye on the British outsider. Mercer knew it would take time to earn his trust. However, time was a precious commodity. He'd have to find a way to speed it up. He remained near the rear of Flynn's pub, watching Aaron and Donal shoot pool.

Eventually, he offered to play the winner, and on their insistence that they wager with a hefty sum, Mercer was welcomed into the game. Of course, he made it a point to lose. Winning would have solidified his pariah status. Plus, he knew the Irish. They wanted to dominate the English, if given the opportunity, to make up for the historical mistreatment.

By the end, Mercer made little headway into being accepted by Flynn's crew. Killian and Aglin would be the hardest to convince. After all, Kevin Aglin liked to hold grudges, and Killian exhibited more brainpower than the rest of the drunken fools, who seemed to care little about anything other than shooting pool, chugging beer, and blowing shit up.

Of course, now that Mercer signed on to Flynn's crusade, the rank and file would eventually fall in line. But until they were convinced Flynn hadn't gone daft, several refused to let Mercer out of their sights. Mercer heard the whispers and saw the surreptitious glances. No one trusted him, which meant they would never talk openly or confide in him. Even when they were piss drunk, none of them would answer his questions. At this rate, he'd never find out where Flynn kept the chemical weapons, what target he planned to hit, or the timetable for the intended strike. And he'd never find out what became of Owen Shepherd.

By three a.m., most of the lot couldn't even walk straight. Mercer tried asking about previous members and fallen comrades. But no one mentioned Owen. As far as Flynn's men were concerned, everyone was present and accounted for. This wouldn't be easy, but Mercer didn't realize it'd be this hard. He should have been better prepared before confronting Flynn in the pub that first night. Now he was stuck behind enemy lines. He needed his team. Hopefully, Bastian got his message.

This same routine went on for days. Each morning, Mercer attempted to lose the tail. The first day, a few of Flynn's men tried to follow on foot when he went for a run, so Mercer made it a point to make their attempt tedious and difficult. After the third kilometer, his muscles loosened, and he hit his stride. Flynn's men were in decent shape, but they weren't prepared for a fifteen kilometer run.

The next day, one intrepid bastard tried to follow in a car, so Mercer took to a walking path through the botanical gardens. After that, he didn't notice anyone tailing him, so he left a message at a dead drop. It was innocuous enough that no one outside his team would notice, let alone realize what the code meant. If all went according to plan, they'd rendezvous tomorrow.

The next morning, Mercer woke energized and optimistic. Truth be told, he missed his team and needed the support. Another day surrounded by terrorists would drive him mad. He laced his shoes, stretched, and set out at a brisk pace.

After a few kilometers, he lost the tail and headed for the river. The loop was the perfect spot to prevent Flynn's men from sneaking up or observing the exchange. That's why he chose this location. He just hoped Bastian was able to get away.

Mercer slowed. The analyst was waiting at the designated point along the River Lagan loop. Mercer stopped and stretched his calf muscles against the railing. Despite the seven kilometers he'd already run, his heart kept a steady beat. Only his left side burned, but that was normal under the circumstances. After all, didn't the doctors say cardio was good for the lungs?

"You all right?" Bastian asked.

"Fine."

"It's been days. I found the coin. Had I not, I might have thought you were dead."

"Flynn thought about it."

Bastian squinted into the horizon. "What happened?"

"To be honest, I'm not entirely sure. He laced my drink with a wicked cocktail. I just remember bits and pieces. But the next morning," Mercer's focus remained on untying his left shoe, "Flynn acted like I was a kindred spirit."

Bastian recognized that tone. "You told him about Michelle?"

"I don't remember, but I must have."

Bastian turned around and posed for a few selfies. "She's always on your mind. Under the circumstances, you had to say something. And you went with the best option."

"It doesn't matter. All that matters is I didn't compromise the team, but I can't be bloody sure of anything."

"Well, I am." Bastian turned to the side and

snapped a few more photographs before examining the screen. "We knew that would be your in with Flynn. Have you made any progress on locating the chemical weapons or Shepherd?"

"No. I take it neither have you." Mercer stared across the water, watching the periphery for signs of Flynn's men. It took more effort than it should to get away from them. Mercer never took the same route. He kept his destinations random. He left at different times, varied the distance and lengths, and kept an eye out for a tail. But it might not be enough. "Did anything shake loose on the gold paper?"

"A civilian office manager purchased it for social purposes."

"PR stunts."

Bastian lazily leaned one arm on the railing as he scrolled through the content on his phone, doing his best to appear touristy. "Anyone inside MI5 has access to it. It's in the bloody supply closet. I found it when I was looking for staples. I'm digging up as much as I can on Liam Partridge, but I'm not making much progress."

"Keep trying. Flynn trusts me, or he's starting to. He told me he had someone inside MI5, but the connection's supposedly dead."

"Do you think he meant Shepherd?"

"I don't know what to think. For all I know, it could be a lie. Or a test. He knows MI5 approached me. Maybe he thinks I'll go running back to them."

"Clearly, Flynn has a lot to learn."

"Indeed." Mercer went to work on the other shoe. "How are Hans and Donovan faring? Has there been any progress on their end?"

"You're not going to like it."

Mercer checked his watch. "Talk fast."

"Someone inside the government removed the car

from impound. The DNA results on the blood came back classified."

"Classified? How is that possible?"

"I don't know. Yancy is looking into it. I've contacted our mates at Interpol. I thought they might be a safer bet considering our current predicament. I'll let you know what we find. Well, I would if I had a way to contact you."

"Enough, Bas. I need you to perform a threat assessment on Mathias Murphy."

"Don't you think dealing with one terrorist cell is more than enough?"

Mercer stretched against the rail. In case someone was watching them, he didn't want anyone to realize he was talking to the sightseeing bloke taking selfies near the water. "I told you Flynn interrogated me. I had to say something."

"And starting a blood feud seemed like a good idea?"

"He left me no choice."

"Jules, what exactly happened?"

Mercer tightened his laces a final time. "It doesn't matter. I'm in. We should assume Shepherd's dead, but I will find out precisely what Flynn did to him. And I will find the chemical agents. What I need you to do is figure out which MI5 agents are in Flynn's pocket. We have to flush them out. Start with Partridge. Flynn had Shepherd's briefing notes. The op runner had the easiest access to that information. He could have copied it inside his office, slipped it into his coat, and passed it off to Flynn." Mercer removed the rudimentary sketch from his pocket and surreptitiously placed it on the railing. "Here are a few additional locations to scout."

"I'll look into it."

"Do that. If things go tits up between Murphy and

Flynn, MI5 will have to intervene. I don't care if they kill each other, but innocents might get caught in the crossfire."

"Anything else?"

"I need equipment. Make sure the stash houses are stocked. Guns, radios, everything. I don't know where I'll be or what I'll need, but I want to be prepared."

"I'll take care of it."

"Bas, watch over the team. Keep everyone alive and be careful. I have to go." Mercer hit the timer on his stopwatch and sprinted off in the opposite direction.

SIXTEEN

As per the instructions, Bastian remained for another fifteen minutes, taking more photographs before grabbing something from a vendor's cart and eating lunch on a nearby bench. Operatives at meets didn't hang around for fear of being spotted, but if Flynn's men were following Mercer, Bastian had to make it clear he wasn't hiding or rushing off. It was the only way to ensure Flynn wouldn't realize he and Mercer had exchanged intel. And after firing on Colin Flynn, Bastian didn't need to make anyone inside the faction suspicious. His life and Mercer's depended on it.

When Mercer emerged at the end of the loop, Killian was waiting. The bodyguard leaned against the car, his arms crossed over his chest. When he spotted Mercer, he waved him over.

"C'mon, it's time you get your feet wet. Colin has a job for us." He tossed Mercer a towel and climbed into the car.

Mercer wiped his face and opened the car door. He glanced over the roof, but he didn't see anyone watching or catch the glint reflecting off a scope. The timing couldn't have been worse, but something told him he and Bastian hadn't been compromised.

"Where are we going?" Mercer checked the weapon at the small of his back, the one he kept beneath the jacket he'd tied around his waist.

"You'll see."

"Answer the bloody question."

Killian snickered. "Afraid I'm taking you back to the warehouse to finish what Kevin started?"

"Colin wouldn't appreciate you knocking the shit out of me, so no, I'm not afraid. And for that reason, you shouldn't be either. I have no desire to anger him or Alana."

"Pisser." Killian's gaze drifted to the rearview mirror, but no one was following.

"You realize we're on the same side. We have the same goal in mind. The same endgame." Mercer wondered if Killian knew of the real reason Flynn was keeping the former SAS operative around. "We want to fuck with the powers that be as much as possible."

Killian would be hard to crack. He didn't speak much, but from his posture and commanding presence, he knew more than the others. However, it could be a bluff. Projecting an air of superiority was often enough to convince others that you were someone important. It was the basic alpha-beta mentality. However, the real alpha was Colin Flynn, and Killian knew it. Mercer snorted. In that scenario, he was the omega.

Over the last few days, Mercer had spent time with Flynn's inner circle, at the pub, at the dinner table, and at the warehouse, where they loaded weapons into the back of a truck. But aside from a few exchanged words when necessary, Killian made it clear he loathed the Englishman. The only reason any of them tolerated Mercer was because Flynn forced them to. They didn't trust Mercer after the stunt he pulled the first night at the pub and with good reason. He would have to do something to change that. He needed them to talk to him.

The car came to an abrupt halt, and Mercer stared up at a large cross. "I should have realized you were a religious man." Mercer eyed the tattoo on Killian's arm.

"Shut your mouth."

Mercer stepped out of the car and followed Killian to the side of the church and down the steps. Surprisingly, Flynn's errand boy trusted Mercer enough to walk in front of him. That was a step in the right direction.

The smell of burning candles and incense assaulted Mercer's senses. He blinked a few times, waiting for his eyes to adjust to the hazy, dark interior. A doorway carved into the wall caught Mercer's attention, and he crossed to it. Opening the door, he found nothing but a narrow staircase.

"Over here," Killian called. "Grab this."

Mercer lifted one side of the heavy box, and the two men carried it out of the basement and up the steps.

"What's inside?" Mercer asked.

"You'll see soon enough."

They loaded it into the boot and got back in the car. Mercer stared out the window. He'd have to tell his team about the church.

When they hit a pothole, Mercer cringed. "Should I be concerned that whatever's in the box might blow us to kingdom come?"

"Nothing's going to blow up unless Colin wants it to."

"What are we transporting? Are we moving bomb materials?"

"Not today. Just guns. Does that go against your sensibilities?"

"No." Belatedly, Mercer wondered what an actual MI5 agent would do in this situation. Is this how Owen Shepherd was caught? Or was Shepherd smart enough to let it go to maintain his cover?

"Good. We'll be delivering the shipment to some buyers and collecting our fees. Colin thought it'd be a good way to introduce you to the operation. He says you don't mind getting your hands dirty."

"Brilliant."

"Some people get squeamish around guns. They see it as killing their own kind, but you're not one of us. You couldn't care less. The more we shoot each other, the happier you'll be, eh?"

"You're right. I don't care." Mercer knew he had to stick to the script, but he heard the disdain in Killian's voice. "You disagree with arming your countrymen?"

"Enemy of my enemy and all. But once our mutual goal has been reached, they'll turn the weapons on us. And it'll make it that much harder to kill them. The bloody cockroaches."

"Have you shared this view with Colin?" Mercer asked.

"It doesn't matter. I do what I'm told. Just like you should."

"Is this how Colin finances his operation?"

"Partially." Killian turned to Mercer. "You're awfully chatty today and, might I add, a bit too inquisitive for your own good."

"I'm just trying to sort some things out."

"I'm still trying to figure out what you could have said to Colin to make him trust you. He only trusts his own kind, and you are not one of us."

"Because I don't bleed green?"

"Like I said, the enemy of my enemy."

"That philosophy works both ways. You're the enemy of my enemy, as well." Mercer stared out the window. "You were there that night. You know what happened. Colin asked the questions. I was in no condition not to be forthcoming."

"Just because Colin trusts you, doesn't mean I do. I know you filled his head with lies, telling him someone inside the faction is betraying him. It's the only reason he'd even consider outside help, but you're wrong. From where I'm sitting, you're the problem, Julian. Before you arrived, we didn't have problems. Now we do. It won't take Colin long to figure that out. Make no mistake. Your days are numbered."

"Is that right?"

"Aye."

Mercer rubbed the stubble on his cheek. "Someone blew up Colin's SUV right outside his pub. You don't think that was a problem?"

"I think that was you."

"Really? I've seen his security. The way you bloody lot hang around that pub at all hours of the night. You and I both know no outsider could have gotten near Flynn's car without you or another one of his guards noticing. If I had done it, mate, you would have bloody well remembered seeing me." Mercer turned in the seat, switching to interrogation mode. "The way I see it, either someone from Flynn's inner circle blew up his ride or made it a point to look the other way so an outsider could get close enough. Which is it?"

"You're daft."

"Were you there that night? Are you sure Colin doesn't think it was you? I've seen you with the men, the way you give orders. Now, you've made me aware of your loathing of this filthy gun business. I'm starting to think maybe this is why Colin wants us to spend some quality time together."

"Don't be a fucking nutter. I had nothing to do with it. I wasn't even there when the SUV blew."

"Convenient. Did someone ask you to step away?"

"Piss off. I love Colin. So does my sister. We'll be family soon enough." Killian's neck reddened. The flush crept up to his ears. If Mercer didn't back off soon, Flynn's second-in-command would put two in Mercer's chest and toss him out of the car.

"You're right, mate. I was out of line. I apologize." Mercer waited for Killian's normal coloring to return before he said, "We should have a think about this."

"No."

"Colin said one of his men was killed that same night."

"Brody wasn't killed. He fell off the bloody roof."

"Men don't fall off rooves."

Killian turned, his eyes cold as ice. "There was a storm. He must have lost his footing."

"Whatever you need to tell yourself, but the timing seems suspect to me. According to Colin, the explosion and the accidental death happened the same night. Could this Brody chap have leaked intel to someone with a vendetta? Maybe Brody's accident was meant to keep him from confessing his sins. I know for a fact Colin can get anyone to tell him anything he wants to know at any time. Whoever's working against him would know this and be forced to tie up loose ends."

"There's no way. Brody never went to the pub. He always stayed at the house."

"Where were you that night?"

"At the house."

Mercer let out a scoff and turned his focus to the windshield, an idea forming in his head. Killian would make the perfect fall guy, which would make it that much easier to turn him into an asset. Mercer could leverage Killian's position and disdain for gunrunning and use it to his advantage.

"Oi," Killian shoved Mercer's shoulder, "what are you thinking?"

"Maybe Brody was given a slow-acting poison. Something time-released to mimic a heart attack."

"He fell. End of story."

"What did the autopsy say?"

"We handled it in-house, as we do with the rest of our difficulties."

"Fine, but MI5 has information on Colin. The Security Service knows he has something big planned, and they're watching him." Mercer checked the side mirror again. "Maybe they sourced that out to the police. Are you planning on losing the tail? Or do you intend to lead them straight to the drop?"

"I know what I'm doing."

So do I, Mercer thought.

"They're always up our arse. That's nothing new, and neither is Mathias Murphy's rivalry with our faction. These are constants." Killian turned down another street, and the police car continued going straight. After another two turns, Killian parked the car and turned in his seat. "How do you know so much about what MI5 knows? Are you working for them? It would explain a lot."

"Like I told Colin, an unknown party approached me to do a job, but I never agree to anything without doing my research. I spent over a decade in Her Majesty's service." Mercer emphasized it by spitting on the floor, just like he'd seen Flynn do. "Even after everything military intelligence put me through, I keep my enemies close. I know what they know, and with the way they're keeping tabs on Colin, I'd have to be insane to make a move against him. Either you and the rest of his boys would hunt me down and kill me, or MI5 would lock me away for murder. I told Colin this when he asked. I'm not loyal to anyone but myself and my boss, and right now, that's him. When this job's done, I'll move on. Any allegiance I have will evaporate."

"You have no loyalty. No honor."

"Just to myself." Mercer watched Killian's hand drift closer to his hip. If he pulled his gun, Mercer would kill him. "Colin knows precisely who I am, and now you do too. So are you going to help me determine who betrayed him, or are you going to continue to ask idiotic questions and get in my way?"

"The only thing I care about is Colin and our mission."

"Brilliant." Mercer jerked his chin toward the windshield. "What are we doing here?"

After a moment of deliberation, Killian let out a sigh. "Come along."

SEVENTEEN

Mercer remained near the basement door of the public library. Above, schoolchildren listened to the story of *Peter Rabbit*. The fact that this was going on beneath their feet sickened him. This was a library, a sanctuary for the public, and Flynn had perverted it for his own gains. Should any of his enemies, be they rival terrorist cells or policing agencies, learn of what went on in this room, the place would be raided. The two heavily armed men covering the door would open fire. Casualties would be unavoidable.

It was an unacceptable price, and one Mercer refused to pay. He and his team would have to think twice about sharing this piece of intel with the authorities, unless they had a guarantee the building would only be secured after normal business hours. That point was non-negotiable.

Mercer watched the women in nothing but their underwear and face masks count the money. They slid the bills into the machines and removed them once the band was secure. Each band boasted a small printed four-leaf clover with a pale blue spade superimposed over it. As with other businesses, it was about branding. The clover and spade indicated this was Flynn's money. Mercer had seen the symbol on flyers and posters around town, but he hadn't known it signified the faction. This new knowledge might prove useful. However, he had only seen it printed on advertisements for pubs and clubs. It must indicate where Flynn conducted business.

Flynn ran a diversified operation and kept everything spread out. Based on what Killian had said, these women didn't know about the church or the drop-off, and whoever left the crate of guns at the church didn't know about this. Mercer snorted, amused by the separation of church and state. Flynn's paranoia meant only his most trusted and loyal followers were privy to day-to-day operations. It would have made Owen Shepherd's job nearly impossible, unless Shepherd had infiltrated Flynn's inner circle. Perhaps Shepherd failed, and that's why MI5 lacked the proper intel, but more than likely, Shepherd had been sold out by someone he trusted.

However, since only a handful of people, Killian, Kevin, and a few others, knew everything about Flynn's business, Mercer would use that to his advantage to turn Flynn against his own men. He needed to make sure the faction leader was consumed with the possibility of inner strife and mutiny. It was the only way to delay whatever attacks Flynn had planned.

Killian crossed the room, handing two heavy duffel bags to Mercer. "Take those to the car. I'll be along in a second."

Mercer crossed the straps over his chest while an armed guard unlocked the door. He nodded to the guard and went up the steps and through the library, catching one inquisitive toddler staring at him. The child waved, and Mercer waved back, even as he internally cringed. Flynn didn't give a shit about his own people. He was a selfish bastard, and if left to his own devices, he'd destroy everything.

Mercer had known plenty of terrorists who called themselves freedom fighters. In some instances, they were desperate farmers and townsfolk who'd become guerillas when their lands had been usurped by warlords or powerful governments. They'd lost everything and were indeed fighting for their freedom. That wasn't the case here. In fact, it couldn't be further from the truth. Flynn was a greedy bastard who'd maim and kill his own people to finance his personal vendetta. Mercer would find a way to persuade Killian to turn on his master or make it appear that he had.

Killian joined Mercer, exchanging the money inside the bags for the guns in the crate. "Ready?" Killian asked, sliding behind the wheel.

"For what?"

"To make the rounds."

After a quick stop to deposit the crate of cash, they continued to their next destination. When they parked outside a club, Mercer spotted Kevin Aglin and Duffy O'Brien, Flynn's lieutenants, waiting near the doors. Aglin puffed on a cigarette, flicking it away as a shit-eating grin erupted on his face.

While Mercer unloaded the bags, Killian whispered something to his colleagues. When Mercer joined them, Aglin took one of the heavy bags and slung it over his shoulder. "Colin says you need to learn the business."

Mercer felt as if he were being observed. He didn't spot anyone, but after the abrupt way he had left the park, he didn't put it past Bastian to have found a way to track him. "Shouldn't we take this inside? Or are you hoping to attract some nosy bobby's attention?"

"Aye." Killian held the door, waiting for everyone to step inside.

Aglin cut in front of Mercer and slapped him in a seemingly friendly gesture against his right pec. "After me," he teased, but the hit was far from friendly. The gaudy ring he wore cut into the barely healed lash wound.

Mercer didn't react to the sting. "Of course."

"You're a fast learner. Stick with me, mate. In the event we encounter trouble, I expect you know how to deal with it."

"No problem." The only problem Mercer could see was standing in front of him. Turning, he gave the sidewalks and passersby another glance. They were under surveillance. He just didn't know who was watching, but he'd find out before the night was through.

It didn't take long for Killian to go into a back room and exchange the contents of one of the bags, a dozen MAC-10s, for stacks of cash. In the dimly lit club, Mercer couldn't tell what else was exchanged, but he kept count as the money was loaded into the bag. There had to be tens of thousands zipped inside the black duffel. The guns weren't worth that much.

"Are you taking that back to Colin's?" Aglin asked as they left the pub.

"Yeah, unless there's a reason I should stay." Killian eyed Aglin, his eyes darting to Mercer. "Is there any reason the four of us need to stick together?"

"None." Aglin hooked his free hand around Mercer's neck, pulling him close. "I'll take good care of our new friend. I'll make sure he makes it back to Colin's in one piece."

"Guess we'll split up then, eh?" Killian looked at

Mercer, who silently agreed.

One down, two to go, Mercer thought as he followed Aglin and O'Brien across the street to a pub. Unfortunately, the rest of their stops were not as simple as the first. The guns and munitions were divided and sold to over a dozen different men at a dozen different establishments. Duffy O'Brien held onto the cash while Mercer and Aglin carried the guns.

It was best to diversify. Drug dealers followed the same model. No one person held both the cash and the product. In the event they were caught, it would be more difficult for the police to prove they were arms dealers. Aglin emptied his bag first, leaving Mercer with the contraband. Should they be arrested, Mercer would be facing decades in prison, and Aglin made sure to point that out.

"You mean Flynn doesn't have the police in his pocket?" Mercer asked.

"Who said he'd call in a favor for you? Give me the bag and wait here," Aglin said.

Mercer did as he was told, watching Duffy struggle beneath the weight of the cash. Unlike Killian and Aglin, Duffy lacked physical strength. He had the sinewy muscles and jitteriness of an addict. He must have been Colin's connection to the underworld. It made Aglin's choice to let him carry the cash seem suspect. Addicts couldn't be trusted. They were victims of their disease.

Movement at the end of the bar caught Mercer's eye and cut his musings short. He turned, catching a glimpse of a dark-haired woman. She'd been watching him. Mercer moved toward her. Could she be an undercover cop or MI5 agent?

"Eh," Aglin grabbed Mercer's shoulder, "where do you think you're going?"

"The loo."

"Piss on your own time."

Mercer watched the woman scoop a drink off the bar and head toward a crowded table. She kept her face turned away. Under normal circumstances, no one bothered to do that, and Mercer didn't believe it was a coincidence.

"Are we going, or should I order a pint?" Duffy asked.

"We're going." Aglin yanked on Mercer's shoulder. "After you, Julian."

Mercer maneuvered around the barstools and made his way past a boisterous group of football fans. Outside, dusk had turned to dark, and the cool night air chilled his skin. The lights and architecture served as a constant reminder he was in enemy territory. This was the last place on earth he wanted to be, but that decision was taken out of his hands the moment he discovered the materials hidden in Flynn's basement.

Setting off in the direction of their next destination, Mercer felt another presence. His eyes darted across the street, scanning for danger. He didn't spot the woman from the pub, so someone else must be watching.

Then again, Mercer had been under constant scrutiny. Flynn's men wanted his head on a pike, even more now that Flynn trusted him. Mercer had to watch his every step. He couldn't risk losing favor with the faction leader. Doing so would be his death, so he'd do whatever was necessary to remain in Flynn's good graces until he knew when and where the attack would happen.

Heading down a side street, Mercer followed the others at a brisk pace. At the end of the street, Duffy cut away to speak to a pusher working the corner.

That's when he heard footsteps. They weren't just being watched. They were being followed.

Alone with Kevin Aglin, Mercer slowed, grasping the wall as if on the verge of collapse. He needed an excuse to look behind them without tipping whoever might be in pursuit. Plus, it was best to appear vulnerable, both to Aglin and the unknown third party.

"You all right?" Aglin asked. "Bag too heavy for you?"

Mercer squinted as if in pain and nodded. A shadow ducked into an alcove, but in the dark, he couldn't make out much more than a human form. He didn't want to say anything until he knew who the person was. It could be a member of his team or some bloody moron from MI5. Or perhaps, Flynn sent Killian or another of his minions to keep an eye on them.

Donovan or Bastian would only make an approach like this if something were about to pop off, and since Mercer had no idea what kind of progress the team had made, he couldn't discount the possibility. If the person following was a member of his team, they'd make an approach at the next stop. Mercer was sure of it. Until then, he wanted Aglin distracted. However, if it turned out their tail wasn't friendly, Mercer would mention it. After all, this might be another of Flynn's tests. And the fastest way to build trust was to fight side by side.

Mercer coughed and clutched his chest. "Must have overdone it with the run." He coughed again and straightened. "All better."

"Right. It was the run."

Shifting his weight to the other leg, Mercer felt the heft of the Sig Sauer on his right hip. "Are we almost done here?" He cast another look across the empty alleyway. Duffy tucked something into his pocket and shook hands with the man.

Aglin looked at Duffy and tapped his watch. "Almost."

"Why does Flynn trust him?" Mercer asked.

"For the same reason he trusts you. You both have something he needs, but he won't hesitate to end you if you no longer serve a purpose. Duffy knows that. I'm just not sure you do."

"You did your best to enlighten me."

"Aye, and if you cross the line, I'd be more than happy to end you myself. There are no second chances."

Mercer smiled. "It looks like we're finally in agreement."

Duffy skittered across the street to join them, and the trio continued to the last club on the list.

Aglin nodded to the bouncer and went to the side door. He pulled it open. "After you."

Mercer didn't want to turn his back on the man who nearly beat him to death, but he didn't have a choice. He entered the dark room, counting the intervals of the strobing neon lights. The duffel bag on his shoulder contained the last five machine pistols. Belatedly, he wondered if MI5 would bother to get him out of the mess should the tail prove to be an overzealous cop. Truthfully, they would probably disavow any knowledge and hang Mercer and his team out to dry. After all, isn't that why they hired outside contractors?

Aglin took the bag from Mercer's shoulder. "Go ahead and order yourself a pint. We'll be here a while."

"Sure."

Aglin and Duffy headed to a private VIP lounge and disappeared behind a heavy velvet curtain. Mercer kept his eyes on the front door, confident their shadow would reveal himself. A few minutes later, a group entered. Mercer didn't spot any familiar faces, so he went to the bar and ordered a drink. Taking the glass, he stood at the side, his back to the wall.

His team would have seen him and made contact by now. Whoever tracked the faction members from club to club wasn't on Mercer's side. That left an unlimited number of possibilities. None of which were appealing. Glancing around, he removed his phone.

Any police activity in the entertainment district? He sent the message to an unregistered burner in Bastian's possession. The number was secure, untraceable, but Mercer didn't know if his own phone had been compromised which is why he hadn't used it since the night Flynn drugged him.

Twenty seconds later, his phone vibrated in his palm. *None. Should there be?*

Negative. Mercer waited, but Bastian didn't make contact again. The analyst knew they were running radio silent. He wouldn't initiate communication, but that wasn't enough. Deciding to send one final text, Mercer typed, *Lose the phone.*

Fifteen seconds later, Mercer cracked open the back cover on his device, removed the SIM card and battery, and dropped the phone into the pint. From across the room, bright blue eyes watched him leave the glass on the bar and disappear onto the crowded dance floor.

A moment later, Mercer appeared behind her. He pressed the muzzle of his gun into her low back. "Who are you? Why are you following me?"

EIGHTEEN

"You noticed? I hoped you wouldn't."

"I noticed." Mercer's gaze went around the room. The club was crowded. No one had any idea he was holding the woman at gunpoint. "Are you alone?"

She laughed and did the unthinkable. She spun away from the gun, pivoting to the right and leading with her forearm. She batted the gun away and punched him in the face. Surprised by the punch as much as her brazenness, he stumbled back a step. However, she didn't retreat. Instead, she launched herself at him, two kicks in rapid succession. The first landed solidly to his already battered chest. The second, he stopped, catching her leg and tipping it up, causing her to lose her footing. She slid backward on the waxed floor, her leg still in his hand.

"You bastard." She scissor-kicked at his other side, but he blocked it with his free hand as he crouched on the ground over her. He pinned her legs with his body, and she punched him again. He moved with the hit, letting it glance off his cheek. Something sharp cut into his skin. For a moment, he thought she had a blade, but it was her ring.

"Stop fighting me."

She let out a string of curses, but her voice was drowned out by the music. That's when he finally got a good look at her.

"Lara?"

She blinked, stunned that he knew her name. "Where's my brother?"

Mercer hauled her to her feet. He kept his chest against her back and his arms tightly around her, pinning her arms to her sides. "I'm a friend."

"You're a fucking liar."

He dragged her, kicking and screaming, down the hallway toward the bathrooms. He pushed her inside, giving the men using the facilities a dirty look. "Get out." They didn't move fast enough. "Now."

Lara tried to scream, and he spun her quickly, covering her mouth with his. The men inside would either think they were lovers or Mercer was about to commit a heinous crime. Based on the chuckles and how quickly they exited, he hoped they believed it was the former. She bit his lip hard enough to draw blood, and he pushed her away. He turned to flip the lock on the door, and she jumped onto his back, clawing at his eyes.

"Fucking listen to me." He couldn't buck her off. Despite her diminutive size, she was trained, probably by her brother. He rammed her against the wall. She left him no choice. He had to fight back. When her grip loosened, he flipped her off of him. "Stop attacking me. I don't want to hurt you." He held up his palms and stepped out of striking distance. He let his hand rest on the Sig, which he'd holstered at the beginning of their fight.

"You're not Irish, but you're with Colin Flynn's

men. Who are you?" she asked.

"I'm not the enemy. I'm here to help. I was sent to find your brother."

"Bloody bastards. You're with MI5?"

"Not exactly." He didn't have time for this. Duffy and Aglin would be finished with their meeting soon. He couldn't let them find her. "What do you know about Owen's mission? What did he tell you?"

She stared wide-eyed at him. "How stupid do you think I am?"

Time was running out. "Give me your phone." She didn't move, so he pulled his gun. "Give me the bloody phone."

"I don't have one."

He grabbed her crossbody bag and pulled it over her head. He unzipped it, finding nothing inside but cash and keys. He tossed the bag back to her, surprised when she caught it in mid-air. "Lock the door behind me. Wait here until we're gone, and stay away from Colin Flynn and his friends. Do you understand? I will find your brother. Do not get in my way."

"Who are you?"

She took half a step toward him, and Mercer aimed at her. He had no intention of shooting her, but he needed her to believe he meant business. If she disobeyed his orders, Flynn's men would kill her, and that bastard Aglin would make it as unpleasant as possible. Mercer wouldn't allow that, even if it meant he had to convince her he was one of the bad guys.

"I'll chain you to the pipes if necessary." He gave her a hard look, wiping the blood from his cheek with his fingertips. "Is that going to be necessary?"

She stepped back. "This isn't over."

"It better be." He unlatched the bathroom door and stepped out, seeing a line starting to form. "Sorry, lads, the loo's out of order. You'll have to use the ladies'.'" He kept one hand on the door handle while he grabbed the mop and caution sign from the cart at the end of the hallway. He shoved the mop stick through the door handle. Since the door pushed in, it would make it more difficult for Lara to get out. Then he put the caution sign in front of the door and headed back to the bar.

On his way, he brushed against a man on the dance floor and nicked his phone. He sent a text to Hans, *The bird's been spotted,* followed by the approximate coordinates of the club. No one should be able to intercept the message, but if they did, Mercer hoped it was cryptic enough to cause some confusion. Since Flynn claimed to have had someone inside MI5 and Partridge and Flynn shopped at the same stationery store, Mercer feared MI5 might be monitoring his team's communications. Since he didn't know who to trust, he didn't want Lara anywhere near the Security Service.

Mercer had just ditched the phone when Aglin clapped him on the back, asking, "What happened to your face, mate?"

"A misunderstanding with a woman." Mercer eyed the duffel bag. "We should get that back to Colin."

"I thought we were getting a pint first," Duffy said.

The mop jerked wildly. "Is that really a good idea under the circumstances." Mercer wiped his face with a napkin. "The police might be on their way."

"He's right," Aglin said, "but you owe us. After we drop this off, you're buying."

"Sure," Mercer agreed.

At the exit, he stole a final glance toward the bathrooms. The mop stick was gone. Hopefully, Lara would keep her distance, but he had seen the fire in her eyes. Lara Shepherd would not be easily dissuaded.

Outside, the streets were dark. Groups waited in line to enter the popular clubs. Dealers and other nefarious characters conducted business on street corners and in alleyways. While most of the city boasted low crime rates, this one block was responsible for most of the reported crimes in Belfast.

Casually, the three men walked down the street. The van remained parked outside the first club they visited. While Aglin and Duffy exchanged friendly banter, Mercer tried to take up the rear. However, Aglin hooked an arm around Mercer's neck and pulled him against his side.

"Where do you think you're going? Planning to disappear with Colin's payday?"

"No."

"Keep up then." Aglin eyed Mercer's cheek. "What kind of misunderstanding did you have?"

"The kind that involves being slapped. Her ring caught me. Does it look bad?"

Duffy chuckled. "It might be an improvement."

Mercer forced a smirk onto his face, resisting the urge to glance behind them. "We should hurry it up. The sooner we get back, the sooner I can get this taken care of, and the sooner we drink."

"Aye." Duffy smiled. "Now you're talking."

Aglin narrowed his eyes, distrust reflected in his irises. As they approached the van, Kevin Aglin unlocked the side door, and they loaded the bags of cash inside. Mercer kept an eye out for trouble. When this began, he thought trouble might be an inquisitive cop or a rival faction member. Now, he knew trouble came in the form of a petite woman. And from the ripple in the crowd, he had a feeling she had found them.

"We need to go," Mercer said as Lara's scream cut

through the otherwise tranquil night.

Duffy tugged on the door handle and climbed behind the wheel, but Aglin had other plans.

He recognized her. "Not yet. We have one more thing to collect. Colin will be pleased." He nudged Mercer in the ribs. "This ought to be fun."

Aglin reached for his gun, and Mercer grabbed his wrist. "Who is she? What does she want?" Mercer asked.

"Is she the bitch who struck you?"

"Yes."

"How the hell'd you find her, mate?"

"I didn't. She found me," Mercer said. "Who is she? What does she want?"

"Colin's been looking for her. He'll be pleased by this turn of events. No wonder he wants to keep you around. You're lucky, and you're not even Irish."

"I doubt he'd be pleased by you shooting her. Is she a cop?"

"Don't worry about who she is. All you need to know is we're going to take her to see Colin. We'll take her alive, more or less."

What was she thinking? Mercer told her to stay inside. He told her to wait. Now she was literally racing toward her death. The woman was clearly suicidal. A gun materialized in her hand. *Where the hell did she get that?* Mercer wondered, not having time to complete the thought before she opened fire.

NINETEEN

"Shite." Mercer pressed his back against the brick as dozens of people screamed and fled.

The once busy street had emptied in a matter of moments. The police would be responding soon. From the determined look on Kevin Aglin's face, he had no intention of being around when they showed up.

Lara fired again, and Aglin took refuge along the side of the van while Mercer ducked down the nearest street. From here, he couldn't see Lara, but he kept Aglin and Duffy in his sights. Duffy opened the driver's door and crouched behind it. He aimed, shooting in her direction.

"Don't," Mercer yelled. "Colin wants her alive." He peered around the corner, but she had taken cover across the street. He prayed she'd find a cross street and disappear, but he doubted she would retreat. The word wasn't in her vocabulary. This woman had a death wish, and for Mercer to notice, it was serious.

Duffy gave Mercer a sideways glance. "I'll just wing her."

Aglin said something to Duffy that Mercer couldn't hear and crept along the side of the van. When he made it to the end of the bonnet, he ran to a cover position behind a mailbox. Aglin knew where Lara was hiding. He and Duffy planned to box her in.

She fired another few shots, the bullets impacting against the steel of the mailbox. They perforated the outer shell but didn't break through the second layer. Aglin poked his head up, and she fired again, missing by mere millimeters. Lara Shepherd was a fighter and a decent shot. Maybe she stood a chance.

Headlights approached from the other end of the street. Aglin used the vehicle as cover to get closer to her position. As soon as the car passed, he straightened. Mercer caught a glimpse of Lara a few meters from Aglin's new position. At that distance, he doubted Colin's lieutenant would miss, so Mercer fired. His bullet hit precisely where he intended, grazing Aglin's gun hand before hitting the brick a meter from Lara's head.

Aglin dropped his gun, and Lara fired. But she was out of bullets. Aglin ignored his bloody hand, retrieved his gun, and aimed directly at her. Duffy pointed his gun at Mercer and pulled back the hammer.

"Want to tell me what that was?" Duffy asked.

"I was aiming for the girl. Thought I'd slow her down a bit, but Kevin stepped in front of my bullet. The bleeding idiot." Mercer kept his eyes on the alley. Another gunshot sounded, and Lara fell to the ground. Mercer took a step forward, and Duffy blocked his path.

"We'll let Colin straighten it out, but it's best if you walk away, mate."

"What the fuck are you talking about? Kevin needs help. I just shot him. Look." Mercer jerked his chin toward the alleyway as Aglin dragged Lara into the street.

Despite the blood dripping from his hand, Aglin maintained a tight grip on her wrists. She fought back, and he struck her. She crumpled to the ground and didn't get back up. He hefted her over his shoulder and carried her the rest of the way. Duffy opened the sliding door, and Aglin tossed her inside.

"Are you all right?" Mercer asked, the desire to shoot them both and save the woman nearly overriding every other thought in his head.

"Get on your knees." Aglin pressed the barrel of his gun against Mercer's forehead.

Mercer raised his palms and lowered slowly to the ground, a dozen disarming techniques running through his mind. "You stepped in front of my shot."

Aglin huffed a few times, cradling his hand against his stomach. He pushed the muzzle harder against Mercer's skull, forcing his head back. "Is that what happened?"

"You don't believe me, pull the trigger, but have fun explaining that to Colin. Duffy saw the whole thing."

"Did you now?" Aglin turned on his friend.

Duffy stood there, flummoxed. "I don't know, man."

The sound of approaching sirens filled the air. "Why don't you stay here and get this sorted?" Aglin kept his gun trained on Mercer as he returned to the van, slid open the door, and climbed in beside Lara.

The van door whooshed closed, and Duffy got behind the wheel. The van barreled down the street.

Mercer ran after them. Screw the mission. He couldn't leave the woman to die. He'd kill them all before he let Colin Flynn get his hands on her.

Mercer was in the middle of the street, gun aimed, when he was blinded by headlights from an oncoming

SUV. The vehicle beeped angrily but didn't slow. He jumped backward, but the truck clipped him hard enough to send him sprawling to the ground. He rolled a few times before coming to a standstill. Somehow, he kept a tight grip on his weapon.

Blinking away the darkness, he watched the SUV come to a halt. The driver had stopped to check on him, and Mercer didn't waste a second. He struggled to regain his footing and sprinted toward the vehicle.

"It's an emergency." Mercer shoved the driver out of the way and knocked the truck into reverse. He gunned the engine, holding it steady as he raced backward after the van. He kept one hand on the wheel as he leaned out the window and fired at the van's tires. He needed to slow them down, but at this distance and angle, it was an impossible shot.

The van lurched to the right, but it didn't slow. Duffy jumped the curb in his haste to get away from the gunfire and popped the back tire. But he accelerated, even as the rim scraped against the asphalt and spit sparks into the air.

At the intersection, Mercer whipped the truck around. He needed to catch them before they got back to Flynn's compound. He had to save her. It was the singular thought in his head. He fired a few more times out the window, but the vehicle didn't slow.

Mercer ejected the empty magazine and reached into his pocket for a spare. Using the steering wheel, he slammed the new magazine into place and aimed out the window, firing again at the vehicle. He was closer this time and took out the other rear tire. The van swerved. Duffy turned the wheel sharply to compensate and rolled the van. After several revolutions, it came to a dead stop on its side.

After what just happened, there was no mistaking whose side Mercer was on. If Duffy or Aglin called

Flynn, Mercer's cover was blown. He'd have to deal with the situation accordingly. Lives depended on it.

Knocking the SUV into park, Mercer threw open the door and crept toward the disabled vehicle. Duffy hoisted himself out the window and aimed at Mercer. This time, the terrorist didn't hesitate to fire, but Mercer dove out of the way. The faint sound of Lara's screams penetrated the sealed interior of the van, igniting the barely contained rage that lived inside him. The flying bullets and the sound of a woman screaming were more than he could take. His vision clouded. He saw red.

Without a thought, Mercer put one in Duffy's heart and a second in his head, never breaking stride as he moved to the back of the van. The van was on its side, preventing the sliding door from being used. That left only the back doors. Mercer opened the door, lifting one side up.

Aglin fired, launching a barrage of bullets at Mercer who barely registered the searing sting as the lead grazed his ribcage. Aglin held Lara in front of him like a shield. "I knew you were lying."

"Brilliant." Mercer ducked against the wheel well as more bullets flew in his direction. He couldn't risk firing back for fear of hitting Lara. "At least you'll die knowing you were right."

"You're the one dying tonight, Julian."

Mercer watched the reflection in the door's rear window. Lara struggled against her captor, so Aglin turned the gun on her. The moment he did, Mercer stepped out of cover and fired. His bullet impacted between Aglin's eyes. It took the terrorist a moment to drop, as if his body didn't understand his brain relocated to outside his skull. Mercer shoved his way into the vehicle, firing a second shot into the dead man's chest.

"Are you okay?" Mercer extended a hand to help Lara out of the sideways vehicle.

She jerked away, kicking into his knee. She grabbed Kevin's gun and aimed at Mercer. "Who are you? And this time, you're going to give me a bloody answer."

"Julian Mercer. I'm a kidnapping and ransom specialist. Former Special Air Service. MI5 hired my team to locate and extract Owen."

"Why should I believe you?"

"I just killed two men on your behalf."

"Lives don't mean much to Colin Flynn, and if you're one of his men, I'm sure they mean nothing to you either." Her gaze drifted to Kevin Aglin, and she cursed and spit on his body. She was angry. Clearly, she was a fighter with a temper.

"Take his phone," Mercer instructed. "Has he made any recent calls?"

"No."

Mercer nodded, a sense of relief washing over him. He'd have to check Duffy's phone, but he needed Lara not to shoot him first. "Then verify my story. Call MI5. The main line. Ask to speak to Bastian Clarke. They'll patch you through. It's the fastest way to prove my identity. We don't have time to waste." He clapped his hands together twice in rapid succession. "Now, darling. The police are on the way."

She narrowed her eyes, pondering this new tidbit of information.

"Do you know the number?" Mercer eyed the gash at her temple.

Her eyes fluttered, and she blinked hard. "Yes," she dialed, "don't be cheeky."

"I wouldn't dream of it."

Mercer counted the seconds during their exchange. The police would find them soon. They couldn't stay here. They had to move. He didn't have time to wait.

Since she was distracted, he edged out of the sideways van on his hands and knees. Once outside, he went to the front and searched Duffy's pockets. The screen was shattered, but Duffy hadn't placed any calls or sent any messages. Mercer was in the clear, but that would change the second the police arrived.

Something to the side caught his attention. He turned to see headlights approaching. He aimed at the vehicle but resisted the urge to fire. Civilian casualties were never acceptable, albeit inherently inevitable. As the car swerved around the accident, Mercer caught the briefest glimpse of the two occupants. The sight of his gun kept them from stopping, but it didn't matter. The sirens were growing louder.

Mercer moved back to the rear of the van, coming face-to-face with Lara. She held the gun, her hand shaking. He didn't make a move toward her. Frankly, he wasn't positive she wouldn't shoot him just for affiliating with Colin Flynn's crew. She appeared unsteady, her movements jerky.

She held the phone out. "He wants to speak to you."

Mercer took half a step forward and reached for the offered phone. "Bas?"

"Jules, what's going on?"

"I need full containment to this location. Monitor the police frequencies and calls. I need you on top of this. I'm heading to the safe house. I'll make contact again soon." He disconnected. "Lara, we have to go now. Either shoot me or put the gun down."

She teetered, her eyes vibrating back and forth. She put a hand out to steady herself, and Mercer feared she might black out. From the looks of things, she had a concussion. Her strong will was the only thing keeping her off the ground, that and adrenaline.

Several people watched from their windows, so Mercer holstered his weapon. The last thing he wanted was some nearsighted tosser telling the police he was responsible. It was time to go. He'd just have to make sure he made everything appear convincing.

He crawled back inside the rear of the van and grabbed the duffel bags. He opened one and yanked out some cash, leaving it around the body. Then he crisscrossed the bags over his chest, wiped the prints off the phone, pressed it into Aglin's hand, retrieved Lara's firearm, and exited the van.

Mercer reached out to help her, but she jerked away. Lights flashed in the distance. The police would be here in fifteen seconds.

"I mean you no harm." Mercer grabbed Aglin's gun from her hand in one quick move. "But I don't have time for niceties." He reloaded the weapon, wiped it, and tossed it into the van. Then he dragged her by the elbow across the street, where they ducked down an alleyway.

"I'll be the judge of that." Her speech was slow and slurred. Mercer feared how serious her injury might be. Maybe it'd be best to leave her for the police to find. But he didn't know if he could trust them with her safety. Flynn controlled part of the police force. Leaving her behind might save her life or be her death sentence. It was a gamble he wasn't willing to take.

He tugged on a side door to a restaurant, but it didn't budge. Aiming, he turned his head and shielded his face before firing at the lock. He tugged again, opening the door and leading her inside. He kept a hand on her elbow as they went down the corridor, past the kitchen, and into the ladies' room.

"What is it with you and the loo?" she asked.

"We have to get out of here." Thankfully, the restroom was empty. He locked the door and propped her up against the sink. He removed the torch from his pocket and shone it in her eyes. He held up his hand. "How many fingers?"

"Fuck off."

"Answer me."

"Three."

It was two, but he didn't correct her. The adrenaline would keep her moving for the next few minutes.

"Are you good to walk out the front door?"

"Better than you." She pointed at the growing bloodstain at his side.

He went to the dispenser on the wall and broke the lock off with the butt of his gun. Reaching inside, he removed a sanitary pad, unwrapped it, and pressed it against the length of the wound. He didn't have time to deal with that now. "Happy?"

"Do you expect me to believe you're just a helpful bloke with a gun?"

"I'm a security specialist."

"You're a mercenary. Are you with them?"

"No. We've already been over this."

"Did my brother send for you?"

He didn't answer. Nothing he said would satisfy her, and he didn't have time for this. The police were outside. The nearest safe house was half a klick away. If they could find an alternative route that didn't lead directly to the waiting bobbies, Mercer could get them to safety.

"Wait here." He left the bags with Lara and stepped into the hallway. He kept his head down, grabbing a dark jacket off a hook as he entered the kitchen. As predicted, kitchens in popular restaurants were always busy. No one noticed him walk through the area and duck into the supply room. He grabbed a roll of plastic wrap and secured the makeshift bandage in place. After a quick search, he found a rear exit near the freezer and a few spare chef jackets.

He returned to the bathroom, once again finding the business end of her gun in his face. "This is getting old." He regretted having returned it to her when he exited the bathroom.

Her grip faltered as the shock took hold. Carefully, he placed his palm over the barrel of the gun and pressed down until it was no longer aimed at his chest. She let go, and he caught it before it dropped to the ground.

"Lara, we have to move. Put this on." He helped her into the jacket and buttoned it. He put on the other white jacket and grabbed the bags. "Stay close. Don't speak to anyone."

They slipped into the kitchen, and Mercer led the way to the rear exit. When he opened it, the sous chef turned around. "What are you doing?"

"Late delivery." He attempted an Irish accent. "Be right back."

Lara followed behind, and they stepped into the cool night air. A chain-link fence separated the delivery area and extra parking spaces from a parallel street. Mercer shed the jacket and helped Lara out of hers. Bright white camouflaged them inside the kitchen, but it would draw attention out here.

Mercer opened a dumpster and tossed the jackets inside. He cautioned a glance back the way they came and spotted two more police cars heading toward the scene of the accident. He pulled his shirt over his holster and tucked Lara's gun in the waistband at his hip. He checked to make sure they were both concealed.

"Up and over, darling." Mercer knelt down, folding his hands over his knee.

Lara gave him an uncertain look. "We need to talk."

"We will, but in order to do that, we have to get out of this mess alive."

TWENTY

"You live here?" she asked in a semi-coherent daze.

"No." Mercer locked the door behind them and checked for intruders. Even though he'd only given Bastian instructions to stock the safe houses earlier this afternoon, the analyst had done his job.

The first thing Mercer did was open the linen closet, remove the middle shelf holding stacks of towels, and slide the false back out of the way. He grabbed the frequency scanner and turned it on. He did a quick sweep of his body and belongings before checking Lara. She was clean and hadn't lied about not having a phone.

He moved on to the bags, checking the duffels and the contents. She dropped onto the couch, holding her head in her hands as she watched him. "Bloody hell. Is that real?"

Mercer used his gloved hands to flip through one of the stacks of cash. "Appears to be."

"What are you going to do with it?"

He put the money back into the bag and zipped it.

"I haven't decided." She needed medical attention. "How do you feel?"

"Like I should have shot you when I had the chance. You still haven't told me much."

"Neither have you." His mind was in overdrive. Like the negotiations he worked, he was coming up on a deadline. Colin would realize something had gone wrong when no one returned to his compound. Mercer had to get back there, but he couldn't leave her, and he wasn't sure Flynn would believe the lies.

"What do you want to know?" She attempted to focus.

"I went to your apartment. Two men were waiting outside. They tried to kill me. Do you know who they are or what they want?"

Her shoulders moved skyward.

Mercer couldn't determine if her lack of cooperation was intentional or a result of what occurred over the last hour. "You have a loose floorboard in your bedroom."

Her eyes darted from the floor to his face. The sudden shift made the room spin, and she fell back against the couch cushion. "What did you find?"

"Nothing."

She nodded, as if remembering something. "Where is Owen? Do you even know?"

"I'm working on it."

"So am I."

"Your brother disappeared. You decided to do the same. Care to explain?"

"Owen sent me a message. He told me to leave everything and go. We were supposed to meet at the train station in North London, but he never showed. I knew something was wrong."

"So you decided to come to Ireland and wage war against a terrorist cell?"

"I came looking for my brother. The last I heard, he had infiltrated Flynn's faction. I've been keeping tabs on them, monitoring their movements, but I haven't seen Owen." She jerked upright, pressing her fingertips against the bridge of her nose. "I just want answers." She blinked several times, but she couldn't force her eyes to focus. "Bollocks."

Mercer went into the bathroom and returned with a medical kit. He knelt in front of her, checking to make sure neither of her pupils was blown. "You have a wicked bump."

He pressed his fingers around the welt, surprised to find only a small laceration. He cleaned the wound, but it was no longer bleeding. The swelling might have been keeping it at bay, but he didn't like the way it looked. She might have a skull fracture.

Her eyes teared, and she hissed in pain.

He withdrew his hand. "My apologies."

"The arsehole you shot was a real sadistic bastard."

"Indeed." Mercer helped her lie down. "I need you to stay awake."

"Not a problem."

He left the medical kit beside her and went to the closet. "How did you know Owen was involved with Flynn?"

"What?"

"His mission was classified. Top secret. How did you hear about it?"

"Owen told me."

"When?"

"I don't remember." She rummaged through the medical kit. "Do you have any aspirin."

"Don't take those. You could be hemorrhaging." He reached for a radio, turned it on, and tucked the earpiece into his left ear. "Anyone reading me? This is team leader. Respond."

"Jules, what the hell's going on?" Bastian asked.

"We're at echo site. Lara Shepherd's here. She's injured and needs medical attention. I don't know who we can trust. How quickly can you get here?"

"Twenty minutes."

"Make it fifteen. I need to get back to Flynn's, and I don't want her left alone that long. If she falls asleep, she might not wake up."

"I'm on my way." The radio grew staticky while Bastian took the lift. Neither man spoke until the static cleared. "Since you located Lara, I'll call off the search in London. We'll need Donovan and Hans here, unless there's a reason they need to stay behind."

"Send for them." Mercer winced. Now that he wasn't in any immediate danger, his body made him aware of the pain. He removed the makeshift bandage, finding it soaked in blood, more dribbled down his side with no sign of stopping. He thought about stitching the wound, but he had a decision to make. "Bas, what are the police saying?"

"They received reports of gunfire. Some witnesses said there were six men. Others said two. One said a crazy woman attacked three people. Nothing's clear." Bastian started the engine. "I plugged into the government surveillance and obliterated everything. I'll have to address the private CCTV feeds separately. The ones on wireless networks have already been handled. I'll have to do a physical check for others."

"We went through a restaurant." Mercer gave Bastian the address. "Make sure you scrub their footage. That's your priority, second only to Lara." Mercer knew what he had to do. "Colin Flynn can't find out what happened. Is that clear?"

"Yes, Jules. But I'd like to know what happened."

"It's a long story. Lara left me no choice. I had to

eliminate Kevin Aglin and Duffy O'Brien. They would have killed her and outed me."

"Shit."

"Lara used Aglin's phone to call MI5. She directed it to the main line, and I left the device with the body. I wiped our prints, so the call should link directly to Aglin. I'm hoping I can use that in my favor. And I took the money."

"What money?"

"Gun money. Flynn's an arms dealer. We delivered a few dozen MAC-10s tonight. I'm not sure what else. We're looking at half a million dollars. He sold something big, but I don't know what. I don't know if I've been compromised." Mercer's thoughts went to Killian. "I don't know if Flynn was monitoring me, but I'm hoping he wasn't." He grabbed a new burner phone, entered the relevant data from the previous phone in order to have the number transferred, and tucked it into his pocket. "I'm heading back to Flynn's now. Get to Lara as soon as you can, and keep her safe. Owen made contact with her a few weeks ago. She knows about his mission. She might know where he is or what Flynn has planned. And Bas, she's been trained. She might be an asset." Mercer let the alternate implication remain unsaid. Bas would know to be careful in case it turned out Lara wasn't on their side. They'd been burned before, and Mercer wouldn't let that happen again.

"How are you going to explain yourself to Flynn?"

"It was an ambush. Duffy and Aglin were killed. I fought them off as best I could, but the assailants got away."

"Do you think he'll buy it?"

"We'll see."

"Julian, you don't know what you're walking into. Going back is suicide. We'll come up with a new plan.

We'll figure this out from the outside. We have Lara. You don't have to do this."

Mercer went to the locked cabinet, entered the combination, and removed a dagger and a garrote. He placed another set of lockpicks in his pocket. "I'll be fine, but I can't walk in with the radio. I have to go. We'll meet up tomorrow at that spot by the water."

"And if you're not there?"

"I will be." Mercer removed the radio and returned to the main room. "Hey," he said gently, "keep those eyes open."

Lara blinked. "You look like shit."

"Thanks to you." He struggled to hoist the bags over his shoulders.

"You're still bleeding."

"I know." He stared at the droplets he left on the floor. Bastian would clean that up. Mercer ripped one of the sleeves off his shirt and pressed it against the wound. He couldn't suture his side or grab any bandages because he'd have to explain how he got them to Flynn, and the less detailed the lie, the better off he'd be. "Help is on the way. Don't shoot him when he arrives."

"How will I know who he is?"

"Ask him for the codeword. Morningstar."

She nodded weakly and closed her eyes.

"And your eyes stay open." With one final look, Mercer went out the door. He checked the walkway to the flat, making sure he didn't leave any traces of his presence or drops of blood. Nothing could link him to this location or her.

He trudged down the street in the direction of Flynn's compound. When he was a good distance from the safe house, he dialed Flynn.

"We were ambushed," Mercer huffed as if out of breath. "The police are everywhere. Kevin's dead. I think Duffy is too. There were four of them at least, maybe six. I saw three men and a woman. They were waiting for us at the van. Where's Killian?"

"He's here." Flynn sounded suspicious. "What do you mean they're dead?"

"They were shot." Mercer continued down the street, keeping his head down. Luckily, not many people were nearby. "I have to get out of here. The police are searching everywhere. I have the money. I grabbed what I could. That's what they wanted. They disabled the van and broke into the back. By the time I climbed out, Kevin was dead. I exchanged fire with one of them. I might have clipped him. I know I hit the woman. She was across the way in an alley. That's where the first volley came from. She shot out the tires. Shit." Mercer lowered his voice, his breathing becoming more frantic. "Who knew what we were doing?"

"No one."

"Bollocks. Killian knew, and he left before any of this happened. That's convenient."

"We'll talk about it when you get here. I don't want to discuss this over the phone."

"The van's disabled. Cops are everywhere. How am I supposed to get back?"

"You're resourceful. Find a way."

Mercer continued down the street, checking the row of car doors as he went. When he found one unlocked, he slipped inside. After a few seconds, he hotwired the vehicle. The last thing he needed was to leave blood evidence in a stolen car, but he had to sell his story. And the blood loss was making him woozy. He didn't know if he'd last the lengthy walk, particularly when carrying two heavy duffel bags. He didn't know what to expect when he arrived at Flynn's compound, but he needed to have enough strength left to be prepared for anything.

TWENTY-ONE

Mercer left the stolen car outside the fence with the engine running. He pushed the intercom and waited. Any minute Flynn's bodyguards would open the gate and surround him. He had one bag crossed over his chest. The other he held in his left hand. His right kept pressure on his side. He waited, hoping to time the theatrics just right.

Beams of light bounced off the ground as the men approached. The gate slowly opened. Mercer took a step forward, dropping the bags and falling to his knees. By the time he hit the wet grass, the guards had circled him. Colin Flynn stood directly in front of him.

"Check the bags," Flynn instructed. One of the men obliged and held up a stack of cash. "Donal, bring those inside." Flynn crouched beside Mercer, observing the blood soaking through his shirt. "Where'd you get the car?"

"Some bloke left it unlocked." Mercer noticed the gun partially concealed behind Flynn's thigh. "I needed it more than he did."

"Looks that way." Flynn turned to another man. "Aaron, lose the car. Get rid of any evidence inside."

"Aye."

Flynn tucked the gun into his waistband and offered Mercer a hand. "To be honest, I'm surprised you didn't steal my money and disappear. Isn't this just about a paycheck, or have you decided my cause is more than an assignment?"

"I thought about it, but that's not how I work, especially now. I don't take kindly to being shot."

"From the looks of you, you wouldn't have made it far on your own." Flynn glanced toward the house. Killian stood a few dozen meters away, near the front door. "Get Maura."

Killian got into a car and drove down the path past them. Mercer watched him go, suspicion playing across his face.

"After Killian left, we were ambushed." Mercer hoped repeating this information would solidify the suspicion in Flynn's mind. "Did you tell him to leave us? Was that the plan?"

Flynn didn't respond. Instead, he led Mercer into the house. They went into the kitchen, and Mercer took a seat. Alana came down the steps with another bodyguard in tow.

Flynn glared at her. "I told you to stay upstairs."

"So more of our friends can die tonight?" She went to the stove, filled a pot with water, and set it to boil. She washed her hands and stood in front of Mercer. She forced his head back and examined the cuts and bruises on his face. "Oh my." She tugged his shirt open. "He'll need stitches."

Flynn removed the gun from Mercer's holster, finding the magazine empty. Mercer intentionally left it that way, so Flynn would believe he expelled the entire magazine in the firefight. His other side was covered in a dark bruise from being sideswiped by the SUV, which Mercer explained as having happened in the accident.

"Killian's fetching the nurse. Maura's on her way," Flynn said.

Alana's brow furrowed in concentration. "Clear off the table. She'll need room to work. I'll clean his wounds while we wait."

"I'm fine," Mercer said. "I've had worse."

"That you have, but I don't think that will matter if you bleed out. The bullet might still be inside you. It has to come out, unless you want to go septic."

Mercer ran his fingertips against his ribs, and she smacked his hand. He gave her a confused look. "It's merely a graze."

"And this?" She poked at his ribs, sending a flash of white-hot pain through him. "Then it's a piece of bone. Either way, it has to come out."

Flynn let out an audible sigh. "Alana, I'll take care of this. Go upstairs."

"Fine, Colin." She cast one last look at Mercer, wiped her hands on a towel, and stormed out of the room.

Grabbing a bottle of bourbon, Flynn poured it into a glass and offered it to Mercer.

"No."

"Fucking hell, you still think I'm trying to poison you?" Flynn knocked back a swallow. "I thought you might want something to dull the pain."

He topped off the glass and offered it a second time. Mercer took it, nodded his gratitude, and swallowed.

"How'd that happen?" Flynn asked.

"One of them surprised me coming out of the back of the van. If I'd only been half a second faster. I should have had the bloody wanker." He finished the glass, and Flynn refilled it.

"Tell me about them."

"They were covered in blackout gear. Head to toe. I didn't get a look at any of them, but this bastard, the one who shot me, he's the arsehole who killed Kevin." Mercer shook his head, as if something didn't compute. "Duffy was already on the ground. The bastards shot him first."

"For a team to get the drop on Kevin, they must be good." Flynn grabbed the bottle and a glass, poured a drink for himself, and poured one out for his fallen friend.

"I don't know. Maybe the accident knocked him senseless. We lost the rear tires. Duffy tried to compensate, and he shoved the wheel too hard. We flipped several times." Mercer looked away.

"What aren't you telling me?"

"Nothing."

"Lie to me again, and the next bullet that goes in you will be straight to your heart."

"When I heard sirens, I knew I had to get out of there. So I grabbed what I could. I didn't see Kevin's gun, just his phone in his hand. Did he call you?"

"You're sure you don't know who's responsible? Could it be the police or MI5?"

"Whoever attacked us came for the money. There's no way that was sanctioned by Her Majesty." The security system beeped to alert them someone was at the gate. Killian was back with Maura. Mercer stared into Flynn's eyes. "I'll only ask this once, but are you absolutely certain it wasn't Killian?"

Flynn maintained eye contact, but he didn't answer. A few moments later, Killian and Maura entered the kitchen, and Flynn leaned back and finished his drink. Mercer's gaze darted to Killian, who took up a position near the doorway.

"Now what have you done?" Maura scolded, examining the fresh wound. She opened her bag, disinfected the area, and removed a scalpel and suture kit. Mercer sipped on the bourbon while she removed the bone fragment and stitched up his side. None of the men spoke. When she was finished, her hand brushed against his belt buckle, and he grabbed her wrist. "Your trouser leg is covered in blood. I need to check for other injuries."

"You don't need to check inside my trousers."

"Fine, but let me do something about that cut on your cheek. You don't want a nasty scar to ruin your good looks."

"What good looks?" Killian mumbled, earning an amused snort from Flynn. "If you don't need me here, Colin, I'll see what the police have learned."

"Not tonight. I'll handle that personally in the morning. You should contact Kevin's family. Duffy didn't have anyone except us, but the Aglins need to know they lost their son. We have two funerals that need arranging, and I don't want the police knocking on their doors with the bad news. We take care of our own."

"I'll take care of it."

"Tell the Aglins I'll be by in the afternoon with anything they need," Flynn said.

"Aye. That I will." Killian waited for Maura, and the two left together.

Flynn sat across from Mercer, taking in every visible injury on his body. "Only a handful of people knew the exchange was happening tonight, and two of those people are dead, according to you. I have to know who is responsible." He glanced at the bags of cash sitting on the floor in the living room. "I believe you're right. I'm being attacked from the inside out, and now two of my friends are dead. You will find the person responsible, or you will face the same fate."

"What do you think I've been trying to do?" Mercer spat. "I need your cooperation. Who knew we'd be stopping at the clubs?"

"I'll let you figure that out on your own. Why didn't you steal the money? I'd expect nothing less from a soldier of fortune."

"This isn't about the money anymore." Mercer peered into the living room, but they were alone. "You know the truth, Mr. Flynn. One of your men is responsible." Mercer placed his empty glass in the sink. "You have the stolen car with my blood in it. Use it as insurance if you like, but for now, I'm knackered. Can I get a ride to the inn?"

"You'll stay here tonight. Alana made up the spare bedroom. Until I decide what to do, I want you close. You're one of the few people I trust."

"That's probably for the best. You might need the extra protection."

"I'm not sure you're in any condition to provide protection." Flynn stood. "I'll show you to your room."

TWENTY-TWO

The next morning, Mercer found his belongings outside his bedroom door. Flynn had sent someone to the inn to collect his things. Mercer showered and changed, unsure if he'd be able to rendezvous with his team in a few hours. He wondered what Bastian would do if he failed to show up. Hopefully, the analyst wouldn't send an extraction team.

Mercer stared at his reflection in the bathroom mirror. His cheek had started to scab. His eye was black, his jaw painted with a matching bruise, and his entire body ached from being struck by a moving vehicle. But none of that compared to the internal turmoil.

Mercer killed two known terrorists the previous night. Kevin Aglin and Duffy O'Brien. They were no saints. Each was responsible for taking several lives, and Aglin enjoyed torture. Mercer experienced it firsthand. It was no secret the world was a better place without the likes of them. But for better or worse, Kevin and Duffy were Flynn's friends, his family, his teammates. Flynn would want payback, and should he discover the person responsible had slept under his roof, all would not end well.

Mercer had to be careful with every word he spoke and every lie he told. Deciding to play up his injuries, he hobbled down the steps. It'd be best if Flynn and the others underestimated his capabilities in case their relationship soured. Mercer had no intention of dying here, but it might not be up to him.

Flynn waited at the dining room table, Alana and Killian at his side. Catching sight of Mercer, he dismissed his breakfast companions with a flick of his wrist.

"Sit down."

Mercer pulled out a chair and filled an empty cup with tea.

"An hour ago, I received this." Flynn slid a copy of a confidential police report across the table. "Kevin didn't even have a chance to return fire. His gun was fully loaded."

"I suspected as much."

"When I find who's responsible, they'll regret having crossed me."

"Do the police have any leads?"

"No." Flynn pushed away from the table and stalked the kitchen. "The stories they heard are unreliable. I trust what you said is true."

"It is."

"At least Duffy fired back. Did he hit any of them?"

"I can't be sure. I went to help Kevin, and the next time I saw Duffy, he wasn't moving." Mercer put the teacup down and skimmed the police report. "How did you get this?"

"That doesn't matter. Killian stayed with the Aglins last night. When he returned this morning, he said Mathias heard the news and delivered flowers, along with his condolences."

Mercer raised a confused eyebrow. "How did he know?"

More than likely, Murphy also had people planted inside the police department. The flowers were meant to rub salt in the wound. Mathias Murphy had no idea how paranoid and delusional Colin Flynn was. Or the rival faction leader didn't care and wanted to launch the first volley while Flynn's faction was at its weakest.

"Mathias is behind this. I know it."

"He can't be working alone," Mercer insisted. "He turned one of your men, and that person gave him the info on your gun deals and money drops. I'll ask you again, Mr. Flynn, who is privy to that information?"

"I know what you think. But I don't believe Killian would do this."

"I hope you're right. Who else has access? Is this a routine run? Perhaps your suppliers or buyers are to blame."

"Could be." Flynn mulled over a few things. "Look into it and get me answers. I'd do it myself, but today, I'll be preparing to bury my friends."

"As you wish." Mercer reread the police report, but he didn't see anything damning. His cover remained intact, at least for now. "I'll need names or access to your records. I might be good at my job, but I'm not a mind reader. I need a starting point. It'll save us both time if you tell me where to look instead of forcing me to ask around. But I can do it either way."

"Fine."

Flynn led the way upstairs, nodding to Killian, who was helping Alana pick out a dress to wear as they went past one of the smaller bedrooms. He hit the light switch inside the master suite, and Mercer looked around. It was the same room he'd infiltrated that first night, but the map was no longer on the wall. Instead, it was spread out on the desk with six bright red Xs.

Mercer gave it a cockeyed look. "What's this?"

"Don't worry about that." Flynn pushed a bookcase out of the way and spun the dial on a safe. He turned around to make sure Mercer wasn't looking before entering the combination. "Here."

"What is this?"

"The schedule, including names of suppliers and buyers. Isn't that what you wanted?"

"I thought you'd have a few names to offer. Are you sure it's wise to have details like this lying about?"

"This is a business. I run it as such. And it isn't lying about."

Mercer glanced back at the open safe. Two thin folders lined the shelves. Several stacks of cash in different currencies filled the top, along with a handful of passports and several guns. Colin Flynn had an exit strategy. He was no martyr. He had no intention of dying for his cause.

"Do your men know about this?"

"I don't know."

"What about your home security system?" Mercer asked. "Any cameras or internal surveillance devices? If someone accessed this room, they might be caught on tape."

"Even if they came up here, they wouldn't be able to get into my safe. No one has the combination."

"Are you certain?"

"I'm not a fucking idiot. It's only secure as long as no one else has the combination, and they don't. And before you ask, no one could have gotten the combination off the security feed because I don't have cameras in my room. I like my privacy. Alana insists on it."

Mercer thought for a moment, realizing she wouldn't want her brother to watch her being ravaged by the faction leader. He looked around the room but didn't spot any of Alana's things. Did she even share a bedroom with Flynn? Or was he too paranoid to sleep with someone? Perhaps the bastard feared she'd slit his throat in the middle of the night.

"I need your word, Julian."

"You have it. I'll find out who betrayed you. I won't stop looking until I have a name." Mercer rubbed his cheek. "You could say I have skin in the game."

"I know your suspicions, but don't be too quick to judge. Killian's like my brother. I don't believe he'd do this, but I'll put him down like a dying dog if I have to." Flynn stared into Mercer's eyes. "The same goes for all of them, including you. Whoever killed Kevin and Duffy will suffer."

"I'll see what I can do."

"Don't see. Just do what I ask. And if you can't, I'll find someone who can."

"Very good, sir." Mercer took the folder, relieved to have an excuse to disappear. "I'll get started right away." Thankfully, Bastian wouldn't be manning a rescue mission anytime soon.

"I want answers by tonight. Meet me at the pub."

TWENTY-THREE

"Jules," Bastian let out a sigh of relief, "after what Lara told us, I wasn't sure you'd make it. I half expected the note you left to be a carefully laid trap."

"You think Flynn's that smart?" Mercer asked.

"It might not have been Flynn."

"You have intel?"

Before Bastian could say anything, Hans and Donovan entered the room.

"It's good to see you," Donovan said.

"What the hell happened to your face?" Hans asked.

"Lara."

The reconnaissance expert laughed. "It's good to have you back." Hans pulled Mercer in for an unexpected one-armed hug, and Julian winced. "Are you sure you're field ready?"

"Bugger off." But Mercer couldn't help cracking a smile, a rare occurrence for him. He had missed his team. Being surrounded by IRA members left him drained. Glancing around the room, he asked,

"Speaking of, where is she?"

Bastian jerked his chin toward the rear bedroom. "She's asleep. She's been in and out since I found her. The doctor said that's normal. She needs rest. We have to wake her every few hours, but she should be okay in a couple of days."

"What doctor?" Mercer asked. "Flynn controls the whole bloody town. You can't trust anyone."

"Don't worry, mate." Hans offered a smile. "The doc's one of mine. After some groveling, I convinced her to help. We took a helo and arrived last night." Before Mercer could voice how dangerous such a stunt was, Hans continued, "Don't worry. We put the doc on the ferry first thing this morning. She's already back in England. She's safe. Flynn won't touch her. He won't even know she was here. And we won't let him get his grubby paws on Lara either."

"You better make damn sure." Mercer rubbed a hand over his mouth.

"You look like you could use some patching," Donovan said. "From what I hear, I missed quite the firefight."

"Jules?" Bas's expression softened. "Best you start at the beginning. Lara said you were shot."

"Grazed." Images of the previous night played through Mercer's mind. "Is she okay? When I left, I feared she might not survive."

"She more than survived. She nearly blew my bloody head off the second I entered the flat. Why did you give her a loaded shotgun?"

"I didn't."

"Obviously, she made use of our stockpiled weapons."

For the next half hour, Mercer told his team everything that happened since he approached Flynn at the pub. It had been nearly a week since they were together, but it felt like a lifetime. Normal retrievals and recoveries didn't require undercover work and only the occasional infiltration. This was something else. They handled extractions often enough, but nothing like this.

"You're sure you got all the nearby footage?" Mercer asked. "Flynn read the police report. If they discover a camera feed you missed, this is over."

"I handled it," Bastian assured him.

"What about plonkers with cell phone cameras?" Mercer asked.

Bastian grabbed the computer and placed it on the countertop. "That will be harder to control, but I have spiders searching the internet. If anything gets posted online, I'll find it and obliterate it."

"It could be too late."

"You should have thought about that before you shot two of Flynn's men in the middle of the street."

Mercer glanced toward the bedroom door. "She didn't leave me much of a choice. Kevin Aglin nearly killed her. He would have done much worse if I allowed him to remain locked in the back of the van with her. And once they made it to Flynn's compound, she would have been tortured and killed. I was out of options. I couldn't let them take her. I couldn't let her die."

Donovan clapped Mercer on the shoulder. "We would have made the same call."

"It sounds like it worked out for the best. Flynn finally trusts you. Look at what he gave you." Hans lifted the folder. "This is serious shit. His supply lines. His buyers. It's enough evidence to lock him up for the rest of his miserable life."

"If any of it is even true." Bastian took the folder from Hans' hand. "And that would also be assuming Flynn doesn't have resources inside the government.

My guess is he gave Jules this packet of intel as another test."

"What have you found?" Mercer's insides twisted. "Do you know who's compromised?"

Bastian clicked a few keys. "I found the full, unedited recording of Owen Shepherd's last check-in with his handler. Partridge didn't give us this."

"Partridge is dirty," Mercer said.

"Just listen." Bastian pressed play. When an unfamiliar voice sounded, Bastian said, "That's Shepherd."

Mercer nodded, squinting into the distance as he listened.

"I don't have much time. Flynn's on the warpath. His stash house was breached. I don't know exactly what they took, but Flynn's out for blood," Shepherd said.

"Slow down." The second voice belonged to Liam Partridge. *"Whose blood?"*

"I don't know. I didn't know about any of this until now."

"Any of what?"

"Flynn's plan. He was building a dirty bomb or a biological weapon. I don't know, but it's a bloody WMD. And it's gone."

"What? That doesn't make any sense. How did he gain access to those materials without us noticing?"

"I don't know. Shit. I have to go."

"Wait. I thought Flynn trusted you. Why didn't he tell you about this sooner?"

"He doesn't trust anyone. According to the records I found, Flynn's been stockpiling materials. He has a plan, a vendetta. His family's dead. He wants everyone to pay. His enemies, the government, everyone who played a role in their deaths. He wants to kill us all. He's planning for mass casualties, but

the materials are gone. Once he finds out what happened to them, who took them, he's going to retaliate."

"When? Who's the target?"

"I don't know. Fuck. We need to act now."

"Calm down, Owen. Take a breath. I need you to keep it together. Do you think Flynn told anyone about this?"

"I don't know." Owen's tone changed. "No one would dare rip off Colin Flynn. Are you sure another agency isn't running an op?"

"Nothing's crossed my desk."

"Find out. I have to go."

"Owen, wait." The line went dead. "Owen?"

Bastian hit a key. "That's the part omitted from the briefing notes we were given."

"So Partridge lied. He knew but acted like he had no knowledge of an impending attack. He has to be Flynn's inside man."

"Or he's covering his own arse."

"I've been trying to stop a terrorist plot, and the bloody terrorist doesn't even have the weapon any longer."

"Actually," Bastian exchanged looks with Donovan and Hans, "it isn't that simple."

"Make it that simple." Mercer waited. The calm he felt when he first entered the safe house dissipated the moment he heard Shepherd's voice on the recording.

"As you know, soon after this communication, Shepherd disappeared. The truth is Flynn never lost the bomb materials. It was misinformation. Flynn knew Owen was spying on him, and this was a test to prove it." Bastian grabbed a stick of beef jerky and peeled off the wrapper. "Owen failed, and it probably cost him his life."

"Who tipped Flynn?" Mercer asked. If it was

Partridge, he might already be compromised.

"I don't know. I've been going over the internal communications and outgoing messages inside Palace Barracks, but I can't draw a line between any one agent and Colin Flynn. They aren't using the company lines to make contact. I've narrowed down some potentials based on the agents involved in Shepherd's op, but I haven't flagged any of them for suspicious activity."

"Flynn said his connection was dead. Who's been killed?"

"No one."

A stray thought crossed Mercer's mind. "Kevin Aglin said Flynn wanted to speak to Lara. He wanted her brought to him alive."

"Probably so he could kill her himself," Hans muttered.

Donovan's brow furrowed. "You think Shepherd left something inside the slick that Flynn wants to reclaim?"

"I don't know. The only person who can answer that question is asleep in the next room." Mercer's eyes went to the door. "Let's wake her up and ask."

Bastian grabbed Mercer's arm. "We've tried, but getting her to focus is a lost cause. She needs rest. She got hit pretty hard. Her brain's jumbled. She needs time to recover."

"We don't have time." Mercer thought about his efforts to question her the previous night, but he hadn't gotten anywhere with her. And that was when she was running on fear and adrenaline. "What do we know about her?"

"You've read her profile. That's about it," Bastian said.

"That can't be it. How did she find me? Why would she risk everything by coming here?"

"She's looking for her brother," Hans said, as if that explained everything.

"But she's been trained," Mercer insisted. "There has to be more to the story."

"We'll get to the bottom of it the next time we wake her," Hans promised.

"In the meantime, I found this on Flynn's desk." Mercer plucked the map off their vinyl sheet and added the same red Xs Flynn had drawn. "I'm guessing those are targets."

"X marks the spot," Donovan said.

"I need you to scout these locations and see what you can find."

"Aye."

"Need help?" Hans asked.

"Sure. Just don't blow out that shoulder. I'm not carrying your sorry arse back to the car," Donovan said.

Hans wrote down a time. "If we're not back, make sure you wake Lara. If we forget and she slips into a coma or something, Maggie threatened to string me up by the balls."

Bastian looked at the slip of paper. "Will do, though it might be fun to see that."

"Piss off," Hans mumbled.

The men collected their gear and exited the safe house.

Taking a seat at the counter, Mercer grabbed a laptop not currently in use and powered it on. "Flynn's convinced Mathias Murphy is to blame for last night's debacle. He asked me to investigate, but after hearing that phone call, I believe you might be right. Flynn's trying to set me up. He's testing me, or he's setting a trap."

"He's still on the Murphy kick?"

"Yes."

"There must be a reason." Bastian pulled up the data they'd compiled on the rival faction. "I have hard copies from MI5's records over there." He pointed to the kitchen table. "There's been bad blood between them for years."

"Why? What happened?"

"They started out as colleagues, I guess. I don't know. Friendlies." Bastian shrugged. "They were conducting business. Murphy sent his men to pick up a shipment from Flynn, but the authorities caught on. Murphy's men pulled out, leaving Flynn's men to take the fall. Several were killed."

"That would make Mathias Murphy a target."

"I believe so."

"That's why Flynn's been so adamant Mathias Murphy is responsible for his recent string of bad luck."

"The real question is if he believes you. Frankly, Jules, you made quite the first impression. Do you really think Flynn believes a word you've said since?"

Mercer thought about the interrogation. He couldn't recall all of it, but he'd spoken at length about Michelle and the pain of losing her. He probably shared more with that psycho bastard than he had with any other living person. The thought left him nauseated but convinced of one thing. "This isn't a test. Flynn trusts me. He wants me to flush out the leak."

"Are we mixing metaphors?"

"Bollocks."

Bastian cocked an eyebrow. "You could be wrong, Jules. Are you willing to risk your life on a guess?"

"It's not a guess."

For the next hour and a half, Mercer and Bastian searched every database and file for details on Mathias Murphy. Fortunately, Murphy kept his activities limited. He and his extended family ran their faction the same way the Italians ran organized crime. It was about family obligation and taking care of one's own. Compared to Flynn, Murphy was small potatoes. And to the Irish, that was a massive insult.

"Jules," Bastian said as they neared the end of their research, "what are you going to do?"

"I'm not sure. But I need to buy some time."

TWENTY-FOUR

"You're not going to like it," Donovan said the moment he returned to the flat. "Those six locations are all soft targets. We're looking at potentially hundreds of civilian casualties, depending on the device and materials used."

"And the disbursal system." Hans placed a high-powered camera equipped with a telephoto lens on the counter. "We actually spotted a few suspicious blokes in the area. You might want to take a look."

Mercer flipped through the photos on the viewscreen. "Aaron."

"Who?" Bastian leaned over his shoulder to see.

"Aaron. He's in the file." Mercer pointed. "Flynn had him ditch the car I stole."

"You stole a car?" Hans grinned.

"Yes," Mercer didn't bother to mask the irritation, "we've been over this."

"Right." Hans glanced at the bedroom. "Guess I should wake sleeping beauty."

"I want to speak to her." Mercer continued to flip

through the images on the camera. "That's Killian." He showed the photo to Donovan. "Different location?"

Donovan pointed on the map. "Yes. Here and here."

Mercer scrutinized the map and photographs. "Flynn's moving ahead with his plans to attack. I can use this." His thoughts went to ways of manipulating the information. "I have to turn Killian into an asset or flip the intel on its head. Is there anything I can use? Anything you noticed? Even the smallest piece of intel might prove useful."

"I'm not sure."

Mercer thought back to earlier this morning. The map was laid out on Flynn's desk. He must have ordered Killian and Aaron to scout locations. Time was running out. "The wheels are in motion. I'll have to find some way to delay Flynn's timetable." Mercer had to convince Flynn that Killian was the informant. He couldn't come up with any other viable options. "What about the other locations? Did you check all of them? Did you locate any devices or delivery systems?"

"No, we searched, but these aren't secluded areas. There are dozens of buildings, churches, parks, theaters. Any one of them could be a target," Donovan said.

"Or none of them," Bastian volunteered. "He could just load up a lorry and boom."

"Bas, whatever happened with the church and tracking the drop-off?" Mercer asked, his thoughts splintering in a million directions.

"Hang on. I've got that here somewhere." Bastian shuffled through the growing pile of paperwork.

"Do you recognize anyone at the other four locations?" Donovan asked.

"No, but our timing could be off. I'm surprised you noticed anyone skulking about," Mercer said.

"They weren't hard to pinpoint. They were the only other chaps casing the place. It looked like they were firmly planted. Neither of them had any intention of leaving his perch." Donovan took the camera and zoomed in. "I'd say the theater would be the most likely target. Wait for a show to begin, place the device somewhere inside, possibly in the ventilation system, and secure the doors. No one would get out. It'd be a massacre."

A chill went down Mercer's spine. They'd seen attacks like that before. "What about the other five locations? What are the best targets?"

"None of those were as clear-cut. Killian had eyes on the theater, but this other wanker, Aaron, was it, he observed everything. Hans and I were unable to make out his target."

Mercer blew out a breath. "Flynn's planning to strike soon. Within the next day or two. He wouldn't leave his people exposed if he didn't need them to monitor traffic and security to finalize their plans." With twelve devices and only six potential known locations, there were too many what-ifs. Flynn might not attack any of these targets, or he could attack them all and several others. Or he might focus his firepower on one vulnerable area to inflict maximum damage. "Dammit."

Bastian handed Mercer the vehicle records and a blurry still taken from traffic camera footage. "This man delivered the crate to the church. I traced his route back to that boathouse we explored. I'm guessing that's where the deliveries are left."

"Where did he go afterward?"

"I don't know. He ditched the car in a parking garage. No internal cameras, and we didn't get a good enough shot of him to put a name to his face." Bastian held up a finger before Mercer could ask the next question. "The vehicle is registered to Flynn's pub. It's listed as a company car."

"That doesn't help us. He's going to attack, Bas. We have to do something."

"We should go back to the profile. We need to figure out what's driving Flynn's motivation."

"Revenge," Mercer said.

"Yeah, okay. Against who?"

"Mathias Murphy. The government agents who raided his compound. Possibly the agency itself." Mercer turned, catching a glimpse of Hans lingering near the now open bedroom door.

"Lara, darling," Hans repeated a little louder, knocking gently against the door, "it's time to wake up."

"That sentiment is usually followed by thanks for the shag. Don't let the door hit your bum on the way out." Donovan smirked.

A muffled, feminine voice sounded from within, and Lara emerged. Her gaze flicked around the unfamiliar flat. Briefly, her focus came to rest on Mercer. "The loo?" she asked, stumbling. She threw an arm out to catch herself, and Hans swooped in to steady her.

"It's just over here," Hans said.

She righted herself and ducked inside. An intrigued expression crossed Hans' face. He patted his pocket and glanced at the commander, who pressed a finger to his lips.

Listen, Mercer mouthed.

Hans stepped closer to the bathroom door, but all he could hear was running water.

"Did I miss something?" Bas asked.

"She just nicked Hans' phone."

"You're serious?"

"Trace it."

Bastian entered a few commands. As a general rule, he kept trackers on the team's phones, along with a programmed trap and trace. "Jesus. You're not going to believe this."

"Are we compromised?" Donovan's hand moved to his holstered weapon.

"No, but she is."

Mercer leaned over. He recognized the number. "Bloody hell. She's with MI6. Find out everything you can on Ms. Shepherd, but let's play this close to the vest for now. I don't want any more surprises."

When she emerged from the bathroom, she stumbled again. Hans caught her, offering a reassuring smile. "Easy, love." She slipped the phone back into his pocket. "Let me help you back to bed."

"I thought you had questions," she said.

"We do, but they can wait." Mercer hoped that was true. They didn't have much time to waste, but he didn't want to interrogate the woman without knowing more about her first. "Are you hungry? We're about to pick up dinner. We can talk then, yeah?"

"Okay." She disappeared behind the bedroom door.

"Do you mind?" Mercer asked Hans.

"I thought being included would involve more than taking photographs and running to the nearest fish and chip place." Hans placed his phone on the counter. "Is this location burned?"

"We'll let it play out for now," Mercer said.

"At this point, if the SIS tries to conduct a rescue mission, we'll ask if they wouldn't mind helping us out with our Flynn problem," Bastian said.

"You all better be alive when I get back, and you better be here. I'm not traipsing across Ireland searching for our next base of operations. It's not safe out there, particularly when Flynn's looking to ruin everyone's day." Hans grabbed a jacket to cover his weapon and went out the door.

"Donovan, keep an eye on her," Mercer said. "Is there any other way out of that room?"

"No windows, mate. No other exits. Same goes for the loo. The only way she's leaving is through the bedroom door."

"She's wily. We need to be cautious." Mercer reached for Hans' compromised phone. "Let's see if our mates at MI6 are in a talkative mood."

*   *   *

"Courtesy of MI6." Bastian typed with one hand while the other tapped a beat on the granite. "Her background's classified. All mention of her being an operative was erased. But after a few calls to old friends, I've pieced some things together. Ms. Shepherd worked with an elite unit. They won't talk about it. So I don't know if she wanted out or if she was compromised. Either way, they disavowed and wiped her for her own protection. I'm not sure any of it is relevant to us."

"That's how she tracked Flynn's operation." Donovan picked up a highly redacted file and passed it to Mercer. "It's why she came looking for her brother as soon as he made contact."

"Owen would have trusted her before the plonkers at the Security Service." Mercer scanned the documents but didn't find any additional details that his teammates hadn't already told him. "What about the men outside her flat in Islington?"

"Even though they officially denied it, I can tell you someone at the SIS made the green sedan disappear from police impound. I'm guessing the men who pinned you in Lara's bedroom were her old mates, not spies, just desk jockeys," Bas said.

"They knew how to shoot, but they didn't know how to do much else. It's how we maneuvered around them so easily," Donovan said.

"And before you ask," Bastian said, reading Mercer's mind, "I verified this directly from the source. Partridge doesn't know anything about it."

"Why didn't MI5 tell us Owen's sister worked for the Secret Intelligence Service?" Mercer asked.

Hans unpacked the takeout containers from inside the bag. "Do they even know?"

"Probably, but it's need to know. And Partridge doesn't think we need to know anything." Bastian stepped away from the counter and rummaged in the fridge. With a bag of carrot sticks in hand, he returned to the computer. "Ever since you mysteriously vanished, Jules, he's been keeping me inundated with Shepherd's old reports and case work. It's how I found the misplaced recording. I've read everything, listened to everything, seen everything. Nothing indicates what happened to Owen, but he was getting close to something. I noticed a shift in his tone over the course of the two years. Flynn went off the rails after losing his family. That's when matters started to escalate. Owen delayed or thwarted several attempted bombings and a few shootings. He's a bloody hero."

"Why would Partridge think he turned? After doing all that, how is that even possible?" Mercer asked.

"How dare you?" Lara entered the room, squinting against the harsh lights. "My brother isn't a traitor."

"No one said he is, love," Bastian replied, not bothering to turn around.

From the look on Bas's face, Mercer knew his friend didn't quite care for the woman or her deception. For the record, neither did he. "Still sore about the shotgun?" Mercer mumbled so only his team would hear.

Bastian shot him an annoyed look. "In case you've forgotten, we're here to find your brother, Ms. Shepherd. And that would be easier if you would be forthright with us."

"So you say." She took a seat and put her elbows on the counter. She reached for the box of takeout, noticing Mercer's cheek. "Sorry about that, mate."

"You are not."

"You're right. I'm not." She rested her head in her hands. "What do you know so far? Have you seen Owen? Is he okay?"

"Tell us what you know."

"You first." Her eyes stared fiercely into his. She wouldn't back down. She was headstrong and stubborn. Even the concussion hadn't knocked that out of her.

"We don't know much. We've barely been at this a week. Jules infiltrated Colin Flynn's faction, but trust is a hard commodity to come by." Bastian hoped that would be enough to get her to open up. She hadn't shared any details concerning her brother or her identity since he picked her up last night.

"You went back to Flynn after everything that happened?" she asked. "I'm surprised he didn't kill you."

"I didn't have a choice. Flynn's planning an attack." Mercer studied her expression. She knew, even though she did her best to hide it. "Did Owen confide in you? You said he made contact a few weeks ago. We ran your phone records. We know he called you from a public phone. Whatever he said to you, that's what caused you to flee, isn't it?"

"I wasn't fleeing."

"Then what did you do? Why are you here?"

"I'm looking for my brother."

"Did you ask your old team for help?"

"What are you talking about?"

"We know you're MI6," Bastian spat.

She opened a container and speared a morsel of food with her fork. She popped it into her mouth and chewed. Every muscle in Mercer's body tensed. He took a step forward, but Hans put his palm on Mercer's chest.

Lara swallowed, watching the exchange. "I'm no longer with the SIS. Haven't been for three bloody years. I'm retired. More or less." She climbed off the stool and filled a glass with water. After gulping down half of it in a few swallows, she turned back to them. "I told you Owen never arrived at the train station. According to MI5's surveillance records, he never even left Ireland. Something happened here, and he couldn't come home. Either he believed Colin was on to him and didn't want to risk my safety, or one of those arseholes at Palace Barracks sold him out."

"Owen knew MI5 was compromised. That's why he called you. He needed outside help and your connections to stop Flynn. That's why those two men were staking out your flat in Islington. You didn't tell them where you went, did you?"

She didn't speak, her expression unreadable.

Hans cocked his head to the side. "You don't trust us, love?"

"How do I know you're any different from the rest of the plonkers at the Security Service? For all I know, you're the corrupt ones." She sneered at Mercer. "I've been watching you. I've seen you with Flynn at the pub, with his mates, with that woman. How do I know you didn't do something to my brother?"

"We weren't here when he vanished," Mercer said.

"Convenient."

"Convenient or not," Bastian said, "we can prove it. And we aren't your enemy. But you know it. Deep down, you know you can trust us. That's what you were told when you phoned your agency contact, wasn't it?"

She eyed Mercer, as if he was the only one she wasn't quite certain about.

"You don't know who to trust, but you can't do this alone. You need our help, and we need yours. Don't be coy, Lara. You have a pretty good idea of who we are. You know what we do." Mercer shoved the phone in her direction. "Call whoever. Ask whatever you want. Ask about me. You'll find out that I despise MI5 as much as you do, but that doesn't mean I'd work with a terrorist. Working for them in this instance is a necessary evil, and one I willingly undertook in order to find your brother. When they contacted us, I didn't know about the terrorist plot or the WMDs, but I do now. We want to get your brother back, but we have to save lives too."

"Wouldn't Owen want that?" Bas asked. "He risked his life to stop Flynn. Shouldn't we continue his work?"

"You make it sound like he's already dead," she said.

Mercer blew out a breath. "We don't know."

Hans reached for her hand, but she pulled away. "That's why we're here. You phoned your mates earlier after you stole my phone. Really, you didn't think I'd feel your hand in my pocket?" He winked at her. "You wanted to make sure we were who we claimed. What did they tell you?"

"That doesn't prove anything."

"It should." Hans withdrew his hand.

"If you won't help us, there's the door." Mercer pointed. "But Flynn will find you. And he will kill you.

I won't have that on my conscience, so if you leave now, we better not cross paths again. I risked everything for you last night."

She considered his words. Maybe she finally understood. "You're right. Flynn is planning an attack. Something massive. Owen found out about it, but he didn't report it. He hoped I still had enough friends at the SIS who could intervene. He gave me coordinates and shipping numbers. I made some calls. A few days later, I received a package in the mail. It was from Owen. It was an empty canister, hermetically sealed. I had the lab run it. They found traces of VX."

TWENTY-FIVE

"What else was in the package?" Mercer asked.

She turned her head away, biting her thumbnail. The temperature in the room must have dropped ten degrees.

Bastian closed the computer and took a seat beside her. "Owen sent more than an empty canister. Whatever he sent, that's what you hid under your floorboards. What was it, love? More weapons? A map? What?"

"It was nothing like that." She hesitated.

"It's gone now. We didn't find it, and I doubt the blokes guarding your flat removed it. What was it?" Mercer asked.

Fear shone in her eyes, but she shook it away. "Owen sent me his credentials. His government ID. His passport. That's when I knew he wasn't planning on making it back home." Her mouth had gone dry. "Are you certain you didn't miss them?"

"We didn't find them," Donovan said. He shot Bastian a worried look and slid the phone to Lara.

"Why don't you call and make sure one of your people didn't recover them?"

While she did that, Mercer and Bastian exchanged a few words in private. If MI5 knew Owen surrendered his ID, they'd use it as proof he turned or intended an unsanctioned suicide mission. The more troublesome question was whether Flynn could have tracked the package, broke into Lara's, and stole Owen's credentials. It would explain how Flynn determined Owen was a traitor and his obsession with questioning Lara.

"Owen found the chemical weapons," Mercer said. "He knew where Flynn was keeping them."

"But the canister was empty. Flynn must have conducted a test run or loaded the disbursal system. We know he's not bright enough to wait," Bastian surmised, thinking of the premature explosion.

"Flynn has other locations I haven't been made privy to yet. Killian's the key. I'll play them both. One of them has to crack," Mercer said.

Lara hung up the phone, shaking her head.

Mercer eyed her. "Did your brother know who Flynn turned inside Palace Barracks?"

She shook her head. "I have some contacts looking into it, but they haven't found anything concrete."

"Maybe we have." Bastian slid the piece of stationery to her. "Have you ever seen this before?"

She read the words, but they were of little consequence. "No. What's so special about it?"

"Flynn has a list of components, bomb materials, written on the same letterhead. We noticed this piece of paper in Liam Partridge's inbox. We're not sure where it originated, but it can't be a coincidence they're using the same paper," Mercer said.

"Partridge is my brother's handler. Do you think he's involved?"

"We don't know."

Lara traced her finger over the embossed design. "You think they're passing notes?"

"There is no electronic communications between Flynn's faction and any of the agents at MI5. They might be utilizing dead drops to leave messages," Bastian reasoned. "You have expertise in this area. What would you do?"

She didn't answer.

"Flynn told me he had a contact within MI5, but he didn't say who." Mercer glanced at his teammates. "Flynn said his connection's dead."

"No one from Palace Barracks has been killed or died recently." Bastian watched the wheels turn in Lara's head.

Abruptly, she slammed her palm on the counter. "No. You're wrong. Owen knew someone on his team was compromised. It's why he came to me and asked for help. It's why we were supposed to meet. Flynn must have discovered Owen's true identity. The turncoat probably ratted him out. Flynn must have done something to Owen." She glared, her rage winning out over her concern. "Owen is no traitor. He would have died for the service before he'd share secrets with a mass murderer."

"I hope you're right," Mercer said. "That's why we need your help."

She blew out a breath, a barrage of curses flying from her lips.

"We want the truth," Donovan said, "just like you do. And the best way to get it is to find out what happened to Owen."

She crossed her arms over her chest. "What do you have in mind?"

Bastian looked at Mercer. "I was wondering the same thing, Jules."

Mercer leaned against the counter, his eyes on the intel taped to the wall. "None of the known locations have yielded results. We haven't gotten eyes on Owen, and no one in Flynn's rank and file has mentioned Owen's name to me. I've checked Flynn's compound. Owen isn't there. What about the church and the symbol Flynn has printed on his cash?"

"The symbol pops up in a lot of dodgy areas," Donovan said. "I scouted a few locations this morning, but they're fronts for Flynn's less legitimate businesses."

"Colin Flynn's an international arms dealer." Lara grabbed a pen and went to the map on the wall. She circled two ports and a private airport. "Interpol and the SIS believe he controls these areas and allows his overseas suppliers to use them."

"Donovan and I have already checked those locations and the old boathouse," Hans said. "We didn't find any signs of your brother."

"I know. That's where my search began. I just happened to be there when a large crate was picked up. I followed the driver to a church and caught sight of you and your pal." She stared at Mercer. "I followed you to the library and the clubs."

"You might have had better luck sticking with Killian," Mercer said. "I don't know where he rerouted."

She grinned. "Pity."

"What did you do?"

"I put a tracker on his car."

"The suspense is killing us," Bastian deadpanned. "Where did he go?"

She held her palm out to Hans. "Your phone, please." After entering a few commands, she handed the device to Mercer.

"He returned to Flynn's compound. He didn't

deviate. He didn't make any questionable stops. He followed orders."

"He had to deliver the money," Lara said.

"How long have you been monitoring Flynn's activities?" Bastian asked.

"Since Owen missed our rendezvous. The only place I haven't been is inside the hornet's nest, and quite frankly, I was prepared to march through those doors last night." She gave Mercer a dirty look. "But you interfered."

"I saved your life."

"You did a real bang-up job."

Mercer's fists clenched until he realized her animosity and sarcasm were a result of her worry. Like the rest of their clients, she feared for her loved one's safety.

"Where is Killian now?" Mercer handed the device to Bastian.

"Still outside the theater. It looks like Donovan and Hans are right. Flynn has his men monitoring the area."

"He's going to strike soon." Lara turned the angry intensity on Mercer. "What are you going to do about it?"

"What can you tell us about Mathias Murphy?"

"He's Colin Flynn's biggest rival. They've been fighting over Ireland's black market arms trade for the better part of a decade now."

"And this morning, Julian turned their cold war hot," Bastian mumbled.

Lara shook her head. "What does any of this have to do with Owen?"

"Flynn's fighting a war on two fronts. I've convinced him Murphy has sleepers inside the faction in addition to MI5 nipping at his heels." Mercer thought for a moment. "Flynn already knew MI5 was on to him, whether from a leak or Owen slipping up, but after you attacked us last night, I told Flynn it was an attempted robbery. Coupled with a few other lies and unfortunate mishaps, Flynn has no reason not to believe me." A dark thought flitted through his mind. He knew how to prove himself once and for all to Colin Flynn, but he couldn't take the risk. He'd use that method only as a last resort.

"So take me to Flynn," Lara said, coming up with the same idea.

"You don't want that, darling," Hans said.

"Oh, I do."

"Love, did you not hear what Jules said. He doesn't want your death on his conscience, and neither do I. We're in the business of saving lives, not sacrificing them," Bastian said.

"Even for the greater good?" She circled the kitchen. "Trust me, boys. I can handle myself."

"You don't know Colin Flynn, but I'll consider it." Mercer tossed a sharp look at Bas when the analyst opened his mouth in protest. "Killian abandoned us last night. And despite what Flynn has told me, he still trusts his second-in-command. So we need to do something to change that."

Bas grabbed his computer and placed it on the countertop. "This would be a lot easier if I...right. We know where the bastard is and what he's doing." Bastian reached for the camera and ejected the memory card. "I can doctor some photos. Create a fake account. Transfer funds. This is doable. I need six hours. The account will be tricky. It needs to be backdated and traceable."

"I can help," Lara offered.

"About damn time," Mercer mumbled. "Radio the moment it's done. Right now, I have to get to Flynn's pub. He doesn't like to be kept waiting."

"Jules, be careful," Bastian warned.

Mercer nodded and went out the door. His team knew how to take care of business, and despite his words, none of them would let Lara leave. She might be trained, but she didn't stand a chance against three former SAS operatives. And no one, not even Mercer, stood a chance against the army Colin Flynn controlled. She was just one person, albeit one who caused a lot of trouble. Maybe together, they'd have a fighting chance.

TWENTY-SIX

Mercer made sure the radio was tucked into his ear. It was small and flesh-colored. Flynn wouldn't notice it, at least that's what Mercer was counting on. Every cell in his body was poised to strike. The only thing he wanted to do was beat the answers out of Colin Flynn. But the attack wouldn't be stopped by Flynn's death. In fact, Flynn's loyal followers would take their anger and sorrow out on even more innocent people. For a moment, Mercer missed the military and precision airstrikes. But he could do this. After all, he didn't have a choice.

Pushing through the pub door, he noticed the establishment was practically empty. Even the bartender was gone.

Flynn sat at the corner table. Four of his guards were positioned around the room.

"Julian," Flynn waved him over, "grab a glass."

Mercer ignored the suggestion and took a seat. "My mind needs to be clear. Where is everyone?"

Flynn took a gulp directly from the bottle. "We

have two wakes to plan."

"And Killian?"

A grin pulled at Flynn's lips. "You're obsessed."

Mercer looked around again. "We should speak privately."

"Whatever you have to say, you can say here."

Mercer couldn't be positive, but there was a strong possibility Colin Flynn was drunk. It could be an act. So Mercer proceeded cautiously. "I've spent most of the day scouting the scene of last night's attack and checking into Mathias Murphy's strongholds. He has a restaurant and pub, both fronts to clean his money."

"Tell me something I don't know. Can you name the traitor? Or are you wasting my time?"

"I'm getting close." Mercer glanced uneasily behind him, sensing a tension building among the guards. Despite the emptiness of the room, he felt claustrophobic. "I told you a woman was part of last night's attack. She shot out the tires. She's the one who set everything in motion. I didn't get a look at her, but I found some blood drops in the alleyway where she hid and followed them."

"You're a blooming bloodhound," Flynn retorted, clearly drunk. That made him unpredictable and even more dangerous, but his condition could be advantageous.

"She broke into a restaurant. I spoke to the staff. She was with a man. They disguised themselves as cooks and went out the back. That must be how they evaded the police. I already checked the security footage, but they were clever. They either stole the footage or wiped it. They didn't want to leave a trace."

"So you still have no idea who they are?"

"I didn't say that. There's more. But I'll have that drink first." Mercer sauntered over to the bar. "Bas, is the photo ready?" he whispered.

"Sending it to you now."

Mercer grabbed a bottle of cognac, figuring Flynn wouldn't have dosed all the bottles, and poured some into a glass. In the mirror, he watched Flynn signal to his guards. It was now or never.

"I did find one other thing." Mercer spun, catching two of the guards as they edged closer. He returned to the table and sat down. He pulled the phone from his pocket and enlarged the photo. "You want to tell me what Killian's been doing all day?"

"I sent him on a few errands."

"Really?" Mercer glanced back at the guards, who were now seated at the bar. "Did one of those errands involve catching a matinee?" He pushed the device across the table. "If I'm not mistaken, Mathias Murphy saw the same show."

Flynn fought to keep his expression neutral, but Mercer could see the surprise in the terrorist's eyes. The alcohol impacted Flynn's ability to appear cold and detached. Instead, rage boiled to the surface.

"When did you take this?"

"Several hours ago. Did you send Killian to broker a truce? Or did you ask him to look into the matter because you didn't believe I was capable?" Mercer waited, watching the flush creep up Flynn's neck and color his ears. "I said Killian betrayed you. Is that enough proof, or do you need more?"

Bastian's voice in Mercer's ear reminded him it would be several hours before the fake bank account was up and running.

Flynn tossed the phone down. "You two," he gestured to the guards near the door, "pick up Killian and bring him to me." Flynn pushed away from the table, grabbing the bottle by the neck and throwing it across the room. It shattered on the floor. Flynn swore, his breath becoming ragged. He was practically hyperventilating when he grabbed Mercer by the collar and hauled him to his feet. "You better not be lying. I want the truth."

Mercer fought his instincts to fight back, sensing the snake would strike. "It's a bloody photograph. There is no lie or truth. It's simply what is."

Flynn's grip tightened, and he shook his head from side to side, trying to make sense of the words. He released Mercer and dropped back into the chair. The anger was barely contained. Mercer knew from experience Flynn couldn't think straight, let alone see straight.

Within moments, Flynn was up and moving again. He grabbed another bottle from behind the bar, took a swig, and slammed it down. He couldn't sit still. Part of him was filled with disbelief. The rest with righteous anger. Someone would die tonight.

"Prepare for an extraction. Flynn's pub," Mercer mumbled into his hand, hiding his words behind a cough. "Wait for my order." He coughed again and rubbed his side, reminding Flynn and the two guards he was wounded. A fight was brewing, and being outnumbered and outgunned meant Mercer needed every advantage possible. He didn't know how long it would take his team to get in place or when the other two guards and Killian would arrive, so Mercer had to prepare for the worst and think on his feet.

"Mr. Flynn," Mercer began.

"Shut up. We're waiting for Killian, and then we'll have this out." Remembering Alana, Flynn dug out his phone and dialed. He paced back and forth, draining the bottle as he went. "I need you to stay at the compound, darling." They exchanged a few curt words, and he dialed another number.

Shit, Mercer thought. Had he overestimated Flynn's affection for Alana? As far as Flynn was concerned, his girlfriend was guilty by association. Mercer would have to do something to change his opinion.

"Colin, you do realize she's nothing more than a victim," Mercer interrupted. "Killian betrayed her too."

"This is my business."

"She didn't know. He tricked everyone. You. Her. Everyone."

"Not you." Flynn jerked his chin at the two guards who grabbed Mercer by both arms and lifted him from the chair. "Want to explain that one, mate?" Now that he found somewhere to focus his misplaced rage, Flynn forgot all about whatever punishment he planned to inflict upon Alana.

Mercer made a half-hearted attempt to tug his arms free, but the guards held tight. "You want to hit someone, Mr. Flynn? Colin? Then fucking do it."

That's all Flynn needed to hear. He pulled his arm back and struck. Mercer shook off the blow, working his jaw and tasting blood. He was getting tired of being punched in the face. The terrorist struck again, moments away from losing control.

"It doesn't matter how many times you hit me. I'm not your enemy," Mercer said softly.

Flynn blinked, the words penetrating through the anger. "Let him go."

Mercer glared at the two men and reached for a napkin. He wiped his mouth. The guards remained poised near Mercer. If the situation were different, Mercer would have them on the ground in a matter of moments, but he had to appear submissive. It was the only way, even though the thoughts running rampant through his mind involved various methods of resolving the current dilemma through violent and bloody means.

For the next thirty minutes, an uncomfortable silence permeated the bar. No one spoke. Flynn had been flexing his hand nonstop. Mercer checked the time. Bastian had to stay at the computer, which meant Donovan and Hans would be performing the extraction, but with both of them gone, Lara might try something stupid.

The pub door opened, and Killian stepped inside. The two men who'd been sent to fetch him remained at the door. One of them flipped the lock. Killian turned, raising a confused eyebrow.

"Colin?" Killian asked.

"Where have you been all day?"

"At the theater, like you asked."

"With who?"

"No one. You told us to split up." Killian glanced in Mercer's direction. "I thought we weren't discussing this in front of him. This morning you said—"

"I know what I fucking said." Flynn stormed toward Killian, forcing the other man into the back corner of the pub. "Explain this." Flynn shoved the phone in front of Killian's face.

"What the hell is this?" Killian started to laugh. "This is pathetic. You can't honestly believe this rubbish? Clearly, it's been doctored."

Flynn didn't smile or laugh. He stared with cold eyes. "Who killed Kevin and Duffy?"

Killian's smile fell, and he glared daggers at Mercer. "You fucking did this. I'm going to kill you." He reached for his gun, but Flynn grabbed it out of his hand and tossed it onto the pool table. "Colin, you know me. We're practically family. We're like brothers."

"Tell me the truth."

"It's him." Killian pointed. "You know it. You know you can trust me." His pleas were becoming more frantic. "I loved Kevin and Duffy. How could you accuse me of being involved?" Killian put his hands on the sides of Flynn's face. "Listen to what I'm saying. Look at me, Colin. Really fucking look. You know me. You know I didn't do this."

Flynn jerked out of Killian's grip and took a step back. He reached for the bottle to collect his thoughts. Torn between loyalties and seemingly irrefutable proof, Flynn didn't know what to think. Before the faction leader came to a decision, Killian lunged for Mercer.

Desperate men did desperate things, and Killian was in dire need of Mercer's confession. He shoved Mercer, pinning him against the wall.

"Tell him the truth," Killian spat.

Mercer brought the backs of his forearms up against the inside of Killian's arms and broke out of the grip. Following through with a headbutt, Mercer forced Killian back and delivered a right cross. The blow made Killian falter.

Keeping one eye on the four guards and Flynn, Mercer charged at Killian, throwing the man onto the empty pool table. Killian's gun slipped off the table and clattered to the floor. Mercer threw a few more punches, the tension in his back and arms dissipating as he swung. He reached for the cue ball, planning to knock out his victim with a well-placed hit to the temple.

But Killian kicked Mercer in the solar plexus and used the momentum to launch himself off the table. He drove his shoulder into Mercer's chest and knocked him backward. Mercer hit the wall hard enough that his ears rang and his breath whooshed out. Somehow, Mercer managed to duck before Killian threw a fast jab that landed solidly against the cinderblock wall. The resounding crunch indicated the

Irishman's hand had broken.

"Anytime now," Mercer said.

"You bastard." Killian swung again, and Mercer dropped him to the floor with a sweeping kick.

"Who's the target?" Hans asked in Mercer's ear.

"Killian," Mercer bellowed.

"And you want us to take him alive?" Hans asked, disbelief in his voice.

"The men who attacked me last night. The masked men who killed Duffy and Kevin, you sent them, didn't you?" Mercer hit Killian again with his empty fist. "Admit it. Admit that they're part of your team. That you orchestrated this. Tell Colin the truth."

"Copy," Donovan said, understanding Mercer's cryptic message. "Keep your head down. Flashbang in three."

Mercer pulled back with his right. The cue ball concealed by his fingers, and he struck hard. Killian's eyes rolled back. His limbs went limp.

At that same moment, the two guards blocking the exit with their backs to the door died instantly. They dropped simultaneously. The sound of the bullets dampened by the silencers on Donovan's and Hans' handguns. Mercer saw the guards collapse. No one else in the room noticed. All eyes were on the brawl, as if this were a prizefight.

But when the canister broke the front window, Flynn and the remaining two guards turned to see the cause. Mercer rolled beneath the pool table, squeezed his eyes shut, and covered his ears. It wasn't enough to nullify the effects of the stun grenade, but it helped him maintain his senses.

By the time Mercer could see again, two figures clad entirely in black were hauling the unconscious Killian out the door. One of Flynn's guards fired. Donovan killed him in the same style Mercer used the previous night. Mercer pulled his gun. He had to make this look real. He fired, narrowly missing. Donovan returned fire to the left, as he always did, and Mercer rolled to the right.

Once Donovan and Hans were out the door with the target, they sprayed the pub, forcing Flynn, Mercer, and the one remaining bodyguard to take cover behind the bar and tables. When the shooting stopped, Mercer was the first to race outside. He fired at the retreating car. Flynn came up behind him, grabbed the gun, and fired several more shots until the Sig clicked empty, but Hans and Donovan were safely away by then.

Flynn yanked at his hair, screaming curses into the night sky. With his face red with anger, he shoved the empty gun back into Mercer's hand. "Find him. Find his team. I'm going to kill them all."

TWENTY-SEVEN

"Those were the same men who attacked last night." Mercer watched Colin's crew clean the pub. No one reported gunfire, but since the entire town knew this was Colin Flynn's business, they must have known better than to call the authorities. "Same tactics." Mercer looked down at the dead guard. "Same spread."

Flynn watched the men get zipped into body bags. By the time the pub opened, no one would know three homicides had occurred.

"You should be somewhere secure," Mercer said. "We don't know what else they might try, but it's clear you're their target."

Flynn glanced at the cut on his forearm. He'd been grazed. Mercer wasn't sure if it had been intentional or accidental, but he knew his teammates wanted to put an end to Flynn's reign of terror as quickly as possible. However, they wouldn't risk killing the terrorist.

"Those were Mathias' men." Flynn exited the

broken front door and warily glanced at his parked SUV. "You drive."

Mercer understood. For once, Flynn was afraid. It was about damn time someone terrorized him. Mercer led Flynn to the rental and unlocked the doors. He checked for bombs and started the engine. They didn't speak again until Mercer pulled up to the wrought iron gates.

"Does Alana know?" Flynn narrowed his eyes on the golden glow coming from the bedroom window.

"No."

"Are you certain?"

"I have no way of proving it, but I did find this." Mercer held out his phone, showing the fake bank account. "Killian was paid handsomely for his deception. Her accounts are clean. Honestly, Colin, I've seen the way she looks at you. She's in love with you. She'd just as soon cut her own throat than betray you. You know that to be true. She'd forsake her family for you."

"I thought the same of Killian, and I was wrong."

"Let me speak to her," Mercer said. "I will get the truth." Flynn would torture the poor woman, possibly even kill her. Mercer wouldn't stand by and let that happen. He'd protect her, even if it seemed she'd dedicated her life to shagging a terrorist. Maybe she couldn't control who she fell in love with, or maybe she was no better than Flynn or Killian. But since MI5 didn't have a file on her and neither did Interpol, Mercer was willing to give her the benefit of the doubt.

"You should get cleaned up first. I'll send Maura. You've ripped your stitches, and I could use some patching."

*   *   *

"You're sure?" Flynn asked.

"As sure as I can be." Mercer examined the staples in his side. "How's your arm?"

"Better than your side." Flynn watched Alana through the open doorway. "I do love her." Her cheek was slightly swollen from where Mercer slapped her. It was the only way to stop Flynn from taking over the interrogation and doing something much worse, but it left Mercer feeling icky inside. As a rule, he didn't like to hit women, unless they hit first. "She cried herself to sleep."

"I didn't hit her that hard."

"It wasn't that. She doesn't believe Killian would betray us."

"So you believe she's not involved?"

"I'm coming around to the idea, but I'm having my men keep an eye on her."

"Probably for the best. You should monitor her calls. Killian might reach out. It'd be the fastest way to track him and find out what Murphy is planning." Mercer pulled a shirt over his head.

"I asked her to call Killian last night, but he didn't answer."

"I can trace his phone."

"It's turned off. Probably destroyed. Killian's been doing this a long time. He knows how to stay off the grid and avoid getting caught. I never thought he'd use those techniques against me."

"Are you sure the rest of your men are loyal to you and not Killian?"

Flynn didn't answer. "I've deposited the other fifty into your account. You have your orders."

Mercer holstered his weapon, nodded, and left the compound. He drove to the center of town, ditched the car in a parking garage, exited through a different entrance, picked up a waiting rental, and swept his person for bugs. After that was done, he activated the radio.

"Flynn made another deposit," Mercer said.

"It's a good thing he likes to pay up front. It's the only way we had the funds and accounts set up to create the fake one for our new pal," Bastian said.

"Where is he?"

Bastian gave Mercer the address. "Donovan's with him, but our prisoner isn't talking. I don't expect he'll speak to you either."

"How's Lara feeling?"

"Are you sure that's wise, Jules?"

"I don't know, but why don't the two of you join us? Tell Hans to hold down the fort. We'll meet up and figure out the play."

"I hate it when we do things on the fly."

"Where've you been, Bas? We always do things on the fly."

When Mercer pulled up to the safe house, Bastian was waiting at the front door.

"He's only slightly worse for wear." Bastian pointed at a locked, soundproofed room. "He can't hear us."

"Good."

Lara appeared steadier on her feet. She fidgeted with the hem of her shirt. She was itching to get answers. "What's the play?"

"What has he said so far?" Mercer asked, catching Donovan's eye.

"Aside from detailing precisely how he plans to get revenge on you, he hasn't said a word. He doesn't know we're connected. It's best we keep it that way. You shouldn't go in there."

"Flynn trained him to resist torture. Hell, living with Flynn is daily torture. Killian will break, but we don't have time for a typical rendition."

"He doesn't know who's behind this," Donovan said. "He's been trying to figure it out. At the moment, he thinks we're MI5. We could convince him otherwise. Maybe we should convince him Flynn orchestrated this, that Flynn betrayed him and the cause."

Mercer thought for a moment. "Killian objected to the sale of machine pistols. He was opposed to arming his enemies because he knew they'd turn against him."

"His enemies, yes, but not Flynn." Bastian flipped through the profile. "He's loyal to Flynn. It won't matter who we claim to be. He'll never betray his leader. He won't give up the targets."

"What if you convince him to give up his enemies?" Lara asked. "We know who Flynn hates. Specifically, we know who his prime targets would be. MI5. Mathias Murphy. And anyone involved in the deaths of Flynn's family." She studied Mercer. "You've convinced Flynn that Murphy is waging war, but I take it Killian didn't buy it."

"Of course not. I played him against Flynn."

"Right, so we continue the charade. How's your Irish accent, lads?"

"He knows I'm English," Donovan said.

"Maybe you're the hitter Murphy hired when Mercer refused to take the contract." She cleared her throat and spoke with a perfect brogue. "Maybe we use what we know and bluff on the rest. We have six targets. We know the locations of Flynn's operating bases, and we have a general idea who's supplying his weapons. We can make this work."

"Jules," Bastian said, "I can fill in. You and Lara should remain out here and monitor the situation."

"Rubbish," she said. "I possess more intel on this situation and have done this many times before. I'll get what we need."

Mercer turned to her. "You stay focused. You stay on topic. Our priority is finding out about the attacks. After that, you can do whatever's necessary to get the answers you need. But not until then, do you understand?"

"Yes."

"Is he restrained?" Mercer asked, and Donovan nodded. "If something goes wrong, we'll pull you out." Mercer pointed an accusatory finger in her face. "Nothing better go wrong. This is a one-shot deal. I went to a lot of trouble to get him here. You will not fuck this up. Do you understand?"

"Yes, sir."

Donovan remained glued to the live feed while she settled into the room and began the interrogation. Lara Shepherd possessed the same skill set as Mercer's team, but she was also an expert manipulator. Still, Killian would be a tough nut to crack, and frankly, it'd be a miracle if the man left the room with either nut still attached.

"She shouldn't be in there," Bastian said. "Neither should you."

"What do you propose?" Mercer asked. "Donovan's been grilling him all night. You have the profile. Aside from Alana, who he knows is under Colin Flynn's protection, there are no other pressure points to squeeze."

"Lara wants to find her brother. I'm not sure she's seeing any of this clearly." Bastian watched her. "At least she appears level-headed. That's more than I can say for most of the interrogations you've conducted in recent years."

"Get her whatever tools she needs, and let her work him over until we have answers."

"What do we do with him when he cracks?"

Donovan asked. There was no doubt. Killian would break. The only question was if it'd be in time.

"Let her find out what happened to her brother and then pull her out. We'll hand him over to MI5 as soon as we identify the leak." Mercer turned to Bastian. "Any progress?"

"You mean since you asked ten hours ago? And in between having to doctor some photographs and set up numbered accounts that directly link Killian to Mathias Murphy?"

"Yes."

Bastian grumbled to himself. "Lara has more friends than we do. They should be making progress, but I've noted some odd lapses in Palace Barracks' security feeds. I've expanded our hunt to include civilian employees."

Mercer's phone chimed, and he read the message. It was a reminder of Flynn's latest assignment.

Bastian adopted an impeccable Irish accent. "Go. We can handle this. I remember a few things when it comes to effective interrogation techniques. I should really give the lass a hand."

TWENTY-EIGHT

An hour later, Mercer returned to Flynn's compound with the surveillance photos. Scouting Murphy's known strongholds wasn't a good sign. Mercer's actions had started a war. And he was the only person who could stop it.

"You should wait. He'll be expecting this," Mercer cautioned.

"He knows what he did. He knows what will happen."

"Which is why you should take your time. Make him paranoid. Let the fear eat at him. It'll drive him mad. And when he's on the brink, that's when you strike."

"No. We do this my way." Flynn pushed away from the table. "Come with me." He pulled on the gold chain hanging from his neck and removed a key. With the key in hand, he unlocked the basement door, flipped the light switch, and descended the steps. "Close the door behind you. I don't want anyone to overhear what we're planning."

Mercer obeyed, doing his best to appear hesitant. It would not be in his best interest to demonstrate any type of familiarity with the basement or what Flynn housed within the locked room. Mercer surveyed the room, noting several missing crates. Perhaps those weapons had been bought and paid for two nights ago. It would explain the exorbitant amount of money Killian received and why he left the first club so quickly. Mercer just hoped it wasn't because Flynn had sold the excess VX. Ireland already had one psychopath armed with a weapon of mass destruction. It sure as hell didn't need two.

Flynn cocked an intrigued eyebrow at Mercer. "I've decided to trust you, Julian. It's about time you extend the same courtesy to me."

"Forgive me, but I've heard tales of men disappearing. A locked basement seems like the perfect place to make that happen."

Flynn chuckled. "Aye, but that hasn't happened in a long while. Men no longer disappear inside my house. I have a separate facility for that. Apparently, I should have taken Killian there. I would have had he not been rescued last night. I won't make that mistake again. I am no longer in a forgiving mood." Flynn unrolled some instructions and checked the setup on the bomb he was building. He released the paper, allowing it to roll in on itself as he arranged the components inside the pressure cooker. "I need you to make a delivery for me."

"Who's the target?"

"Mathias."

"Which location? You had me scout five of them."

"The pub. He deserves an eye for an eye."

Mercer considered the neighborhood, the nearby shops, the pedestrians present at this time of day, and the innocent lives that would be lost.

"Mathias's men shot at you last night. You mean to tell me you don't want revenge?"

Mercer nodded at the bomb. "What's inside? Explosions are messy. Unpredictable. The fallout is harder to contain." He studied the jars of nails and coins. "I prefer clean kills with minimal fallout and less chaos. It's harder to determine if the target's been eliminated when you wipe out half a city block."

"That's precisely the point. It's why you'll be delivering this." Flynn patted the side of the bomb. "Mathias wanted to rub it in my face. It was a show of force to rescue that bastard traitor from my pub. He wanted to show me he was responsible. So I want to make my move just as obvious. If he wants a war, I'll give him a bloody war."

"This could be taken care of quietly."

"You don't get it. It's not about Mathias. It's about sending a message to Mathias's faction, the fuckers at MI5, and the rest of the bleeding world. No one interferes with Colin Flynn's operation. No one."

Flynn was a megalomaniac who wanted to create chaos. He wanted to cause panic, and he didn't care if his methods resulted in mass casualties.

"Just one question. Why me?"

"You haven't been compromised. And I have matters to which I must attend. This is the first volley. After this, the rest will come in three waves. I have plans, Julian. Big plans. I'll need your help with them. There is no one else. I paid you. I trust you can handle it."

"Very well." Mercer couldn't refuse. Not now. Not when he was so close to learning the truth. He would find some way to minimize casualties. The bomb assembly didn't have an aerosol or disbursal system. It wasn't a VX bomb, but that didn't mean it wouldn't kill plenty of people. He had to do this. This one act would redefine his relationship within the faction, and it would be enough to convince Colin to divulge the rest of his plans for the other devices. "I'll need a few hours to determine the best place to leave the device."

"No." Flynn reached for the industrial-sized container of rat poison, filled a few jars with the liquid, locked the lid, and checked the wires before securing the timer. "Everything is already prepared. Leave this inside Mathias's pub. No doubt, the bastard will be celebrating having Killian back in his grasp. It'll give us the opportunity to inflict maximum damage." Flynn grabbed a sheet of gold embossed paper and scribbled down the address. "Leave it just inside the front door. Once it's placed," Flynn pressed a button, and the timer lit up, "get the hell out of there."

"Someone will notice."

"So distract them. Make sure they are too busy to notice." Flynn's expression hardened as he carefully lifted the bomb and placed it inside a heavy-duty cardboard box. He did his best to keep it level, and Mercer couldn't help but wonder how stable the explosive was. "If he does notice, he'll believe it's nothing more than a late delivery. Either way, by the time he realizes, it'll be too late."

Mercer held the top of the box while Flynn taped it. "It's set to go off around the same time Kevin's wake begins."

"Wake? So soon?"

"No need to waste time. As soon as the bodies are prepared, we tend to our dead and celebrate their lives. No reason to delay. Plus, it's the perfect alibi." Flynn smiled wickedly. "You should go. The clock's ticking."

Together, Mercer and Flynn carried the box up the steps and placed it in the back of a white SUV. Mercer wasn't sure if it was Flynn's vehicle or if it belonged to one of his men, but he didn't bother to ask. The vehicle had a GPS. Flynn would know if Mercer detoured from his route, so Mercer couldn't take any chances. He'd have to figure it out as he went.

TWENTY-NINE

The SUV could be bugged. If not, the bomb's detonator might be sensitive to radio signals. Mercer just hoped cell phone use wouldn't be a problem.

Driving one-handed, he sent a text to Hans. Since the rest of the team was otherwise occupied, he hoped the reconnaissance expert was up for this. The bomb had to go off. If it didn't, the trust Mercer had worked so hard to earn would be lost. He couldn't let that happen. He just needed to make sure the pub was empty.

Time? came Hans' response.

Mercer glanced at his watch. *Twenty-seven minutes.*

Detonator?

Timer with an added cell phone trigger.

He might intend to light you up.

Mercer didn't reply. That was a possibility. If Flynn was monitoring the GPS signal coming from the vehicle, he might detonate the device once Mercer was in range. It'd be one way to clean up the mess and pass the blame, but Mercer was confident Flynn wanted the credit. In fact, he was betting his life on it.

The phone buzzed again. *See you in ten minutes.*

Mercer eased his foot off the gas. His teammate was en route. He needed to slow down to give Hans time to catch up. Since he didn't know Hans' precise location, he wasn't sure how this was going to work, but his teammate would be at the coordinates. Perhaps, Hans could remove the canisters containing the explosive projectiles. It would limit the range of the weapon and decrease the blast radius.

For the next ten minutes, Mercer continued at a crawl. He'd accelerate and slow, attempting to mimic heavy traffic patterns even though his erratic driving was the cause of said traffic. Idly, he wondered how things had gotten so screwed up. This was supposed to be a simple recovery. In and out. But nothing was simple. *Bloody terrorists,* he thought.

He pulled to the curb at the designated intersection. Immediately, Bastian and Hans got into the back seat, and Mercer continued on his way before the rear door even closed. No one spoke until he turned the radio up to an ungodly level on the off chance Flynn had hidden a listening device inside.

"What are you doing here?" Mercer asked Bastian.

"Don't worry about that now. What's going on?" Bastian asked.

"It's in the cardboard box." Mercer glanced at them from the mirror. "It's good to see you."

"I'd prefer if these reunions didn't center around being blown to smithereens. Don't get me wrong. I like getting some action," Hans grinned, "but not like this, mate."

Bas flicked open a knife and cut the tape. "Bloody hell." He climbed over the seat, and Hans followed. "Jules, what kind of liquid is this? VX is amber-colored in liquid form. This is too red."

"It's not VX. It's rat poison."

"Sick fuck," Hans said. "As if maiming wasn't bad enough, he wants them to hemorrhage to death."

"You can't deliver this," Bas said.

"I don't have a choice. Flynn trusts me." Mercer swerved to avoid a pothole, and Hans cursed.

"Might you hold it steady? This thing is highly volatile," Hans cracked a smile, "kind of like you."

After some careful consideration, Bas stopped fiddling with the device. "It's a closed circuit. I can't disassemble any of it without triggering an explosion." He activated a cell phone jammer to prevent a premature detonation.

"Plan B." Hans climbed over the seat while Bastian resealed the box. "Donovan and I have been known to clear a place out. Drop me at the next stop, and loop around the long way. I'll have it taken care of by the time you arrive. How's our timetable?"

"Fifteen minutes." Mercer frowned as a morbid thought entered his mind. "Did something happen to our captive?"

"No. Donovan's keeping watch," Bastian said. "It'll be slow going. I don't expect we'll get results this way."

Mercer's gaze flicked to Hans. "Are you field ready?" Mercer had his doubts, but now wasn't the time to pick a fight. Hans proved himself last night. Plus, clearing an area and dealing with a bomb shouldn't require any shooting.

"Don't worry. I'm right as rain and just in time to pick up your slack. It's nice to know you didn't get your brain scrambled or go over to the dark side." He tapped Mercer on the shoulder. "Drop me off here. I'll get the bar and surrounding area cleared before you arrive."

"It can't be obvious."

"It won't be."

Mercer slowed at the next red light, and Hans jumped out of the car and raced toward their final destination.

Bastian slid into the back seat, analyzing Mercer's appearance through the mirror. They could barely hear each other over the blasting radio, but it was necessary. "Lara's letting our captive stew. She's a firecracker and too bloody creative with the torture techniques, if you ask me."

"She'll do anything to save her brother."

"Reminds me of someone I know."

"Bas, don't."

"No, I think I bloody well will. You realize our friends at MI5 will not see this as a necessary act. In fact, it's enough to get you placed on a watchlist or even a most wanted list. Do you want to spend the rest of your natural life locked in a cage or on the run? You are about to deliver a bomb to a pub. Think about it. What are you doing, Jules?"

That was a good question. Mercer had become so focused on the mission objectives, blinded by them, that he was acting erratically, even by his normal standards. "Two nights ago, we sold half a million in weapons, mostly MAC-10s, but I know Killian sold something else. Something larger."

"Something like a few of these pressure cooker bombs or the VX?"

"I don't know."

"Two of Flynn's men ended up dead, and Killian was taken. Are you sure Flynn trusts you?"

Mercer slowed when the pub came into view. "We'll find out, won't we?" Swiveling in the seat, he faced his friend. "Get out of here. I'll handle this. And if I can't, it's up to you to stop Flynn and find Shepherd."

Bastian opened his mouth to say something, but one look silenced him. Instead, he tapped his ear. "We have radios for a reason."

"Not with that device."

"After. We stay in contact. Things are about to pop off. I can feel it."

"Me too." Mercer looked at his watch. They didn't have time for small talk.

"Don't get yourself blown up. I don't have a spatula handy to scrape you off the brick."

While Mercer unloaded the heavy box, Bastian disappeared down the street. Mercer glanced around as he moved along the sidewalk. A few people were eating at the bistro across the way. He'd have to find something to block the nails and other projectiles from traveling that far. Based on the amount of explosive in the pressure cooker, the device had a fairly large blast radius.

For a moment, Mercer reconsidered his actions. If this went wrong, a lot of innocents would be killed. That would be blood he'd never wash off his hands. He would be entirely to blame.

He pushed his back against the pub door. *Murphy's* frosted the glass in perfect italics. The door was constructed of a solid, thick wood that went to waist height before glass replaced the sturdy construction, boasting the hours of operation and the name stenciled above. Despite Hans' insistence that he would clear the bar, Mercer was surprised to find it nearly empty.

Placing the bomb on the floor next to the hostess stand, Mercer cautiously moved through the establishment. Perhaps he should shove the bomb inside the walk-in freezer. At least in there, it would be less likely to result in casualties, but the lack of destructive fallout would be obvious. What to do?

As Mercer pondered this, he heard voices coming from the back room, one of which he recognized. He ducked behind the bar, checking the time. They had less than five minutes.

"I'm sorry for the inconvenience." Hans' voice grew louder. "Gas leak. You know how dangerous they can be. We'll get you sorted, and you'll be up and running in no time." Hans handed one of the men a business card. "If you have any questions, that'll get you connected directly to the main branch." He ushered the workers toward the rear door. "The sooner you clear out, the sooner we'll get this checked."

Before the rear door even closed, Bastian came through the front with four cinderblocks stacked in front of his chest. He eyed Mercer, who was still hidden behind the bar. "Want to give me a hand? You made this mess."

Mercer grabbed two of the blocks from Bastian. "I told you to leave."

"Pish." Bastian placed two of the cement blocks in front of the cardboard box and stacked the next two on top. "Since this is how you chose to conduct an op on your own, I'm going to have to take over this mission." His eyes sparkled, and he called to Hans. "Grab the other four blocks."

"Aye." Hans dashed out the front door.

"Where did you get these?" Mercer asked as he entered the kitchen. Refrigerators were notoriously well insulated. The door would do nicely. He examined the hinges and reached for one of the metal implements on the counter.

"A nearby construction site."

"Convenient."

"Sheer luck," Bastian said as Hans returned with more blocks. "If that hadn't worked, I was prepared to steal a car and park it on the sidewalk right out front.

Figured it might be large enough and sturdy enough to stop the flying nails and debris." Bastian placed the other four blocks along the side of the bomb, walling it in on two sides while the third side remained flush against the hostess stand which was propped against a row of wooden booths. By leaving the fourth side open, facing into the pub, the blast would act more like a shaped charge, the energy and force moving in the direction of least resistance.

Mercer returned to the front with the refrigerator door. He propped it against the stand and placed it in front of the cement blocks. The pub would be lost, but lives would not. At least, he hoped not.

"Time," Mercer said. "I have to go. Flynn might wonder what's taking so long."

"Give me a sec." Bastian went out the door with Hans and Mercer at his heels. He made quick work of the SUV's GPS tracker, shorting it out by overloading the secondary electrical system. "Flynn will assume it was damaged in the blast." Bastian glanced around. "I'll wipe nearby camera feeds. No one will know we were here."

"What about the gas leak?" Mercer asked, eyeing Hans.

"Work orders have been issued. Paperwork is backdated and timestamped an hour ago. Flynn won't be the wiser." Hans rotated his shoulder, sore from carrying the heavy blocks, and raised an eyebrow at Mercer's bleeding side. "And you were worried I wasn't field ready. You ripped a stitch."

"Staple. It's easy to do when you can't exactly fight back." Mercer climbed into the car. "Stay out of sight." He tapped his ear. "I'll keep the line open so you'll get immediate updates. Let's put this to bed. Thirty seconds, gentlemen. Get clear."

Putting the car into drive, Mercer headed down the

street. He was a block away when he heard the boom. He didn't stop, but he scanned the damage in the rearview mirror.

The entire front of the building had blown outward. The windows shattered, raining shards of glass into the street. The front door had blown clear off, smacking into a parked car and triggering the noisy alarm. Mercer could only imagine what the interior must look like. There probably wasn't much left of the bar or the refrigerator door. Hopefully, it was no longer recognizable, but he couldn't worry about it now. The explosion would be enough to appease Flynn, even though the lack of casualties would be very disappointing.

A crowd gathered around the scene, cell phone cameras aimed at the destruction. With any luck, no one had noticed his teammates or the cinderblocks. Mercer didn't care if they spotted the SUV or noted the plate. In fact, he'd prefer if someone stopped Flynn before it was too late, but deep down, he knew that wasn't possible. And after what just happened, Flynn would escalate. Mercer would have to force Flynn to divulge the details of the attack. Only he and his team could stop Flynn now.

THIRTY

Mercer paced the main level of Flynn's compound. The bombing had left him antsy and frustrated. He tried to block out the jitters and focus on the voices coming from the floor above. Flynn was making preparations for Kevin Aglin's and Duffy O'Brien's funerals. From the sounds of it, Flynn had forgiven Alana. Maybe bombing Murphy's pub had put him in a good mood.

"Julian," Flynn said as he made his way down the steps, "I didn't realize you were back." He glanced around, but the usual bodyguards weren't around. "How did it go?"

"Fine, I suppose." He waited a beat, as if reconsidering his words. Would it be better to tell Flynn up front that the bar was empty, or should he wait for Flynn to find out on his own?

"No trouble, then?"

"None. The place was practically a ghost town. I suppose now it's a morgue."

Flynn cracked a smile. "I'll remember this." He clapped Mercer on the shoulder, eyeing the wet stain on his shirt. "It looks like you have little hope of properly healing."

Mercer glanced down. His mind was so focused on the mission he didn't notice the sting. "Must have happened lifting the box."

"Get that taken care of and get some rest. You've earned it." Flynn reached for a set of car keys. "I'll pick you up later tonight, after I pay my respects." He called up the steps for Alana to hurry, but Mercer grabbed his shoulder before the terrorist could walk away.

"If there are other targets you want to hit, I can scout ahead. Make sure we're in the clear."

Flynn's gaze rested on Mercer's hand. For a moment, Mercer wondered if he overstepped and Flynn would lash out, but instead, Flynn smiled. "No worries. It's been taken care of. Everything is set."

Mercer forced his face to remain neutral, but the muscles in his back tightened. "You mean the first wave is ready? The bombs are in place?"

"Glad to see you were paying attention. Why? Did you want to deliver the bombs yourself? I thought you didn't want to get your hands dirty."

"I'm just offering to help. You paid for my services."

"I see. That's why you're loyal? Because of the money? I thought you were coming around to the cause."

"I might be."

"Excellent. You'll have time to prove yourself. The first wave won't begin until after I lay my brothers to rest. There will be plenty of work for you to do after that."

As had become the norm, Mercer wondered if this couldn't come to an end with a single bullet. He could do it. Right now, he could do it and escape before anyone realized what happened. But the faction would continue to exist. They would still carry out Flynn's masterplan. Maybe that was a risk worth taking, but Mercer shook the thought aside. There were too many unknowns, and he made a promise to find out what happened to Owen Shepherd. He would keep his word.

"We'll discuss the details later." Flynn offered his hand to Alana, who had come down the steps. "I'll give you a ride back to the inn, Julian."

Mercer returned to his room at the inn, put a few new stitches in his side, and waited twenty minutes before leaving. He radioed his team, informing them of his impending arrival, and headed for the safe house.

*   *   *

"MI5 and Interpol are all over the bombing," Bastian said. "They know Flynn's behind it, but they have no proof."

"Did you inform them of our involvement?" Mercer asked.

"Not yet. Partridge is suspicious. I've been ducking his calls." As if on cue, the phone rang. "That's the tenth time in the last two hours. I'll have to speak to him soon."

"We're going to need all the help we can get. Flynn is planning three waves." Mercer pointed to the map. "I don't know the order of his strikes, but they will be coordinated. He might have already delivered the devices. He wouldn't give me a straight answer. All I know is he said he wanted to wait until after he buries his mates."

"The funerals are tomorrow morning. That doesn't give us much time."

"Have you gotten anything out of Killian?" Mercer jerked his chin toward the feed. "Has Lara tried waterboarding or electrocution?"

"Not yet. Please don't give her any ideas." Bastian reached into a bag and pulled out a handful of crisps. He popped one into his mouth and chewed. "We need to come clean about our involvement. If the authorities find out we planted the bomb before we tell them, it'll look like we switched sides. And MI5 already has their hearts set on identifying a traitor."

"It's catching," Mercer remarked. "Fine. As soon as she steps away, we'll brief her, and let her call it in." He watched the woman work. Despite the concussion, she remained focused and unyielding. "I'm having trouble believing she's retired."

"So am I."

A few minutes later, Donovan opened the door, and he and Lara stepped out. Once the lock was secured in place, Mercer told them what happened, concluding with, "Which is why we blew up Murphy's pub earlier today."

"Bloody hell." Lara studied each of the men in turn. "Who are you people?"

"Security specialists with an emphasis on K&R and asset retrieval," Bastian said. "But as you can see, we're deep in uncharted waters."

"Jules," Donovan said, "you realize you might have started a war."

"It started the moment I shot Aglin and O'Brien."

"Are you sure Flynn doesn't know you evacuated the area first?" Lara asked, adding, "Are you sure you got everyone clear and there were no casualties?"

"None reported," Bastian said. "And no one knows we were there. MI5 will be vigilant. They might discover trace evidence. We need to get ahead of this. We were hoping you might do us a favor."

She thought for a moment. "I suppose."

Mercer handed her a satellite phone. "Call it in."

While she spoke on the phone, Bastian read his text messages and played the voicemails from Partridge. "I left an anonymous tip that a turf war was brewing from one of our unregistered burners. Partridge wants us on top of this. He wants to know what kind of progress we're making and where you've been for the last few days."

"Tell him I've been ill. He might believe it," Mercer said. "You need to go back. Tomorrow, all hell will break loose. We'll need the support. We need MI5 and every other agency on alert."

Lara concluded her call. "They're in Colin's pocket. We can't trust anyone."

"Not all of them. Maybe a few, which is why we need Killian to answer our questions. He can tell us what Flynn has planned and what's become of Owen," Mercer said.

Hans dragged a folding table and a large bucket into the room. Over his shoulder was a towel. "Kidnapping has become our specialty as of late. Though, this one isn't paying off. Where do you want this, darling?"

Lara took the towel. "Leave it by the door. The threat is more effective than actual torture. Men will say anything to get the pain to stop, but getting Killian to admit to lies won't answer our questions." She spotted a sealed syringe in Hans' shirt pocket and pulled it out. "This ought to help sell it."

Bastian watched her disappear inside. A moment later, she appeared on the screen and injected the saline into Killian's neck. Then she set up the tools of her trade. "Does anyone else think she's enjoying this a bit too much?"

"Leave her be." Mercer understood the need for answers and the desire for vengeance. A new thought entered his mind.

Bastian frowned. "What now?"

"I have an idea."

"Balls."

Mercer knocked on the door and waited for Lara to step out of the room. "What?" she hissed, annoyed by the interruption.

"Tell him about the bomb. Tell him Colin's already enacted the first wave. It'll come in three waves. I don't know what they are or what it means, but it's something."

"He might let something slip because he thinks it's already done. Brilliant." She ducked back into the room and closed the door. First, she'd convince Killian the drugs would make him unable to resist her questioning. The mental manipulation would start to wear on him, and then she'd tell him Flynn's plan was already underway and a success. It'd explain her rage and anger. Combined with the torture she planned to implement, he might just speak, and then they'd have him.

THIRTY-ONE

Killian didn't crack. Lara went at him for hours, until she was sick and dizzy, but he remained strong and stoic. Donovan brought in high-powered flood lamps and blasted German death metal through the speakers, hoping sleep deprivation and sensory overload would loosen Killian's tongue.

"At least it's soundproofed," Hans mused. "I'm all for rocking out at the clubs, but I'm not in the mood to party."

"You better get going," Donovan said.

"I'll keep in radio contact. Let me know if anything develops on your end with Killian or the blokes in military intelligence." Mercer tucked the radio into his ear, performed a soundcheck, and went out the door.

He arrived at the inn thirty minutes before Colin Flynn. Mercer cut it close, but he wanted to stay at the safe house as long as possible in the hopes Killian would shed some light on the matter. Since he didn't, Mercer would have to get the intel directly from the source.

Flynn wasn't pleased. He stalked the small room, blowing out a frustrated breath. Mercer poured a drink and pushed it across the table. Wordlessly, Flynn picked it up and swallowed.

"Mathias Murphy is still alive," Flynn said. "He's one lucky bastard."

"What are you talking about?"

"There was a gas leak inside his pub, so he wasn't there."

Mercer considered the information. "No wonder there was such a huge explosion."

A small smile crept onto Flynn's face. "He won't be opening shop anytime soon, but he should be dead. That bastard's luck is about to run out."

"Is he the target of the first wave?"

"No, I have a much more valuable goal in mind."

"What is it?"

Flynn poured another drink. "You'll know in due time." After finishing the whiskey, he put the empty glass on the table. "It's been a knackering day. Tomorrow morning won't be much better, but I won't let Kevin and Duffy's deaths be in vain. By this time tomorrow night, everyone will know who controls Northern Ireland."

Mercer tried to delay Flynn's retreat with questions and sympathies, but the faction leader turned a deaf ear to him. The voices in his head were louder than any in the real world. Mercer followed him out of the inn and back to the car.

"Where are you going?" Mercer asked.

Coming out of his daze, Flynn eyed Mercer over the roof of the car. "Back to the pub. My mates are waiting. Stay here. It's not your place to join us tonight. But you will tomorrow."

Mercer watched the car's taillights disappear. Hans would keep an eye on Flynn. Hopefully, the terrorist would keep his word. That gave them less than twenty-four hours to stop the massacre.

They had to figure this out. They had to do something to stop it. Where was Colin Flynn keeping the VX and the rest of the bomb materials? They weren't in the basement. Flynn already dealt with one tragedy by keeping explosives on his property. He wouldn't be stupid enough to do it a second time, especially with a lethal nerve agent.

"Is he talking?" Mercer asked the moment he stepped into the flat.

Donovan looked up from the reports and shook his head.

"Where's Lara?" Mercer didn't see her in the main room. "Is she in there with him?"

"No, Bastian is."

Mercer turned the volume up on the monitor. If anyone could appeal to Killian's humanity, it'd be Bastian.

"We don't know enough. How are we going to stop this?" Mercer asked.

Donovan put the report on the table. "I don't know." He dissected Flynn's dossier. "We should assume it's a soft target. He's not the type to run straightaway at the government with a bomb strapped to his chest."

"He wouldn't make it very far."

"Precisely, so he'd do it in a roundabout fashion." Donovan laid out surveillance photos from the six locations. "Bas compiled a list of events, ceremonies, speeches, anything that will garner a government or police presence. Those would be the best targets."

Mercer read through the list, but they all fell flat. "Are they near any of the target sites?"

"No, but there must be at least six more strike zones, right? He has twelve bombs."

"Eleven. We used one today."

"Right. Eleven."

"He could be using multiple devices at any one location to expand the blast radius. He might not have eleven targets." Mercer sifted through the photographs. There had to be a clue somewhere in this mess.

A few minutes later, Bastian stepped out of the room. "He's pigheaded. Despite everything, Killian believes in Colin and the mission."

"Flynn was going to kill him. We saved his bloody life. Doesn't he see that?" Mercer asked.

Bastian shook his head. "He blames you for that, not Flynn."

"Flynn trusted Killian with everything, and in turn, Killian trusted Flynn with his sister's happiness and well-being." Mercer looked at Bas. "Do you think you can use that?"

"I'll see what I can do. In the meantime, focus on everything Flynn had Killian do. As Flynn's right-hand man, he would have been given the most important assignments."

"The theater. That has to be the primary target." Clicking the mouse, Mercer found the schedule for the next day. "Fuck."

Donovan leaned over Mercer's shoulder. "That has to be the target. It's a sold-out show. Given the actors and the performance, the crowd will be full of men and women Colin Flynn would consider HVTs."

"Let me see that." Bastian pushed his way to the computer. "Dammit, Partridge. You bleeding moron."

"What?" Dread gripped Mercer's innards as he read the internal memo. "That piece of shit. He'll do anything to keep us in the dark. Doesn't he realize this is connected?"

Bastian reached for the phone. "I'll tell him there's

a threat. They need to cancel."

"You can't."

Bastian's eyes went wide. "What do you mean I can't? This has to be Flynn's target. If he releases VX in the theater, we're talking a thousand casualties, and that's just the people inside. Depending on the disbursal method and placement, we could be looking at a few hundred more deaths. We have to shut this down."

"What about the internal leak at Palace Barracks?" Mercer asked. "If Partridge is involved, he'll tip Flynn. And we won't have a chance of stopping this."

"It's a gamble, mate," Donovan said. "It could go either way."

"Fuck." Bastian tapped the pen against the tabletop like he used to do with his cigarettes.

Mercer stared at him. "You know Partridge better than the rest of us, and you know the situation inside MI5. I'm leaving it up to you. You make the call."

Bastian scrubbed a hand down his face, dropping the pen and removing the lighter from his pocket. He flicked the Zippo open and closed repeatedly as he worked through the various ramifications. "It's not just the government officials. It's their protection details. The place is going to be crawling with agents and police. Why didn't MI5 inform us? They must be providing security, along with the local police force. It'll be nearly impossible for Flynn to sneak the device inside."

"Even though they asked for our help, they haven't informed us of much of anything," Mercer said.

"Regardless, an attack on the theater will take out half of Ireland's governing body and the men responsible for raiding Flynn's compound and killing his family. This is what he wants. This is his endgame," Donovan said. "That has to be it."

Mercer shook his head. "This is just the beginning. The first wave of his attack."

"Killian's going to talk. He doesn't know what day or time it is. We'll use that to our advantage. But to be clear, this is a gamble. We're betting everything on the theater being Flynn's target. If we're wrong, Killian will realize it immediately and we'll have no chance of gaining his cooperation," Bas said.

"Then we better be right." Mercer settled behind the computer. "Use Alana. Tell him whatever you have to. She's the only leverage we have."

"Aye."

Hours later, Bastian emerged from the makeshift interrogation room. He glanced bleary-eyed out the window. The sun was starting to rise. Donovan and Mercer hadn't looked up from their research, but despite their best efforts, they weren't any closer to stopping the attack.

"After a shower, I'm heading to Palace Barracks. I'll tell them an attack is imminent and to have a rapid response team ready, but I'm not divulging any hard details. You're right, Jules. We don't know who we can trust. As soon as we have verification of Flynn's target, you let me know, and I'll have units move in. It's the best we can do. We move too soon, and Flynn will change his play. But if we move too late." Bastian turned his head to the side, seeing no reason to finish the statement.

Mercer nodded, watching his friend disappear down the hallway. He and Donovan exchanged sullen looks. They'd failed missions before, but those occasions were few and far between. And those were the ones from which the team never truly recovered.

Donovan pressed the radio. "Hans, anything to report?"

"Nothing. Flynn and his cronies are sloppy drunks.

They dragged themselves home a few hours ago. There's been no movement since."

"Return to bravo site. We're T minus twelve hours."

"I'm on my way."

"Twelve hours?" Mercer asked.

Donovan shrugged. "The show starts at six. Figured that would be the best time to do it. You should get some sleep, commander. You're on point."

"I'll sleep when this is over. We don't have time to waste." Mercer stretched and circled the room, stopping in front of the interrogation room door. "Are we sure he won't talk to me?"

"At this point, you might as well give it a go. We've got nothing left to lose."

THIRTY-TWO

Killian wouldn't break, even though Mercer would have broken half the bones in the man's body had Donovan not dragged him out of the interrogation room. It didn't matter what they did to Killian. He wouldn't give up the terrorist's plans. And they didn't have the weeks or months it would take to convince him otherwise.

"I'll do whatever it takes to get Flynn to trust me. Once I know when and where he's going to strike, I'll radio. Bastian said MI5 will be prepped and ready. They'll need to coordinate evacuations with the local police." Mercer glanced into the closed bedroom. "We'll need her connections."

"I've contacted our friends back in London. They're aware of the situation. Mobile medical teams are prepped and ready to move out," Donovan said.

"Let's hope it doesn't come to that."

Hans looked up from the maps. "I'll continue to scout Flynn's other known locations and any place I find marked with his clover and spade insignia. I'll radio in any suspicious movement."

"Be careful, Hans. Don't let them see you." Mercer palmed a set of keys. "Do the best you can. It's been an honor, gentlemen."

"Jules, don't," Donovan warned.

Mercer nodded tightly and left the flat. So much for a typical recovery. He considered everything he knew about Colin Flynn and the vast amount of progress he'd made infiltrating the faction, but it wasn't enough. None of it would mean a damn if Flynn carried out the attack. Shepherd must have known what was coming. He must have had details, and those details led to his demise.

While Mercer showered and changed, preparing for the hell that was to come, one odd thought remained on his mind. What did Flynn do with Shepherd's body? It hadn't been discovered. Maybe the undercover MI5 agent was buried at sea or cremated. Hell, he could be buried somewhere on the grounds of Flynn's estate for all Mercer knew, but obviously, Flynn had a way of disposing of bodies. And Mercer didn't know what it was.

"What does it matter?" he mumbled to himself. He had to focus on the matter at hand.

When he emerged from the bathroom, he found Flynn waiting. "Where have you been all night?" Flynn asked. He wore a dark suit and sunglasses, either to hide the tears or to deal with the hangover. Possibly both.

"I couldn't sleep. I thought I'd try to track down that traitor, but I didn't have any luck."

"Don't say his name. I can't think about that right now." Flynn took off his tie, rolled it up, and shoved it into his pocket. "No more misery. The rest of the day is a celebration, a tribute to the ones we've lost. We're finally taking action. We're going to get justice." He wrapped an arm around Mercer's shoulders. "Car's waiting. I hope you're ready."

"One minute." Mercer slipped out of Flynn's grip and holstered his Sig. He put an extra two magazines in his pocket and grabbed his phone.

"Expecting trouble?"

"It never hurts to be prepared."

"Aye."

Flynn prattled on about the injustices in the world, the plights he had faced since boyhood, and the more recent tragedies he suffered. Mercer made the appropriate comments and offered sympathetic platitudes, but Flynn didn't hear any of them. He was driven, caught up in his own world. Unfortunately, that didn't include exposing his master plan.

"Where are we going?" Mercer read the unfamiliar street signs. "I thought we were going back to your house."

"No reason. Alana's there, and I don't want to bring any of this near her."

"How is she?"

Flynn's right shoulder inched upward. "Upset. Her only remaining relative abandoned her. He's the reason we buried two friends, two of our brothers-in-arms. He lost his way, and he betrayed us. She may never forgive him or herself for not seeing it." Flynn shook his head. "We're not talking about this."

"Sorry. I didn't mean to bring it up."

"It's okay. Right now, we're preparing to ride into battle. I hope you're ready, Julian."

"What's the plan? Who's the target? Are we striking against Mathias Murphy?"

"No, mate. We're aiming much higher. We're hitting the aristocracy and the pricks they hire to keep us in line. The bastards who force us to comply with their orders and their will. The ones who took away our liberties, killed our families, our friends, destroyed everything we held dear."

Mercer was familiar with the rhetoric, but grandiose speeches and flowery words didn't answer the question. "And the target's location?"

"We're going to spit right in their fucking eye." Flynn stopped the car outside a condemned machine shop. "Now we collect our tools."

Mercer followed behind, keeping an eye out. Several of Flynn's lieutenants were already inside. His personal guards were watching the door. Each of the men was armed to the teeth. It'd take an army to break in here.

"Bloody hell," Mercer said, sounding impressed. "This is incredible." An assembly line built more pressure cooker bombs, but these weren't chemical weapons. These were basic incendiaries, filled with projectiles and rat poison. They'd inflict plenty of damage but nothing compared to what a nerve agent could do.

"That's part two." Flynn patted Aaron on the back. "Make sure you create two concentric circles. They'll clear the area. So a hundred meters around. That'll take out the perimeter. The remaining five will wipe out those who make it to the hospitals. No one's getting lucky today. Make sure the timers are synced. We've estimated the response times. A half hour after the initial blast, and two hours afterward. They shouldn't be expecting that."

"Yes, sir," Aaron replied.

Mercer rubbed his ear, surreptitiously activating his radio. "You're planning to take out the first responders and the survivors at the perimeter? And whoever makes it past will meet their fate at the hospitals? That's brilliant."

Flynn smiled, enjoying the adulation. "You haven't

seen the best part." He led the way past the two dozen terrorists and up a back staircase. Mercer eyed the rusty metal chains and the heavy equipment. "You and I are going to set all of that in motion."

They continued along the metal walkway, turning and moving along the upper level to an office with a rusted door. The first thing Mercer noticed was the stench, a combination of human waste, sweat, and fear with overtones of fetid meat and copper. He breathed through his mouth, hoping not to gag.

Flynn opened the rusted door with an ear-piercing squeal. An aluminum box sat on the worktable. The reinforced interior housed the VX canister and the delivery system. "This is what's going to make everyone come running."

"Chemical warfare? Are you sure about this? VX permeates. It lingers. This is your home. You want to destroy it? Destroy your people? Make everything unlivable?"

"I'm not talking about nuking the place. They'll get it cleaned up eventually. But they'll never forget. This is how I choose to make my stand. Are you with me?"

"I'm here, aren't I?"

"Very well. I'll give you the rest of the details on the way. Right now, I need to get this armed. I hired an expert. He should be here any minute." Flynn picked up the case and gestured at the door.

Mercer stepped out of the office, the stench increasing exponentially. One of the chains hanging from the ceiling shuddered, and Mercer watched it curiously. He went around the side of the office, shocked to find the chain wrapped around a man's stomach.

Mercer moved toward the body, and it moved. "Shit." He jumped, surprised. The man was filthy, covered in sweat, grime, blood, and his own filth. He was barely recognizable, but Mercer would know him anywhere. Owen Shepherd. "Who is he?" Mercer took a step forward to feel the man's racing pulse.

"He's a dead man." Flynn eyed the disconnected IV needle and the nearly empty bag hanging from the side of the office. "Don't concern yourself."

Mercer squinted. "I recognize him. He's an MI5 agent. How did you capture him?"

"I didn't. He came to me." Flynn placed the case gently on the floor and reached for his gun. "I kept him alive for answers, but I don't need him anymore. I should shoot him."

"No. Let me interrogate him. I told you what became of my wife. How these pricks let that psycho bastard kill her. I want to know who's responsible. I bet he can give me a name."

Flynn rubbed his forehead with the side of his gun. "You have until the device is ready. Then you put two in his head. Is that understood?"

"Thank you, sir." Mercer pulled a knife from his pocket. "Let's not waste time." He sliced a shallow cut into Shepherd's cheek, and the man, who'd already been through far worse than anything Mercer could imagine, screamed through the duct tape covering his mouth.

Flynn chuckled, hefted the case, and made his way down the steps. Mercer glanced around, but the office and the slatted metal walkway blocked the view from downstairs. He pressed his radio.

"I've located Shepherd. Do you copy?" he whispered.

He waited, but he didn't hear a response.

"This is team leader. Is anyone reading this?" he asked.

He examined the restraints. Shepherd's wrists were bound together with a cable tie, as were his feet. The chain was looped and hooked around his waist, holding him up. His feet dragged on the floor. The man was too weak to stand.

"Owen," Mercer whispered, "I'm a friend. MI5 sent me. I'm here to help."

Shepherd blinked a few times, his eyes wild and fearful, like a wounded animal. He'd been beaten nearly to death and starved, left to soil himself and rot in his own filth. Mercer moved closer with the knife, and Shepherd cringed, letting out frantic, pathetic mewls.

"Shh. I won't hurt you."

Shepherd shook, struggling to find his footing. He didn't believe a word Mercer said.

"Your sister, Lara, came to find you. We're working together. We captured Killian. She's interrogating him now."

At the mention of his sister's name, Shepherd stopped struggling. His previously unfocused eyes found Mercer's.

"That's better. Listen, I'm going to get you out of here." Mercer hit his radio again, but it wasn't working. As gently as possible, he tugged on the tape. "This will hurt, mate. I'm sorry about that."

Shepherd squeezed his eyes shut, tears dripping down his cheek. He could barely speak. His mouth and throat were too dry. His skin bled from the tape. "Grace?"

"Your wife and son are safe. They were moved into protective custody as soon as they lost contact with you."

Shepherd nodded.

"I'll get you back to them. I promise." Mercer tapped his radio again. "Bloody thing won't work."

"It's the metal. Interferes with the signal."

Mercer cut the bindings from Shepherd's hands.

"Leave me," Shepherd managed, nearly choking on his own tongue. "Flynn, the VX, you have to stop him."

"I will."

"If I get away, he'll know it was you. I have to stay here. You have to kill me."

"No one's dying today, except Flynn and his faction members." Mercer shoved the folded knife into Shepherd's hand, along with his cell phone. It had a weak signal, but it was still a signal. "Palace Barracks is compromised. Do you know the source of the leak?"

"A janitor."

"Are you sure?"

"That's what Flynn said. I saw him right before Flynn put two in his head."

Mercer thought. Maybe it was true. Maybe it wasn't.

Shepherd made a feeble attempt to grab Mercer's hand. "Flynn has a van. Costume design. It's on the list at the theater. He has an ID. No one will stop him. He's going to get inside. He intends to release the VX behind the stage. It'll wipe out the actors and front rows. When the ones near the back run out and call for help, he'll blow up the first responders. Then the hospitals." Even now, barely coherent, Owen Shepherd was still a man on a mission.

Mercer wouldn't let this be his last. "As soon as we clear out, call for help. Tell them what you told me. Can you do that?"

"Yes."

Mercer looked up at the chain and the frail, starving man. "Cover your ears and remain completely still until we're gone. All our lives depend on it." Mercer pulled his gun and fired twice. The bullets tore through the rusted metal wall of the office. Without missing a beat, he turned on his heel and went down the steps.

"Filthy wanker," Mercer spat. "Didn't even remember his own bloody name."

"I'll have someone clean up the mess tomorrow." Flynn waited for a man to finish securing the wires around the canister, handed the bomb technician a stack of cash, exchanged a few words in Serbian, and locked the case.

Mercer looked around the room. Most of the faction had already left to plant their devices. Flynn barked orders to the stragglers about where to rendezvous after the deed was done.

"Come on. We have to switch vehicles." Flynn led the way back to the car and secured the chemical weapon in the boot.

Mercer caught a glimpse of the countdown timer. It'd be a miracle if the device didn't detonate on the way to the theater.

THIRTY-THREE

Flynn drove the van to the loading dock and smiled at the man at the guard station. He held out the fake ID. "Busy night?"

"You caught the last minute rush. Show's about to start. You're cutting it close." The guard handed back the ID and pushed a button. "Go straight. Security's tight tonight. They need to sweep the van."

"Sure, no problem." The van rolled forward. Flynn glanced at Mercer as the men in suits and earpieces swept the undercarriage of the vehicle in front of them with long-handled mirrors. "Should they try to search inside, we'll kill them."

Now that Mercer knew the plan, he only needed to make sure the terrorist remained breathing long enough to respond to the check-in with his faction members. If Flynn didn't respond to the call, Flynn's followers would remotely trigger the VX and the other bombs.

"Doing so would attract too much attention. It's best we do this cleanly," Mercer said.

The guards checked the outside of the vehicle and barely glanced in the back of the van. Since the device was hermetically sealed, it didn't trigger any alarms.

"Good thing I kept you around." Flynn pulled up to the rear door. "Let's get this set up. We don't have time to waste."

"When's the check-in?" Mercer placed the box with the nerve agent on the platform of a rolling cart.

Flynn piled a dozen costumes on top of the bomb and wheeled it inside. "In five minutes. That should be enough time to place it and get clear. We'll watch what happens from a safe distance."

Mercer looked at his watch. Experts were on the way, but having less than five minutes to disarm the device was cutting it close, especially when the theater couldn't be evacuated.

"You keep doing that." Flynn jerked his chin at Mercer's wrist. "Do you have somewhere else to be? Or are you anxious for the fireworks?"

"Both."

Flynn maneuvered through the backstage area like he'd been inside the theater dozens of times. He must have been casing the place for months. According to Bastian, this particular show sold out the day tickets went on sale.

The lighting experts and set designers bustled about as Flynn pushed the rack of costumes behind the thick velvet curtain. He placed the cart beside another two parked racks. He jerked his chin toward the side. "Keep watch."

"Aye." Mercer crossed his arms over his chest and watched the stagehands hurry to make last minute changes. The main actors remained off to the side, running through vocal warm-ups. The nervous energy made the air crackle. Mercer felt it. The hairs on his arms prickled. These people had no idea what Flynn planned. They had no idea these next few minutes might be their last. "Is it set?"

"All done." Flynn took a step back to admire his handiwork. The costume cart did an excellent job concealing the device. The case was open. Mercer could see the digital timer counting down. 6:12. "Let's get out of here."

As soon as they were outside, Flynn reached into his jacket pocket and pulled out his vibrating cell phone. Mercer held his breath, fearful Flynn might detonate the device early.

"Aaron, it's done. Make sure everyone else is in position. The second wave will go off at the perimeter thirty minutes from now. The third wave will target the hospitals, police headquarters, and Palace Barracks. There will be so much confusion, they won't know which way is up. We want them panicked." Flynn paused. "Right. We'll celebrate our victory tonight."

"We're ready to move out," Mercer said, more for his teammates listening than for Flynn.

"Aye." Flynn unlocked the van doors.

"Wait," Mercer said, "did you hear that?"

"Hear what?"

"In the back."

"We don't have time for this." Flynn opened the rear door. "There's nothing here."

Mercer slipped his arm around Flynn's neck and squeezed, but the terrorist wouldn't go down without a fight. Flynn reached behind him, scratching at Mercer's eyes. Heaving himself forward, Flynn forced them into the back of the van.

Pressure against the carotid artery should put a man down in ten seconds, but Flynn wouldn't succumb. Mercer squeezed harder as Flynn rolled on top of him, forcing Mercer onto his back. Flynn elbowed Mercer hard, over and over, ripping the stitches and staples.

Mercer hissed, doing his best to ignore the sudden searing pain as he held tight. But Flynn broke free and straddled Mercer. He wrapped his hands around Mercer's throat and squeezed.

Mercer pulled the Sig from his hip, pressed the muzzle beneath Flynn's ribs and pulled the trigger.

Flynn's eyes went wide. He looked down, watching the deep red, nearly black, blood soak the front of his shirt. He stuttered, and blood poured from his mouth. Flynn fumbled for his phone, but Mercer grabbed his wrist and snapped it backward.

Yanking the phone out of Flynn's hand, Mercer tossed Flynn to the side and climbed out of the van. At least the dying terrorist couldn't remotely trigger the bomb, but it would still go off if Mercer didn't get it out of the theater in time.

Mercer tapped the radio as he raced back inside. "Flynn's down. Where's bomb disposal?"

"The mobile unit is on the way," Donovan said. "They should be there any minute."

"We don't have time for this." Mercer pushed his way backstage, ignoring the confused looks he received as he loaded the device back onto the costume rack and pushed it toward the exit. "The weapon is live. It's going to activate in three minutes and twenty-two seconds."

"Jesus, Jules."

"I'll secure it inside the van. Tell them to hurry." Mercer darted past security, hoping to avoid questions about his bloody appearance. Flynn had men nearby. An evacuation might tip them off, and until the rest of the devices were secure, they had to do this the hard way.

Mercer lifted the case into the back of the van. He

climbed in after it and closed the doors. Flynn stared at him, a gurgling wheeze passing through his opened mouth.

"How do I disarm it?" Mercer asked.

Flynn smirked, his eyes dulling as the life left his body.

Mercer let out an exhale, forcing his shaking hands to still. The deep breath caused him to cough and wheeze. Great, just what he needed. "Donovan, where are our guys?"

"They should be right on top of you. Non-descript vehicle, like you requested."

Mercer glanced out the door. "They're here. How's our progress?"

"MI5 and police headquarters have been swept. Two devices disarmed. Four men in custody. I don't know about the hospital yet. Bastian and Partridge are coordinating the raids to disarm the other eight devices."

"Let me know as soon as it's done."

Mercer moved out of the way as the bomb expert dressed in hazmat gear slid into the rear of the van. He placed his equipment and tools beside him and handed Mercer a roll of plastic sheeting and duct tape.

"We normally have the robot perform the disarming, but we don't have the time. And we're already spread thin." The tech didn't even look in Mercer's direction as he opened the faceplate surrounding the canister and carefully lifted it up to examine the wires and disbursal system. "In case this goes wrong, I need you to seal us in."

Mercer unrolled the plastic and taped it to the side, making sure it was solid around the doors and windows. The canister let out a hiss. "What the hell was that?"

"It's compressing. We have less than a minute."

The tech continued to work, and Mercer found himself staring at Flynn's body. Even though the bastard was dead, he wanted to beat him to a pulp. The device let out another hiss. Mercer's eyes darted to the tech, who had finished detaching the VX just as the disbursal system activated.

The tech placed the chemical weapon into an airtight container and sealed it inside. "I don't know if I made it in time."

"What do you mean?"

"It compressed. When it released, it might have vaporized a small amount. How do you feel?"

"Fine."

"Still, we'll have to wait for containment to arrive." The tech reached for his radio and sent the message. Normally, bomb disposal used radio frequency jammers to prevent remote and accidental detonations, but they couldn't utilize those in this instance with so many other devices across the city still in play. A loss of cell or radio signal would have tipped Flynn's faction.

Mercer rubbed his hands down his face and sunk to his knees. "The chemical weapon has been contained."

Donovan let out a sigh of relief. "Thank god."

"Afraid I wouldn't make it?" Mercer laughed, which turned into a cough. He held his side and covered his mouth. When he removed his hand, there were specks of blood.

"Shit." The bomb disposal expert radioed for decontamination and quarantine. "Try to relax. We'll get through this."

"Jules, what's going on?" Donovan asked in his ear.

"I'm fine. It's nothing."

"It's not nothing," the bomb expert insisted.

"I'm not talking to you," Mercer said.

That made the bomb expert even more concerned.

"Take it easy, mate. We'll get you sorted."

Mercer wiped his hand on his trousers and plucked the radio from his ear. "I'm not daft or dying. I'm talking to my team. I've been coughing up blood for a while now. It's courtesy of this wanker." He gestured to Flynn's body.

Despite his protests, containment was set up around the van. Men in full hazmat suits opened the doors, hauled Mercer out of the van and into the showers. They stripped him of his clothing and belongings, and after full decontamination, they handed him white scrubs to wear, loaded him into the back of a special emergency vehicle, and brought him to the hospital.

THIRTY-FOUR

"At least this place didn't blow up," Mercer said.

Bastian chuckled. "That would have been just your luck. It's a good thing I've got your back."

Mercer watched through the window as the nurses and doctors treated Owen Shepherd. The man had been at death's door. Lara remained at his side. She wouldn't lose him again.

"The rest of the faction members have been apprehended," Hans said, joining them. "Donovan handed over Killian. I told him we'd meet back at bravo site and help with the cleanup."

"In a minute." Mercer waited to catch Lara's eye and gestured for her to join them. "How is he?"

"Alive, thanks to you. He has a long road ahead, but he'll be okay." She held out her hand for Mercer to shake. "I pulled some strings and voiced a protest. Apparently, someone else had already beaten me to it. Every agent at Palace Barracks will be reassigned and investigated. According to Owen, a janitor was on Flynn's payroll. He stole classified documents that were meant to be destroyed, and that's how Flynn learned of Owen's identity."

"At least we found our leak," Bastian said. "Jules was afraid it was Partridge."

"I had the same thought," Lara said.

"Regardless, it's best if Owen disappears for a while. Flynn might have allies operating in the area," Mercer warned.

"Owen and his family will be relocated. My contacts at the SIS will make sure of it," Lara said. "It'd be best if you take your own advice and get out of Ireland while you can."

"We're planning on it," Mercer said.

Bastian smiled. "Take care, love."

She nodded and went back into Owen's room.

"Partridge wanted us for a debrief," Bastian said as they made their way out of the hospital. "But since you had your hands full, I took one for the team."

"What did you learn?" Hans asked.

"The gold stationery is what the janitor used to pass notes to Flynn. Apparently, a terrible secretary bought it, but no one liked it. So there was plenty around for the janitor to use to scribble notes, passwords, intel, whatever he happened to overhear or find in the wastebaskets. That's how Flynn knew as much as he did. According to Partridge, no actual agent or supervisor was compromised. It was the civilian workforce, and they'll take steps to ensure that doesn't happen again in the future."

"What became of the janitor?" Mercer asked.

"Dead. His body washed up on shore a few days ago. The police thought it was the result of a boating accident. The man had been on holiday, so it made sense."

"Flynn killed him," Mercer said.

"That would be my guess," Bastian said. "Our

mates in intelligence have urged us to stay away from Ireland and the rest of the UK for a while, at least until things calm down. We did bomb Mathias Murphy's pub and incite a war between the two most powerful factions. Some affected parties might still have it out for us, Jules."

Mercer thought about it. After everything that happened, he had no love for Ireland. But he would miss home. "We head back to London tonight. As soon as we get our next call, we'll resume our normal K&R duties. Hans has proven he's more than capable in the field. It's time we get back to business as usual."

DON'T MISS HUNTING GROUNDS, THE
NEXT INSTALLMENT IN THE JULIAN
MERCER SERIES

Retaliation

ABOUT THE AUTHOR

G.K. Parks is the author of the Alexis Parker series. The first novel, *Likely Suspects,* tells the story of Alexis' first foray into the private sector.

G.K. Parks received a Bachelor of Arts in Political Science and History. After spending some time in law school, G.K. changed paths and earned a Master of Arts in Criminology/Criminal Justice. Now all that education is being put to use creating a fictional world based upon years of study and research.

You can find additional information on G.K. Parks and the Alexis Parker series by visiting our website at
www.alexisparkerseries.com